A counselor AMONG wolves

LIV OLTEANO

Published by
DREAMSPINNER PRESS

5032 Capital Circle SW, Suite 2, PMB# 279, Tallahassee, FL 32305-7886 USA
http://www.dreamspinnerpress.com/

ISBN: 978-1-63216-922-8
Digital ISBN: 978-1-63216-923-5
Library of Congress Control Number: 2015901362
First Edition May 2015

Printed in the United States of America
∞
This paper meets the requirements of
ANSI/NISO Z39.48-1992 (Permanence of Paper).

Readers love *A Tooth for a Fang*
by LIV OLTEANO

By LIV OLTEANO

LEADER MURDERS
A Tooth for a Fang
A Counselor Among Wolves

Space Files R
The Heracian Affair
Sandstorm Heart

Published By DREAMSPINNER PRESS
http://www.dreamspinnerpress.com

One

"I HAVE to talk to you about something," Herman Weiss stated in his usual steely tone. "Something that should but can't be reported to the Council. Nobody can find out."

I sighed. "I'm the Bureau's counselor. Whatever it is that should be reported by the Council's standards will be. I'm not going to—"

"Doesn't patient-therapist confidentiality apply?"

"Of course. Unless whatever it is you're telling me constitutes a risk to yourself or others, in which case, by the Council's directives, it will be reported. I'm guessing it would fall under those directives, considering you think it does."

"You owe me," he snapped.

"I know."

"I saved your life."

I worked my jaw, then nodded. "You did."

"You do this and we're even."

"The Council won't tolerate—"

He snorted. "The Council isn't your fucking concern."

I lifted one eyebrow. "Pretty sure it is."

He leaned forward in the chair he dwarfed and narrowed those striking icy blue eyes at me. "Your real concern is pissing off an unstable werewolf alpha sitting a few feet away."

Well, shit. Now it was too late to deny any knowledge or involvement. Then a particular word from his little tirade registered. I blinked a few times and my stomach clenched tight. "Unstable? What are you saying?"

Weiss ran a hand through the graying hair that had been neatly combed back just moments before. "Went to see Amanda yesterday. She pushed my buttons, and... it resulted in me breaking the glass divider and flinging five agents through the room when they tried to hold me back."

I scratched my chin. "The extra-strong, super-reinforced glass divider?"

"Yes. They ended up shooting a tranquilizer dart in my ass to stop me. I would've killed her, Sands. Bathed in her blood, painted the walls with it...." He cleared his throat and looked away.

I counted to ten in my head and ran a hand over my face. "Why didn't I hear about this? Incident this big should've been reported by all involved, including the Medical Care Unit."

He smiled. "Hence my request to talk to you about something that should but *can't* be reported."

I exhaled, counting to ten. "You had the five agents, the MCU personnel, and any possible witnesses to your temper tantrum *not* report the incident?"

He grinned, glowing with pride. "I run a tight ship."

I squinted. "That's one way of putting it. Another would be everyone covering your ass is defying the Council," I hissed.

He held a hand up. "Don't go there. They're protective of their alpha, that's all."

"That's a bit backwards, isn't it? Aren't you supposed to protect them?" I muttered.

He growled. "Don't piss me off, Sands. Won't end well with my track record lately."

"Holy dangling lobes," I whispered. "It happened *more* than once?"

"I've been having... shitstorm temper tantrums in the last couple of weeks."

Dear gods and wings, no. "Temper tantrums?" I almost squeaked. "You should've reported that the moment it happened! Alphas don't do temper tantrums out of the blue. That's why you're seeing me now."

"You know what happens to crazed alphas," he said grimly.

I shivered. "It was just a glass divider, Weiss. I'm sure the Council won't put you down, considering the circumstances...."

But I stopped myself there. Maybe they'd put him down especially because of the circumstances. After all, his mate, Amanda—who was going to be executed this week—had started up an antileader movement and killed one werewolf alpha and two vampire sires. Maybe getting rid of Weiss would help the Council place the blame on someone other than them—dead werewolves couldn't really defend their name, could they? Of course, the Weiss family had been providing alphas to the only Council-sanctioned werewolf pack for two generations, so the Council wouldn't go against them simply out of politics. Not when the Weiss of the day played ball with them. Not when the next Weiss in line was barely seven years old. But an alpha whose mate had been held in custody for a couple of weeks having "temper tantrums" now—anyone with half a mind would think it was rages. If they could claim just cause, and rages were that, then things might be different. I'd have to confirm if it was terminal stage or incipient. Incipient was easy to solve; terminal meant execution. If there was any chance of him not getting executed and me not getting blamed for either not knowing or knowing but not reporting, it had to be incipient.

I crossed my legs and arranged my tie, hoping to exorcize some of the restlessness from my system. "Tell me about the… tantrums."

He looked down for a moment, then back up to me. "Happened five or six times since Amanda was taken in. They start out of the blue, and before I know it, I'm in red and itching to taste everyone's blood, break their necks, crack their spines, and—"

I cleared my throat. "I get the picture. Have you tried… diffusing the cause?"

He frowned. "Doing what?"

I squirmed in my chair. "I mean, you know… a conjugal visit. It's why rages happen in mated couples, especially when one of the mates is a leader. They're a side effect of, you know… being without your mate for a while."

Heat crept up my face as I pictured Weiss "diffusing the cause." I swallowed thickly, hoping against hope my years-long teenagerish crush wouldn't show. Not now, of all times. *Sweet flapping wings, not now*, I thought desperately.

Weiss leaned forward and set his hands on his knees, shaking his head. I thought he was about to say something, but then he shook his head again, growled a little, seemed to want to speak—but didn't.

I frowned. "Weiss?"

"Fucking shit!" he snapped.

I froze for a moment. Was he going into a rage now? In a rush, I started to read his emotional grid. If he was going into a rage, I had seconds at best to drain the rage out of him. My skills were rusty, but I could do it if I had to. It went against my principles, though, which was why I'd become a therapist instead. Draining whatever emotional state someone went through was a momentary solution; it did nothing to help the underlying cause. But still, I'd choose being alive over being shredded to pieces by a raving mad werewolf of any kind—let alone Weiss, a mountain wolf, meaning one of the strongest and largest, and an alpha to boot.

As I read his emotional grid, though, the mystery only got thicker. "You're not going into a rage. You're embarrassed. Why would you be embarrassed?" I asked, stupefied.

Weiss was a lot of things, but shy was definitely not one of them. I couldn't actually remember seeing him embarrassed since I'd started working as counselor for the Bureau of Paranormal Investigation, where he was director. I'd been here for about five years.

He rubbed a hand over his face, then finally looked up. "You're not supposed to pull any of that fairy shit," he grumbled.

I cleared my throat. "Fey."

He grinned. "I kind of like 'fairy,' though."

I squinted. "I kind of think I'll report you to the Council if you use it again."

"You're just pissed you can't go tattle on me," he grumbled.

"You're just pissed you go on all fours when you shift, Mister Wolfman," I snapped.

He snorted. "As opposed to staying bipedal, like the lycans? Sorry to disappoint, Sands. I'm very fucking proud of being a werewolf. I'm not saying lycans aren't good, mind you. Travis and Rick are damn good guys, and they've proven that in my time of need. I don't have an issue with my form when I shift, Sands. Need I remind you that it's fey who have issues with us animal-like folks, werewolves and lycans alike?"

"It's not being animal-like that they have issues with. What Kingdom fey have a problem with is whatever they can't control directly. Believe me, I know."

He nodded. "Yeah, you do."

I took a good look at him, noticing how he tapped his foot against the floor. Though it was subtle, the message was clear. He was on edge even now. But it didn't make sense.

"You're asking me for a favor. Why push my buttons?"

"Can't help it," he growled.

I flinched. "Excuse me?"

"Edelweiss," he snarled.

Was his brain so flooded by hormones that he was losing his mind entirely? "What does that have to do with anything?"

"You reek of the shit," he growled.

I was still lost. "And?"

"I'll ask you just this once. Do you mean to convey the message that it conveys?"

I widened my eyes. "I take health supplements with edelweiss. If the message is there are things that could be improved in my system, then yes, I mean to convey that message, I guess."

He snorted. "Bullshit. It means something else when a Weiss is sniffing it," he snapped.

Crap. Why did that never cross my mind? Of course edelweiss would somehow mean something to a Weiss. I hadn't thought of checking the records for these kinds of links when I'd started taking my health supplements. Obviously, I should have. Though in my defense, I hadn't expected to come anywhere near Weiss, since he and all of his agents generally avoided me like a pest. My pulse spiked. I really hoped the scent didn't mean some sort of challenge, or I'd find myself on the receiving end of a prime beating in a matter of seconds.

"What does it mean?" I asked as calmly as I could.

If he were going to attack me here, his secret would get out. He wouldn't do it, no matter what the damn edelweiss meant. That was if he were still sane, which was yet to be determined. Actually, him ever being sane was yet to be determined. And I was positively flipping out of my mind for having a crush on the wacko. I cleared my mind, redirected my focus on him.

He looked up, searched my eyes. "Really don't know?"

I kept eye contact, though it wasn't advisable with an unstable alpha. "I really don't."

"Really?" he rumbled deep in his chest.

Shit. I was starting to get a hard-on. Definitely not the proper response in this situation. I needed a distraction, quickly. "You were going to tell me about diffusing the cause of the maybe-rages."

He growled deep in his chest, the sound crawling up my bones and resonating in my head. "Lack of conjugal visits isn't a factor."

"So you've been having them?"

"No," he snapped.

I frowned. "You lost me. Mated werewolves get incipient rages when they haven't… been with their mates for too long. If you have been, then you shouldn't be having rages—so it's some other cause, which isn't good news, but at least we'll know it won't get you executed. If you haven't been with your mate, then the rages are happening because of that. But they're incipient, easy to get rid of, so you have a conjugal visit, and the problem is solved."

"If not fucking Amanda would've given me rages, I would've been having them for years by now. All right?" he said, looking away.

What? "You mean you and your mate haven't… for years?" I asked, flabbergasted.

"Yes," he growled, squinting at me.

Shit, now I was feeling almost as awkward as he looked. "That's… interesting," I muttered.

"Me not fucking my mate is interesting?"

"No, I mean the fact you didn't get rages because of it. So it's not related to that now either, we might assume."

"Guess so."

I scratched my chin. "Uh-huh. Then where are these bouts of rage coming from?"

"Fuck me if I know," he grumbled.

I kind of wished I could, though it was totally outside the realm of possibility. Crush on him or not, I had no reason to think Weiss was anywhere near a possibility. For all I knew, he was straight, in fact—also impotent or severely blue-balled, and possibly insane. I still wished I could run the tip of my tongue all over his chest and nibble his collarbone, to begin with. I shook my head to clear those thoughts away. "Everything we discuss is in confidence, and it's important that you're sincere with me on this. Rages aren't something to play with," I said as kindly as I could.

He growled viciously. "I fucking know! Almost decapitated a guy on the street the other day. Don't lecture me, fey prince. I'm not a patient guy on the best of days. This isn't the time to goddamn test my patience."

I gulped, trying to ignore the prince jibe. "What I'm trying to get at is... you haven't been with Amanda because you didn't feel the physical need? Or have you been using... a replacement of sorts?"

He lifted an eyebrow. "You asking me if I fuck around or wank?"

My face heated up like crazy, enough to be sure I was blushing. "I'm asking if you've been repressing needs, or if you simply didn't have them. It's important. Hormones are the basis—"

"Amanda and I aren't up for discussion. I haven't been repressing shit, but I do get hard if that's what you're asking. I'm not limp-dicked."

Of course I pictured him hard the next second, because my mind worked in visuals like that. Sweat bubbled up on my temples. He already looked like he wanted to cap me, those icy light blue eyes fixing me with murderous intent. My whole body was tense, muscles full of energy and ready to make a run for it. It was irrational of course, a fight-or-flight response brought on by the intense vibe of doom he was emanating. But if I ran, that would be the end of me. To werewolves, someone trying to run away was like catnip. It only made it that much more fun to catch and kill you, got them all the more excited. I needed to steer this discussion away from my impending doom and more toward safer, less scary topics.

I cleared my throat. "Right. Would you be willing to have Dr. Black do your blood workup?"

He glared for a few moments, then sighed. "As long as my name won't be tied to the blood, yeah."

I nodded. "Don't worry, he's kind of a friend. I think I can ask for a favor."

"He found a replacement for that lab guy already?"

"Show must go on, right? Not like he's going to close up his practice because his lab technician strayed off the path."

"By straying off the path, you mean trafficking marking hormones and fucking with hierarchy," he hissed.

"Yeah. Dr. Black had nothing to do with that."

"I hope this time he picked a lab tech who won't try to start the fucking apocalypse," he commented spitefully.

I wasn't sure what the hell to say. Everything set him off, obviously. Any Amanda-related topic seemed to earn me extra murder points.

He looked up, those gorgeous eyes focused on me like lasers. "Until we sort this out, Sands, you're my new partner."

No freaking way. "What?"

two

"YOU HEARD me," he grumbled. "In case I get a rage, you have to be there to prevent me from lashing out. We both know you can, as fey."

Of course he had to use the right word now that he was angling for something.

"And we both know I'm not allowed to," I added, shaking my head. "The Fey Act prevents us from exercising our... special abilities on Council territory. Going against that would make me a criminal before the Council. I might like you alive, but I like me alive even more."

Weiss stood to his full, impressive height and stepped close to me. I expected some sort of intimidation act. He was Weiss after all—that came to him naturally. His hulking shape loomed over me, his breathing becoming the only thing I could hear. I swallowed and fought the urge to run the hell out of there.

"Look up, Edelweiss," he almost purred.

The tone was so incongruous with everything Weiss was that I did look up, wide-eyed. All the better, since him standing and me sitting gave me an almost cruel close-up with his crotch.

"There's an exception from the Fey Act," he said, grinning crookedly.

"What?" I screeched, shaking my head.

"Think about it, it would fit. You'd watch over my temper, make sure I won't do anything I'd regret later. Buy me enough time to find out what's going on," he added, his gaze turning sad.

This was just too much. "Is this a prank?" I asked incredulously. "You can't be asking me to hook up."

He grabbed my arms and pulled me to my feet. "Listen, Edel. If you report me, they'll put me down. You know they will—it's the law. The Council can't afford to do me—of all people—any favors, not after Amanda. They won't invest the time to look into it. What they will do is write it off as terminal rages and cap me. I'm not asking you to hook up. Just pretend that we're together for a while... until we figure out what's going on with me. If we can't find anything that can be solved in a couple of weeks, I'll go to the Council and turn myself in. Please," he whispered. "Do it for Alf at least, if not as a favor to me."

I gulped. "That's low, Weiss, bringing your seven-year-old into it."

His gaze darkened. "If I get a rage when he's around...." He trailed off and shook his head. "I'm asking you to prevent me from killing innocents. Begging isn't my thing. But I am begging you to help me now. I'm that desperate."

"Must be. Nobody ever comes through the door unless under dire circumstances," I said flatly. "There are other fey around. You could hook up with one of them—for real. They'd level your emotional grid on instinct. Why do you need me?"

"Because I trust you," he stated simply. "And so does the Council. Trusting someone new would be... difficult right now, for everyone."

"I understand that, but if you got a fey to fall for you for real, then—"

"Then I'd make the same mistake I did with Amanda," he said, looking down. "I may have been an idiot then, but I'd like to think I've learned some lessons from the whole fucking ordeal. You're my *only* option, Sands."

Weiss leaned in closer, too close. His scent invaded my lungs, the warmth of his body bringing sweat to my temples again. Blood pounded through my veins, the illusion I could somehow, by some miracle, get to touch his lips getting me high. I focused on my thoughts, ignoring my body. This was when it really mattered that I didn't give myself away. This was when I had to stand my ground, not let my private desires get in the way of my ethics. Ethics were important for a therapist... but Weiss wrapped his arms around me slowly, as if giving me time to bolt. I didn't try, I didn't move... I didn't even dare breathe, waiting to feel his arms close around me. I hated myself instantly for it, but after years of dreaming, and hoping, and stealing glances… the man of my hot, sweaty dreams was going to hold me.

"If I have to actually seduce you, then I will, Edel," he whispered with a grin in his voice.

I flattened my lips. "Oh, because I'm that easy, you think?"

He chuckled in a self-deprecating way. "Because I'm that desperate."

My heart broke a little. Of course he'd think seducing me was such a terrible task that he'd only resort to it out of sheer desperation. I tried to hide my hurt feelings, brush them under the carpet. I looked down, hoping my gaze wouldn't give me away. "You're not my type," I stated coldly.

"You were Travis's boyfriend for a while there, so I know you like the leader type."

Shit, this was just what I needed. His mentioning Travis didn't help at all with my conviction to not do this. I'd broken up with Travis because I'd realized I was actually pining away after Weiss the whole time Travis and I were together. Either Weiss knew, or his killer alpha instincts were pushing him in the right direction. If I balanced his emotions without us being a couple officially, the Council would find out. They had fey consultants to keep an eye out for anyone fiddling with emotional grids. They'd take me in, PBI counselor or not. And Weiss did have a point on the trust thing. He'd have to trust some stranger with a secret that would get him killed, were it to get out.

When alphas got terminal rages, it wasn't treatable. Their hormones turned them into wild, senseless monsters—they had to be put down, for everyone's sake. A raving mad Weiss would be even more dangerous than anyone. His family was known for their incredible genes and strength. The thought alone gave me the chills. If the Council got wind of this, they'd put him down—no doubt about it. I couldn't, in good conscience, turn down his plan, not under these circumstances. Not when a seven-year-old kid—whose mom was going to be executed this week—depended on him.

Weiss was all Alf would have. I couldn't allow the poor kid to become an orphan. Nobody would ever take in a Weiss alpha-to-be, and we all knew Alf had the alpha hormones. Weiss had gotten him tested. Only a matter of time before the kid reached adulthood and the hormones started flooding his system. I couldn't just leave Weiss to his fate, not when he'd saved my life five years ago. Not when the thought of a world without him strangled me.

I looked up. "Don't try to pull that crap with me. I'll help you because, despite this bastard move of yours, you're a good guy. I'll help because you have a seven-year-old son who's about to lose his mother, and you're all he's got. I'll do this because it's scientifically interesting to explore the case. But don't think you can sucker me into it with a grope or a fuck. I can help you right now because I'm half fey. That also means I know when you're pretending…. I know what you feel as you're feeling it. You can't bullshit me, Weiss. And stop calling me Edel."

He chuckled darkly and took two steps back, assessing me with more interest than he'd ever shown. "Well, go figure. Little Edel has some teeth of his own, and he knows how to bite."

"I don't think that pissing me off is what you should go for right now."

"Maybe not. But it's fun."

"Get out of here, Weiss. Go home, think on this until tomorrow morning. If you're set on going ahead with it, we'll start this show then."

He stuck his hands in his pockets and cocked his head to the side. "Oh, no. You're coming home with me. Don't look so stricken, we'll just pretend to be a couple. But we won't pretend the being together part. We are going to be together, all the time, from now until we figure this shit out. I can't take the chance of a rage happening when I'm at home."

I shivered. "You mean you want us to be nose to nose 24-7? Are you insane?"

He snorted. "I don't think therapists are allowed to use the word. Not nose to nose literally, unless your magic trick requires it?"

"We don't have to be too close, but in the same house for sure. I'm not strong enough to pull it off over long distances," I begrudgingly admitted.

It wasn't something to be proud of. The whole couple dispensation had been given in the Fey Act because being involved with someone made fey balance their lover's emotional grid on reflex. We couldn't really help doing it for our lovers—those we actually loved, to be precise. It didn't matter where they were. But for a long-term singleton fey like me, it was a rusty skill to balance emotional grids. My balancing muscles were dusty and flappy from lack of use. The fact I had a crush on him did help, though I hoped he didn't know about it. But it would still be hard work for me.

"There you go," he said. "You're coming home with me until we solve this shitty situation."

"You mean you want us to actually live together while we're pretending?"

He nodded.

"Starting tonight?" I asked in a faint voice.

He nodded again.

"It won't look good. You're still officially with Amanda, even if her execution is just around the corner."

"You think anyone will be outraged because I'm betraying *her*? If anything, it will show my pack that I still have some sort of balls. They might start doubting that fact after what Amanda did. Besides, a mating is just like a human marriage. Putting an end to it officially is more of a technicality when it's clear everything is over. It doesn't keep some from moving on. It wouldn't keep a werewolf alpha from moving on. It won't."

"You're going to use a fling with me as proof of balls? Seriously?"

"Actually, I'll be using it as my chance to keep breathing. But if my pack thinks I'm over Amanda, I certainly won't mind it. Nobody will. And it won't look like a fling at all."

"Sweet flapping wings, what have I gotten myself into?" I muttered, shaking my head and looking at him.

"You're saving my life, Sands. Shitting around aside, I'll owe you big time. I'm sure it'll come in handy to have the PBI director at your mercy," he added.

I breathed out slowly. "Yeah... I can just picture you being at my mercy, totally in character for you."

He laughed—loud, full, and rich. The sound made my heart jump in my throat, and I found myself shaking my head and smiling. I allowed warmth to spread through my heart for a moment. Looking on the bright side, I'd get to spend a lot of time with my crush. He was probably annoying, had smelly morning breath, and farted while he slept. After a week or two of that, I'd finally get over him. And I would earn a lot of favors from him in the long run, provided he didn't end up dead during this experiment—and didn't get me killed either. I knew just the thing his support would work wonders on. He wouldn't like it, I was sure, but that was the funny part about favors: once you owed them, you had to deliver.

All I had to do was spend all of my time with a man I'd been fantasizing about for years, balance his emotional grid, and not give away my stupid crush. How hard could that be?

In my car, I followed Weiss to his home. My poor little car looked as tired and weary as I felt most days, but just like me, she did her job well day in, day out and didn't make any fuss about it either. I tailed Weiss's Beamer, listening to The Cure on the radio and tapping the rhythm on the steering wheel with my thumbs. I stopped at a red light and looked out at a couple crossing the street. They were young, probably in their twenties if I were to guess. Two beautiful young people, holding hands and smiling at each other as rain started trickling down from moody gray skies. It was one of those oddly harmonious moments, the kind that could go on a card and touch you after just one glance. Something about the warmth of their gazes seemed to light up the whole street. The subtle strength of their grip as they held hands created a kind of gravitational force all its own, and their smiles were so bright they merged into the glorious sun of this new planet of their togetherness. But then they melted into the crowd of pedestrians on the other side of the street, and the warmth left with them. Everything shifted, the memory of the harmony of their presence turned cold in my chest, and for a moment I couldn't breathe. I closed my eyes for a second, wanting to smile and hit my head against the wheel at the same time.

After I opened my eyes again, the world looked different. I hated and admired it from my cold, lonely corner of the singledom universe. From my viewpoint, everything now looked gloomy and heavy as rain poured down in earnest, all the extra weight pressing down on my very soul and making it hard to breathe. The street looked like black waters eager to swallow us all down and feed us to the starving monsters underneath. There was no lifesaver, no ship to rescue me from these icy black waters, and I had no idea how to swim. And we hadn't even been pretending to be a couple for a full hour yet…. The future looked bright right now—not.

The light turned green, and I resumed tailing Weiss. This evening I wasn't going to my empty apartment and my empty personal life. I was going to celebrate my lack of a love life by sleeping close to the man I wanked to—oh, the sheer joy. Sure, I had friends. We went out once or twice a month, and spent the time mostly talking about their boyfriends, girlfriends, wives and husbands, their kids, their in-laws, their vacations, or remodeling plans. I was the only single thirtysomething person in my group of friends, and considering my line of work, it often ended in freebie therapy sessions anyway. All friendships went that way, I guessed, only mine included considerably less reciprocity. I didn't talk about my Weiss crush to anyone, not my human friends, not my supernatural ones—nobody. It would do me no good to get the condescending or commiserating glances it would earn me. I threw my own pity parties just fine by myself; no need to invite others to them too.

We finally arrived at Weiss's house. Of course he didn't live in a complex, like the rest of the PBI personnel. The man had a house with gateway security and the works. It occurred to me that I should call the Moonglow complex, the building where my apartment was, compliments of the PBI. Security had to know I was going to spend time somewhere else. After Weiss got in through the gates, the guy covering security there waved me to stop.

"Evening," he said flatly. "PBI registration, please."

Well, wasn't he bright as sunshine. I felt like a teenager caught with a tent in his pants during class as he wrote down my ID details and threw me a few curious glances.

"Spending the night?" he asked, not looking me in the eye.

I cleared my throat. "Yes."

"I'll notify security at Moonglow. Good night," he recited and held out my PBI registration.

I didn't make eye contact either as I took it. My face burned as I went through the gates. I watched in my rearview mirror as they closed. The guard shook his head, seemingly not impressed with his alpha's choice for a fuck-toy. He'd sure be happy to know we were only pretending, but of course the whole point of this act was for everyone to think we *were* sleeping together. I was pretty sure that by the time I made it up the stairs into Weiss's house, half the pack would know I was spending the night with their alpha. By tomorrow morning it would be official—Timothy Sands, Herman Weiss's fuck-toy. I could just add that to my CV, it would be that widely known. Why the fuck had I agreed to this mess? So Weiss wouldn't get killed and I'd get juicy favors from him, right. And he sort of saved my ass from getting Fey Court duty or getting killed. I owed the bastard. I had a feeling I'd need to remind myself of that often.

After I parked, I got out of the car and walked to the front door, where Weiss was waiting for me. And as I climbed the three stairs that separated us, looking up into his bright blue eyes made my stomach clench tight and sent a pang through my heart. *Just remember this is all a game*, I reminded myself. *Don't get carried away. Don't allow the disease of your crush to get any worse than it already is.* Feeling sorry for myself didn't help or change things, but sometimes I couldn't stop that train. Didn't mean I had to ride it for more than the one station, though.

"Safe to talk here?" I asked, looking around.

He nodded.

"How will we do this?"

"You get the spare bedroom beside mine. I've got a cook and a house caretaker, so whatever you need, tell them and they'll get it. Of course, when we go to sleep we'll spend some time together, sell it to the staff too. Then you go sleep in the spare bedroom. They already know I snore bad."

I frowned. "You snore so bad that the staff can hear it?"

He shook his head and looked away.

Oh-kay…. "What about your son?" I asked in a small voice.

He sighed. "He's seven. Don't tell him anything unless he asks about it. And if he does, just tell him to ask me."

"But won't he feel uncomfortable with a stranger in—"

His gaze snapped to mine. "My family is none of your concern, Edel. Keep your eyes on the ball, and everything will work out just fine."

I lifted my eyebrows. "You do remember I'm the one doing you a favor here, right? What's up with the tone and attitude?"

He ran a hand through his hair. "Sorry. I'm just so pissed about it all."

"We could talk about it, if you'd like. I mean, I am a counselor," I added, smiling.

He snorted. "Right. Because on top of this clusterfuck, having a shrink poke through my head is exactly what I want."

The bitterness of his tone stung. "Excuse me for trying to help. Maybe I'll just refrain from it and go home, how about that?" I snapped and turned to walk away.

His arm shot out and grabbed me before I could even register the movement. "You're staying right here," he growled.

It wasn't a playful kind of growl either, not the regular one he regaled the Bureau with on a daily basis. It was the nasty, "I'll go for your throat" kind of growl that meant business—at least that's how it sounded to me.

I flinched. "Weiss…."

"Shut the fuck up and do your magic fey trick, Edel."

I scanned his emotional grid and the blood in my veins turned to ice. His rage was a monumental mass of bright red, burning hot—almost to the point of melting the eyes out of my head. I doused the mass with cool, blue, calming energy for a couple of minutes. I was rusty, that was true—but still, this kind of intensity… it was overwhelming. Frankly, I was shocked nobody had gotten killed yet if all of his rages had been like this. At least, I hoped nobody had gotten killed.

"Done," I said faintly. "Feeling better?"

So much tension had drained away, his face looked relaxed. Fey exchange had that effect: loosened people up, relaxed them, balanced them for a while. How long it lasted depended on the level of skill and practice of the fey doing it, and I figured it would last him until tomorrow evening, more or less.

"Wow," he murmured. "If I'd known it's this good, I would've gotten it done years ago."

"It's not a facial," I snapped as I swayed on my feet.

He gripped me with both hands and held me steady. "You all right?"

Was I? "Yeah. Sorry, it took the wind out of me because I haven't been exchanging for a while."

He frowned. "Didn't know it would hurt you. I wouldn't have asked if I'd known."

I smiled. "I'm just rusty, don't worry about it. I'll be fine after some sleep."

"You sure?" he asked with what seemed like real concern.

"Yeah. We going in or what?"

He nodded.

"You can let go now," I said, trying to extricate myself from his grip.

He snorted. "Stop squirming. I'm letting go when there's a sitting surface under your ass."

"I'm not a child," I said, squinting.

"I know."

"Then don't treat me like one," I said, trying to get free of his grip again.

He pulled me close and shook me a bit. "What, is the physical contact that unbearable? Afraid I'll ruin your outfit? My paws aren't muddy," he gritted out.

"This isn't a rage brewing, it can't be. So what the fuck is up with the attitude?" I asked, wide-eyed.

He looked down into my eyes for a few moments, his icy stare giving me the chills and taking my breath away at the same time. He had that effect on me, like I was dropped under cold, cold water, and the air was slapped out of my lungs for a moment. My heart was beating violently, and I felt my bones almost go liquid.

"Edelweiss," he hissed.

"You keep saying that. What the hell does it mean?"

He let go of me, stepped back. "God fucking damn it, I'm sorry. I'm sorry."

He stormed away, pushing through the front doors and exploding inside like a tornado. I only caught a few glimpses of his grid as he walked away, but what I did see was interesting to say the least—yearning and regret. I walked inside and closed the door behind me, going over the whole thing in my mind. Yearning? He didn't want me. I was pretty sure of that much. Then why would he—?

"You smell like tailup," a tiny version of Weiss said from my left.

three

I JUMPED. The tiny figure that just appeared there had scared the crap out of me. "Ugh, hi there. Didn't hear you coming," I stammered. "Were you standing there for a while?"

He shook his head of black hair. Weiss's icy blue eyes looked up at me from the kid's face, a note of meanness to them, even though the kid wasn't glaring at me right now. At least I thought he wasn't glaring; with Weisses it was hard to tell. For a tiny thing, he looked pretty impressive, I had to give him that. A tiny Weiss, already a striking appearance at seven. Wow.

"What did you say I smell like?"

He grinned. "Tailup." Then he turned and ran away. "Dad's home, *diiiiinner*!" he screamed.

I wasn't sure if it was for my benefit or someone else's. I ran both hands over my face. How was I supposed to handle this? Alf was no ordinary seven-year-old, not that I had too much experience with those either. But still, someone just showing up like this had to be uncomfortable for him, seeing me around in his house.... Weiss didn't strike me as the explaining type either. Didn't he care about his son's feelings? Tiny werewolf alpha or not, he was still a kid.

A plump young man showed up from behind a corner. He frowned, looked at me for a while, then smiled. "You must be the guest Security called about?"

I bit the inside of my cheek. "Yeah. I'm Tim," I said, reaching out to shake his hand.

He sniffed a couple of times, shook my hand, and smiled wider. "Bert. Any particular preference for dinner? You vegan or anything like that?"

He said "vegan" like it was a disease, which would've been almost funny if it hadn't been annoying. "No, I'm not. Why?"

He snorted. "Thinking I should know since I'll be feeding you. It's good that you eat meat. I don't trust anyone who lives off of grazing," he muttered, walking away.

I pinched the bridge of my nose. Brilliant, Weiss's "staff" was just as delightful as he was. It made sense, but I'd been hoping to find easier people to get along with. Hope, it seemed, was foolish.

Weiss walked down a flight of stairs wearing dark sweats and a black sleeveless shirt. His shoulders seemed wider than usual, his arms more muscled and tense, ready to do damage. The impressive length of his legs looked slick and strong even in those sweats, the floppy fabric accentuating the sturdy elegance of his every move. His hair looked wet, like he'd thrown some water over his face before changing. Dear magic wands, the man was gorgeous. My throat went instantly dry. I looked away quickly and visualized sausages—it was my antiboner tactic. No idea what it was about them, maybe the minced meat, but it always killed my friskiness.

"Hope you don't expect formal wear for dinner, your highness," he grumbled as he walked by me.

Yet another jibe at my unpleasant lineage, lovely. Easy to ignore at the moment, though—I swallowed thickly as I looked at his ass— sweet flapping wings, you could bounce quarters off of it. "Just occurred to me that I don't have a change of clothes."

He sat at the dining room table and waved me to join him. "Good, you'll show up to work tomorrow wearing the same clothes you had on today. If you're worried about sleeping and shit, I'll give you something. Not sure what, exactly, you're smaller than Amanda," he said, looking me over with too much attention.

I cleared my throat. "I do have my gym bag in the trunk, don't worry."

He lifted an eyebrow. "Gym? Seriously?"

"What's that supposed to mean?"

"Sit down," he barked.

I did. Bert came out with a stack of plates, set one in front of Weiss and me and an extra three.

"Didn't take you for the gym type," Weiss said as he stretched his legs under the table until his foot brushed mine.

"What, because I'm not a pack of muscles like you?" I asked, irritated.

He grinned. "Thanks, didn't know you were paying attention. No, because I never saw you at the Bureau's gym."

"I go to a regular gym."

He set his elbows on the table and leaned in. "Why the fuck would you do that?"

"Because I like their equipment," I muttered under my breath.

Especially liked Sammy's equipment. He was my personal trainer there. I liked human fuck buddies. They made me feel less like an outcast for some reason. Among the PBI crowd, I was always something of an odd duckling. Fey didn't mix well with others, which meant they usually didn't mix at all. Pretty much a closed-off community, save for some officials and diplomats. Most of the time, I was the only fey around the Bureau.

Weiss frowned. "Some fuck buddy there I need to know about?"

Crap. I widened my eyes. "How's that any of your business?" I hissed.

"Everything about you is my business from now on, Edel."

"Stop calling me that!" I said through gritted teeth.

Alf ran in and plopped into a chair. "Is Tailup your friend?" he asked, looking at his dad.

Weiss's icy gaze landed on his son, and then a miracle happened. Those light blue eyes lit up with warmth as he gazed at his kid. He even smiled, which stopped my heart midbeat.

"His name is Tim," Weiss said, still smiling.

"Tim Tailup?" Alf asked, fluttering his eyelashes.

Weiss grinned. "Just Tim, to you."

Alf glared at me in his so-Weiss way and I wanted to giggle. "Smells like tailup to me," the little guy said in a surprisingly firm tone.

Weiss growled, or more like emitted a strange combo between a growl and a sort of purr. "Don't make me come over there."

Alf grinned, apparently fairly proud of himself, then shrugged. "Okay, but he does smell like it."

To my utter surprise, Weiss snorted, then smiled wider. Alf blinked those long lashes at his dad, then grinned wickedly. The kid had him wrapped around his little finger. Weiss seemed almost like a different man, a softer, kinder version of him that was even more charming. It made me wonder how he might've been if he hadn't been alpha, but then again the thought itself was silly. If he hadn't been alpha, he wouldn't have been Weiss—the Weiss I was so taken with. Watching him with his son didn't help kill my crush, not at all. But it was a thing of beauty to observe them together; I could already tell. They just clicked in a way my dad and I never did, for instance. Remembering him brought me down, and that wasn't a mood I wanted to be in tonight. Sweet gods and wings, this was just too much for a poor fey-slash-elf like me.

I looked between them, totally lost. "What's a tailup?"

Alf grinned. "When you're lifting your tail for a Weiss," he explained cheerily.

My mouth hung open for a moment. "What?"

"Alf, you're gonna get grounded," Weiss warned.

"Fine," the little guy grumbled. He looked at me, wearing this serious expression. "When someone smells like you do, it's an invitation to mate. Tradition and stuff, you know?" he asked, looking up at me. "Aunt Tish calls it a tailup—tail up, see?" he explained, gesturing with his hands.

"Your Aunt Tish is a moron," proclaimed Weiss.

Alf frowned. "I like her. She tells me stuff you don't."

"If I don't tell you, then you don't have to know," his father informed him.

I grabbed a glass of wine as soon as it appeared within my reach. I felt like I was witnessing a weird kind of cheerful family argument, only when I thought things were headed toward the little guy getting grounded, Weiss would throw in some random grin like he was proud instead of pissed. This was a whole other planet, planet alpha, and I had no idea how to speak their language.

"Bert says you won't make me alpha. I make myself," Alf said.

Weiss said something, but I tuned out the discussion for a while because—wow. I looked at this mini-Weiss version and had to admit he was kind of charming even now, at seven. He had a more commanding presence than me, and I was almost five times his age. It occurred to me that Weiss alphas tended to be so tough and respected because in order to become one, they had to survive and outdo their dads, which seemed a tall task. A task that even as a seven-year-old, Alf seemed compelled to achieve. Though he didn't really mean to, everything he did challenged his dad's authority—it was instinct, probably. I didn't envy Weiss the witnessing of Alf's teenager years, that was a damn sure fact. Though it might be funny to watch the two of them from the peanut gallery.

And as I admired the battle of wills going on, I suddenly realized that while Weiss's and my charade was going on, I would be collateral damage in this war of alpha wills. Had Amanda felt this way too? Not so fun to watch from the peanut gallery, maybe—it meant you weren't part of their odd nasty/sweet chemistry. Not that it was new to me, being on the outside. I gulped down more wine.

"You look terrified," Weiss said, lightly, slapping my shoulder.

I looked at him. "What?"

He laughed. "Don't let the little wolf see fear. He'll ride you without mercy."

"I'm not little," Alf whined, frowning.

I thought for a moment about Weiss riding me, which of course prompted another drink of wine. "I'm sure I'll manage," I said, smiling.

Alf sniffed at me and wriggled his nose, then focused on eating. Another two people had joined the table, Bert and a chick who kept giving me death glares. I dug into my food, suddenly eager to do anything but talk. Pack life was a constant game of politics and for an outsider like me, it made things difficult, to say the least. While I knew in theory how to act and react, finding myself at Weiss's dinner table sort of blew all my knowledge to hell. And I realized as I ate that I smelled to all of them like a "tailup," as Alf had so artistically put it. That bastard Weiss didn't tell me, of course; I had to find out from his son. I was sitting at his table with his son and two pack members, smelling like a widely open invitation for him—or someone else—to ride me into this pack. Damn it! I choked on a piece of meat.

Weiss slapped my back and sent the meat flying out of my throat. I watched, horrified, as the bit flew over the table, then hit the opposite wall, falling to the floor. I watched in what felt like slow motion as everyone's gazes trailed its flight and landing, then looked back at me. My face was beet red, no doubt, and I made to get up and clean it away.

Weiss set his hand over mine. "Tricia or Bert will clean that up after dinner," he stated.

Said Tricia gave me a double dose of the death glare she'd been giving me anyway, and Bert only gave me a cursory glance as he bit into a chunk of meat instead of cutting it in morsels. Looked to me more like they wanted to clean up my dead body than the meat I'd choked on.

I shook my head. "Thanks, but I'll—"

"Wasn't a question," Alf snapped at me in his angel-like seven-year-old voice.

I looked between him and his dad, then nodded, mortified. What I really wanted to do was run the hell out of here, but then again, I'd agreed to do this for a reason—or a couple of them. I swallowed down my anxiety and resumed eating, this time paying more attention to each bite. The least I could do was not embarrass myself during this meal—again.

Soon the awkward affair of dinner was, thank the gods, finally over—and without any more embarrassing incidents. Bert took Alf upstairs to bed—after a long and arduous argument that he didn't have to go to bed like a kid, since the rest of us "men" were staying up. The kiddo was cute in an obnoxious-slash-adorably bossy way, kind of like his dad.

Weiss and I were in the living room now, while Tricia prepared the bedroom Weiss had assigned me.

"I don't like having people do things for me," I said after a gulp of wine.

My third glass of the night, and I just barely managed to feel less like I was under a microscope in this house.

Weiss took a swig of his whiskey. "Would've thought you're used to it, your highness," he said, watching me with something very much like malice.

"I wish you'd stop saying that. See a throne under my ass? I'm not royalty, not since I walked out on my father. At which point he sent out assassins after me, and almost managed to kill me. Something I'm sure you remember, since you're the one who saved me."

He took another healthy swig of whiskey. "Tell you the truth, I always thought that might've been staged."

I frowned. "By whom and for what?"

"Infiltrate the Bureau. You do remember fey weren't involved with us back then."

"Why defend me, then? Play into the trap?"

He shrugged. "Best way to see what you were after."

"So you took me into the Bureau for the same reason?"

He grinned over the rim of his glass. "I knew it was for real by then. I could've used a counselor I owned."

Shivers traveled up my spine at the word—owned. "You think you own me?"

"Didn't pursue it in the end. But I could have."

"Owned me?" I asked in the coolest voice I could manage.

"You owed me big. It was a card I had to call in at any time."

"But you didn't, for five years. Didn't find any use for it?"

"Thought I should save it for something… special."

I smacked my lips. "Like endangering my career, which you did help me start out, and possibly getting me in Bureau custody or worse?"

His gaze smoldered. "Like saving my life. Fair trade, isn't it? A life for a life."

We looked at each other over the rims of our glasses in the dim light of his living room. I remembered the night he saved me as if it were yesterday. My father's lackeys had cornered me in an alley. By the time Weiss had come in, I'd gotten three of them down. But they'd gotten at me too, and the remaining one was just about to kill me. Weiss had been in his wolf form, glorious gray coat bristling and his thick growl filling up the whole alley with its intensity. He'd gone for the assassin's throat; one clean jump and the fey was dead. Then he'd sniffed me, licked his snout, and stepped back to change. It was my first and last time seeing Weiss naked, but I still remembered every ridge and curve of his body. The image was emblazoned in my mind, with cinematic special effects like an angelic glow around his naked body and background music in a jazzy mix of trumpet and sax. Each and every time I saw him again after that, for a split second I was back there, in that alley—and he was making a superhero entrance and saving me. Except superheroes didn't come back and ask you to return the favor.

"And after this, you don't 'own' me anymore?" I asked before taking another sip of wine.

He shrugged.

"I still don't like people doing things for me," I grumbled.

"Get used to it. It's politics," he stated simply.

I lifted an eyebrow. "How so?"

"Bert and Tricia are the kids of my father's beta. They had to fight everyone claiming the right to become my betas, and they won. It's a privilege for them to be here, at my service. Doesn't matter if they're ironing my boxers or killing intruders," he said, shrugging.

I blinked. "They iron your boxers?"

He snorted. "Don't take everything so literally, Edel," he said, grinning.

I glared. "Don't call me Edel. How many times must I—"

Within a second he was standing in front of me, pulling me to my feet. My glass of wine clanked against the hardwood floor, the bit of wine it still hosted now drawing a tiny bloodred splash on the floor. His hands held my arms, digging into my flesh hard enough to make me wince. He nuzzled my hair, taking his time, our skin touching here and there as he moved his head. My pulse sped up insanely, muscles burning with the rush. There'd be no way to make this hard-on go away, not without cumming.

"What are you doing?" I barely managed to whisper due to a lack of air.

"Just pretend to enjoy it," he murmured.

"But why—"

His lips touched mine, and the world exploded in bright colors. My heart jumped in my throat, and my stomach tightened in a knot of anticipation as every nerve ending in my body tingled. I shook, a body-wide shiver that I was sure he felt. One of his hands cupped my nape and angled my head back and up as his mouth fastened on mine again with almost deadly intent. I gasped, and despite trying to push down a trembling moan, something of it made it into his mouth. He hummed, a strange mix between a growl and what sounded like bliss. His tongue dipped into my mouth and glided against mine, a tender caress that had my toes curling. Strength left my body, my hands dangling at my sides uselessly. He held me as he wanted, wrapping his other hand around my middle and pressing me against the hard line of his magnificent body. I thought I was going to die—killed by sensory overload and the looming despair of having to deal with this memory for the rest of my miserable life. I'd been an idiot thinking this would be the perfect opportunity to put an end to my crush on him. I was kidding myself, fooling myself into imagining this wouldn't be the worst mistake I could ever make. But it was, by far, the worst. This would hurt.

He released my lips and looked down into my eyes, those bright blue eyes of his now looking dark, stormy, and hot... so hot that my lungs burned. I took in a deep breath, trying desperately to swim in these arctic waters.

"Why did you do that?" I whispered.

He smiled. "This is our first night together, Edel. I want you. I'm eager to have you. What else would I be doing but taking every chance I can to have you close?"

I inhaled sharply, searching his gaze for some trace of truth. But there wasn't anything there now, only the cold arctic planes of his will. Acting. He was acting, but for whose benefit?

"There's no audience for this show," I mumbled.

The sound of glass crashing against the floor came from upstairs, and I thought I heard a woman's voice cursing.

"Tricia?" I asked, frowning.

"Yeah. Surveillance system."

"In the house? We'll pretend even in the house? What... what kind of—"

He rubbed his lips against mine, shutting me up. "Relax, no cameras in the bedrooms and no mikes anywhere. After we go up, you'll take a T-shirt of mine to sleep in, and that will be it."

I frowned. "Why do that?"

"So you'll smell of me," he murmured, grinning.

I swallowed thickly. "You're getting too much of a kick out of this."

He chuckled. "It's a challenge. I like challenges—especially winning them."

"You could've warned me your plan included such a hands-on approach," I gritted through my teeth.

His gaze focused on mine, some sort of curiosity bubbling up in those arctic depths. "You don't seem too displeased with it, if the hard-on poking my thigh is any indication."

My face heated up, and I frowned. "Well, you stuck your tongue down my throat and rubbed against my crotch, what did you expect?"

"Didn't expect anything. It's a pleasant surprise."

I frowned. "That I can get hard?"

He grinned crookedly. "That you get hard for me. Makes it all the more believable."

I pushed against his chest. "Let go of me, asshole."

He wouldn't budge, though. "Don't take it so *hard*, Edel," he said, still grinning.

I squinted. "You mean not as hard as you're taking it? Because it's not your gun poking at my stomach," I shot back spitefully.

"Well, it's a kind of a gun," he said, totally relaxed.

"Did we pretend long enough for your staff? Can you let go of me now?"

He sighed and stepped back, rearranging his hard-on. I turned away to do the same, my eardrums pounding and eyes stinging. I was in the clear for now, the groping and smooching had gotten us both hard so it didn't mean anything. Healthy men got hard when they fooled around, and I could guess we were both just as rusty in the couple department—that had to be it.

"Bedroom's ready," Tricia snapped from the living room's door.

"Thanks," Weiss replied huskily. "We'll go up in a moment. Night, Tricia."

"Night," she grumbled and stomped away.

I turned to face the smooching monster. "What's up with her?"

He shrugged, seeming totally relaxed about the hard-on he sported. "One of those wanting to compete for the spot."

"You mean the job of being your squeeze?"

"My mate."

I gaped. "What, they're putting in CVs or something? Applying for the job?"

He slid his hands in his pockets. "Pack politics. They announce the desire to compete for my attention, fight it out among themselves, unless I tell them they don't stand a running chance."

I pinched the bridge of my nose. "You mean they actually fight it out?"

"Unless I tell them each they don't stand a running chance," he repeated.

"So either you tell them you're not interested, or they get the magnificent reward of plucking their eyes out with the others you are interested in? That's just lovely," I added dryly.

He clacked his tongue. "Barbaric, yes. I know what fey think of our politics."

"It's really annoying when you do that, lump me in with fey opinions like I can't think for myself. Do you see anyone else but me in this room?"

He shook his head.

"Then ask me what I think about things, don't presume to already know. You don't know shit about me."

We looked at each other for a while, the silence growing tense. I'd had enough of his you're-so-fey bullshit. After the whole making-out scene, I was confused, hurt, and turned on—not the most patient state of mind.

He looked at me for a while longer, then said, "You're right. I'm just used to seeing very… like-minded fey."

I snorted. "Right, because you've known so many in your life. How many others outside of my executioners five years ago, and Council lackeys?"

He lifted his eyebrows. "Don't like the Fey King's emissaries?"

"Why would I? Just because I'm fey?" I snapped.

"Didn't know you felt so strongly."

"Well, newsflash: you're not the only one in the world who feels, strongly or not."

"Fair enough," he said, nodding. "Lemme show you your room," he said, turning away and walking toward the stairs.

four

I FOLLOWED, trying to calm down the storm of desire, frustration, and annoyance bubbling inside me. I didn't know what I'd expected would happen, but nothing of what was happening was it. I certainly hadn't imagined choking on food, being molested, and then feeling Weiss get hard after the molestation. Truth be told, the most annoying thing wasn't even his usual lack of tact. The most annoying thing was how everything seemed to affect me, and it was just the first day.

Weiss stood by an open door and cocked his head to the side. "This is you. And this," he said, turning slightly to the side, "is me."

The doors were side by side, so we'd be close enough. I made to go into my bedroom, half expecting him to grab my arm again. Maybe somewhere deep in my heart, I actually wished he would. Because I was starting to get used to the idea I would feel his hands on me, even if it was just to manhandle me... because I desperately wanted to feel him any way I could, and this disaster of a situation was giving me the cruel hope that I might.

But he didn't stop me; in fact he closed the bedroom's door after I went in. I locked the door from the inside, wanting to make a point. The room was spacious, with nice, sturdy furniture and clean, minimalist lines. The bed was made: soft white sheets and plenty of fluffy pillows waiting for me. My gym bag sat by the bed, so obviously either Tricia or Bert had gone through my trunk. I just hoped it wasn't Tricia, or I'd have to worry she'd cut my brakes or something.

I pulled my shoes off, took my shirt off, and shook off my pants. I strolled into the bathroom, delighted to find fluffy white towels waiting for me in there. I still had a hard-on to appease, and after all the tension of the day I really needed a nice long hot shower. Mint-scented shower gel, soap, and shampoo were waiting for me on a shelf inside the shower cabin. My heart pounded as I started the water and felt it glide down my body. The spray had a lovely pressure, the caress on my skin easing some of the stress away. I ran my palms down my chest, then grabbed my hard-on with one hand and stroked myself a couple of times while I cupped my balls with the other. I imagined the hands were his because he was my constant fantasy. Blood pounded through my veins as soon as I imagined him with me, many of the real-life details of tonight filling in the generic lines of my former fantasies.

Now I felt his scent envelop me. I felt the shape of his body against me like I had earlier in the living room. I felt his lips on mine, hot and almost abrasive in his careless hunger. My dick pounded, heavy and weeping precum as I stroked myself harder, faster. I opened my mouth under the spray of water, allowed the sensation of my full mouth to translate into Weiss's tongue invading it with greed. My hand moved faster as I gripped my balls and massaged them inside my sack. My heart skipped a beat, tension pounding into my eardrums. I imaged him grabbing my hair and pushing me face-first into the wall, his hard-on pushing against my asscheeks, his hard body looming over mine. Close, so close to me, his hot breath fanning over my shoulder as his lips rubbed against the shell of my ear. "Ask for it," I imagined him growling. "Please," I whispered brokenly. "Please," I said, as my hand rubbed my dick furiously. I imagined his tip rubbing against my hole, my whole body exploding in a chant of gratitude to whatever gods would've granted me that wish. My heart stopped, and I opened my eyes wide as my orgasm tingled down my spine, buzzed through my balls, and finally exploded out of me in thick, white streams. I let go of my balls and propped my hand against the wall, leaning against the tile as my knees weakened. I gripped my dick harder as the last shivers of my orgasm zinged through my nerve endings.

For that one short moment, I felt relieved. I felt light, almost weightless. I could inhale at full lung capacity, no weight pulling me down to the very bottom of arctic depths. But then the moment was over, and icy water fell over me again despite the shower's warmth. I rubbed a hand over my face, drizzled some shower gel in my hands, and washed myself quickly. By the time I'd rinsed and gotten out of the shower, I already felt heavy, almost too heavy to move. Wrapping the fluffy white towel around my hips, I used another one to pat myself and my hair dry. It looked like a blond mess of strands, but I didn't feel like blow-drying it right now. Shaggy would have to do. Maybe I needed a haircut. Wisps of hair had grown to almost reach the tips of my ears.

I walked back into my bedroom still rubbing my hair dry, the towel hanging almost haphazardly around my hips. And as I entered, I froze. My bed wasn't as I'd left it. It was radically different, in fact. Weiss, wearing only sweatpants, lay back against the headboard and was merrily watching TV—in *my* bed. Okay, technically it was his, but right now it was mine.

"What the hell?" I muttered.

He spared me a glance, running his gaze over me from head to toe and back up again. "Nice entrance."

I put my hands on my hips. "What the fuck are you doing?" I asked, exasperated.

"Watching TV," he said in a general "duuh" tone.

"I mean, why are you watching it in my bed?"

He yawned and stretched his legs, making his muscles bunch and relax again in a mesmerizing way. "Easiest way to make sure you'll smell of me. You'll sleep in that T-shirt," he said, inclining his head toward the lump of fabric resting at the foot of the bed. "Your pillow and sheets will smell of me too, so you'll smell right in the morning."

And they'd smell of him while I'd sleep in them. The bastard... how was I supposed to sleep like that?

"Want to coordinate our stories about how we spent the night together too?" I asked acidly.

He snorted. "I'm a goddamn PBI agent, Edel. Trust me, I've got it covered," he said, smugly pressing some buttons on the remote.

To my endless horror, some porn started playing instead of the game he was watching. Weiss fumbled with the remote and changed channels, but it was too late. I'd already heard some shameless moaning, and it was giving me a rise—especially considering the half-naked Weiss sitting on my bed. God, how his abs flexed with his every move. The hard ridges of his muscles almost choked me, despite trying to look at anything else. And the hair on his chest, going down into a happy trail that was lost under his sweat—

I hung my head in utter defeat and despair. "What the hell is wrong with you?"

He cleared his throat. "The porn wasn't part of the plan."

Good to know. "How did you get in, anyway? I'm pretty sure I locked the door," I snapped.

He held up a hand. "See that over there?" he said, pointing to an open door. "Communicates between our bedrooms."

I was shocked I hadn't noticed it before. Close to losing my patience, I took a deep breath and stared at him. "Is it just me, or are you getting off on this?"

He looked down at his sweats, where there was some response, I realized, looking down on it with him. Then he looked back up at me and grinned. "I'm funny like that," he said.

Okay... okay. I'd had it. "What are you playing at, Weiss?" I asked, feeling defeated.

He lifted his eyebrows. "What do you mean?"

"You're in my bed wearing only sweats after you just groped and molested me down in the living room. Are you sure we're both clear on the fact we'll just pretend to be together? Because it looks to me like you're taking this whole thing a bit too... seriously."

Big mistake. He got up, giving me a full show of how his abs flexed and how his body looked in motion from up close. So much wank material gathering, my brain was short-circuiting.

He sat at the edge of the bed, resting his hands on his knees. "As long as we're having this heart-to-heart, I think there are some things you should know. You might want to sit down."

I sat in the chair beside me, careful not to have stuff hanging out of the towel or flashing him. "Go on."

He sighed. "I'm not exactly sure how to behave."

"Picked up on that."

He growled and looked up into my eyes. "I mean, with you, in this situation."

"Neither do I," I said as kindly as I could. "I hope you understand this is... new to me too."

"I doubt going out with someone is new to you."

"You'd be surprised," I muttered under my breath. "I mean, pretending to go out with someone is a first for me too."

"I guess I am used to pretending."

I frowned. "What's that supposed to mean?"

"Never mind. I do cross lines, even on my best days. This hasn't been one of them. I feel like an ass."

"You are an ass," I quipped.

He growled again and glared at me.

"Sorry," I placated. "Why feel that way?"

"Where's the line between pretending convincingly enough and actually going out together?"

I scratched my chin. "I guess meaning it makes the difference."

"Yeah, but when we were making out downstairs… I meant it. Does it mean that when we were kissing, we were pretending very convincingly, or that it was real?"

Jesus Christ, he was asking me? "I can't answer that for you. But I will ask that we set some limits. I mean, I get the whole convincingly part, but there have to be limits."

He nodded once. "Name them."

"You won't spend time almost naked in my bed, for one thing. No groping, make-out sessions in front of others. If we behave like we're trying to prove something, that's exactly how it'll come through—like we're trying to prove something."

"No groping, making out, or naked visits to your bedroom—where's the fun in that?"

I lifted my eyebrows. "You're having fun?"

He chuckled, something flickering through his eyes. I was mesmerized by the way his abs moved, by how his chest expanded and contracted with breath. I was mesmerized by him. I tried to focus on the discussion instead.

Weiss grinned and stared at me. "You're acting like you're not having fun, but I think you are. You certainly had fun when we made out, considering the boner."

"Both our boners, you mean?" I asked snidely as I tried to cover the growing bulge of my groin with the second towel. Hopefully the move was discreet. "What's up with the sudden interest in me, Weiss?"

"Maybe it's not that sudden. I did find you interesting enough to keep alive five years ago."

His gaze turned hot, burning hot for a moment—but it wasn't desire that burned there. It was something else, a mix of longing and some sort of proprietary sense that had me entirely baffled. Either he was really losing his mind, or I was. One of us had to be insane, though, everything was too freaky at this point for anything else. So I decided it was just as good a time as any to broach a topic I'd been dying to look into.

"I'm gay and single, Weiss. You're hot. After the whole smooching display downstairs, I am turned on. There, happy?"

"Thrilled. Don't lie to me, Sands. I know when you do."

I snorted. "How would you?"

He grinned. "Your heartbeat. It gives you away."

"Whatever. The question is, why did it turn you on? Didn't know you were into guys."

There, I'd said it. I tried to keep my expression as close to "curious but not dying to know" as I could.

He just looked me over, slowly, seeming to take in every detail of my unimpressive body. The lithe bone structure thanks to my mom's elf genes, the very lean muscles thanks to my father's fey gene pool. He probably picked up on every imperfection in the hairless expanse of skin he could see—again, thanks, Dad! Something weird happened. He didn't seem amused or bored, but somehow... curious. Maybe even interested. "Before Amanda, I had someone—someone I didn't mate. Someone who couldn't have birthed me a baby. Someone who wasn't a convenient mate for a future pack alpha. Someone I loved and cared for way more than I cared for Amanda. You remind me of him."

My gut clenched. "How so?"

"It's not the way you look, more your presence. Can't really describe it, but your very presence reminds me of him."

"That's why you helped me five years ago in that alley. I reminded you of him."

"You keep reminding me of him every time I see you. It's why I try to avoid it."

"Because you broke his heart?" I asked in a low voice.

What I really wanted to ask was "Because you weren't man enough to stand by the one you loved?"—but that, I suspected, wouldn't go over very well.

Weiss looked up and studied my face for a while, that strange look in his eyes again. I realized now that it was the resemblance that had triggered all the weird reactions from him. It was all the memory of this guy he'd left because apparently he wasn't convenient for Weiss's political agenda. It was all memory, not me. I didn't even count in this equation, not beyond forcing him to face this memory, or maybe this guilt every time he saw me. Five years ago, he'd saved the memory of someone he used to love, not me.

"I don't care about what you think," he said. "I only told you because it seemed fair you should know. That's why I'm weird around you, maybe why I take more liberties than I should or you want me to."

"Lame excuse for your lack of manners."

"It's the reason, not an excuse. I don't need excuses, Sands."

"Of course you don't," I replied, shaking my head.

For a moment there, I wanted to make a scene. To hurl nasty words at him, to slice through him and draw blood. But I knew I had no reason to. The man owed me nothing. He'd helped me out when I needed it, and now I was returning the favor. Despite my fantasies, there was nothing else there. There could never be, I realized with crushing disappointment. Not because he wasn't into guys, but because I reminded him of someone he didn't want to be reminded of. The kiss downstairs, the yearning I'd caught glimpses of, the strange interest he'd sometimes taken—none of it had been about me. I didn't even exist for him, not beyond being useful. That sobered me up, at least for now.

I cleared my throat. "Don't worry, Weiss. I get it. It's going to take some adjusting to respect the limits of our agreement—a learning curve. Not like we'll be in this situation for longer than a few days anyway. We'll manage. I'm happy you told me."

"Wouldn't have thought it, but I feel better now that I did."

I smiled as my heart broke a little. "Great. Anything you'd like to talk about, I'm here for you."

He cocked his head to the side. "Yeah, I don't think I'll take you up on the offer. But thanks for making it."

A phone started blaring. Weiss leaned back on the bed and reached out for the nightstand. I stuffed the towel down and closed my eyes, imagining sausages. Many, many sausages. My heart was broken right now, true, but my other parts were perfectly functional. Despite me disliking him right now, he did possess a hell of a body. I was a sensitive guy; gorgeousness moved me.

"Someone better be dead," he growled in the phone. "You're shitting me. Text the location." He looked up. "We've got five dead bodies."

I widened my eyes. "Were they…?"

"Together, all of them? Yeah," he muttered darkly.

I bit the inside of my lower lip. "Five in one hit?"

"Fucking hell," he growled as he got up. "Get dressed. Seems like we'll have a full night."

We got dressed and left in a hurry. We took his Beamer, because he demanded it, and I knew better than to antagonize him right now. He drove us out of the city, speed limits apparently not a factor in his thoughts. I gripped the seat, then my knees, and gritted my teeth all the way there. We shot through the police roadblock at the outskirts of the city.

I wasn't sure, but I thought I saw the officers' headgear fly off as we sped by them. If they reported it, dispatch would tell them to ignore the incident anyway. PBI had its hooks into human authorities. While there were some mutual help agreements in place, they generally left paranormals entirely in the Council's and PBI's care. Weiss would never get a speeding ticket, and if by some miracle he did get it, the PBI would fix it without him even bothering with the details. Which was probably part of the reason why his lunatic driving went on unchecked. That, and nobody in the PBI daring to tell him anything about it. Telling Weiss what to do was something of an extreme sport— whoever tried it most likely ended up with something broken, either a bone or an eardrum.

He finally slowed down a little and shot into the Silverline woods. He hit the brakes suddenly, and my face almost smacked into the windshield. Before I could even come up with compliments for his driving, he jumped out of the car and stormed into the woods. In the distance I could see some lights, people moving about—the crime scene, then. I got out of the car and walked toward the small crowd.

"Get a move on," Weiss bellowed from a few feet away.

I reached out and read his emotional grid—dear waving wand, he was pissed. Borderline raging, in fact, which shouldn't have been even possible after I'd drained the rage earlier.

I quickened my step and fell in line with him. "You need to relax, Weiss. You're getting close to red, and I can't drain it again tonight."

He ran both hands over his face, and then one of them glided up through his hair. "Fuck," he hissed. "Five victims, Sands," he said through gritted teeth.

I reached out to pat his shoulder, but he glared at me, so I stopped and stuffed the hand in my pocket instead. "I know," I whispered.

He exhaled in a whoosh. "Let's do this."

He strode over to one of the guys near the site. I managed to reach the outer perimeter of the scene and stayed there for a while. I wasn't squeamish by nature, but this... my stomach turned as the stench of dead flesh invaded my lungs.

"Talk," Weiss growled.

Jackson, one of the more experienced crime scene investigators, looked grim. "Five dead bodies. We have the names of two of them," he said, gesturing toward some IDs lying down in the grass.

Weiss stepped closer to the IDs, picked them up with his now gloved hands. "Why leave us two IDs?"

I stepped closer. "Hey, Jackson."

He nodded. "Sands. What do you make of this?" he asked, looking around.

UV lights showed a pentagram drawn in blood—plenty of it—on the grassy surface underneath the bodies. The five dead bodies were arranged with their heads as points of the star, their legs spread out to form the middle. They'd been dead for a while, if the stench was anything to go by, yet they didn't look bloated or decomposed enough to smell this bad.

"Arranged crime scene," I said as evenly as I could.

Jackson nodded. "This isn't the primary, from what we've seen so far."

"Or one of the primaries," Weiss grumbled, coming to stand beside me. "We could have anything from one to five primary crime scenes."

"Maybe," I said. "The IDs are part of the staging. Whoever did this wants us to follow that lead, control the scope of the investigation. They're sending us a message."

"Don't know what message that is, but it's gonna be a fucked-up one for sure," Jackson said, shaking his head.

Couldn't really contradict him on that.

"Some sort of satanic shit?" Weiss asked hopefully.

"This isn't a satanic symbol," I intervened. "In fact, as it's 'drawn' by the bodies—equal length corners—it's a protective symbol."

"Protective symbol drawn in dead bodies and blood," Weiss gritted out.

"The two we IDed so far are for sure lycan alphas," Jackson said, looking at the bodies.

I frowned. "And we know this already because…?"

"That one over there—Mitchell Banks—was recently reported for abuse by his mate. Abuse team was investigating it when he disappeared. The other one's Christa Salinger. Her mate's been in and out of MCU these last few weeks. Her name pinged on Abuse's radar as well."

Abuse—that was the newly made division consisting, for now at least, of Travis—my ex, lycan extraordinaire, and experienced PBI agent—and Rick—Travis's newly turned mate, the only lycan tracker our Bureau had. After the Amanda situation became clear, the Council agreed to set up an Abuse team, and we were working on a draft for the anti-abuse regulations for leaders.

Weiss shook his head. "Two lycan alphas, both pissing off their mates."

"Abusing," I corrected lightly.

"Allegedly," he said, squinting at me.

I stuck my hands in my pockets and looked at the symbol again. "A protective symbol drawn in blood and dead bodies, two of which are of *allegedly* abusive leaders."

"Don't even fucking think it!" Weiss growled viciously.

Jackson's brows twitched upward. I swallowed thickly. Didn't have to say it, obviously we were all making the same connection—the Leader Murders connection.

"Process the scene 'n' e-mail me the report when you're done," Weiss gritted out.

He grabbed my arm and dragged me out of there in angry strides. I pretty much had to run beside him to keep up.

"Where are we going?" I asked, frowning.

"The fuck out of here."

We reached the car, and he pushed me toward the passenger door before he climbed in. I followed his lead, got in, and froze with my hand on the door before I'd managed to close it all the way. Weiss pounded his fists against the steering wheel and snarled so viciously, I seriously thought I'd shit myself. His face morphed into wolf traits, his eyes went almost white, and he howled long and incredibly loud. The sound exploded out of the car and slid into the dark forest, provoking a series of howls in the distance. Real wolves, some of his pack werewolves? I didn't dare breathe for fear of setting him off. His chest expanded with every breath, air rasping in and out of him. If he was losing control and going into a rage, I'd be the first casualty. The downside of becoming his emotional crutch was I'd be the first to break if he got out of control. Tonight, if he did, I'd have no line of defense. I'd given all my resources to balancing him out at his house earlier.

"Do something," he growled with a lisp, since his teeth had elongated too.

I turned my head slowly in his direction. "Like whip out my magic wand and make it all better?"

He snorted, though it could've been a laugh too. "Funny."

I swallowed and watched the wolf traits recede a bit. "You should see me in my fairy suit," I said evenly.

He snorted louder. More of the wolf traits disappeared. "Might be fun," he said without distorting the sounds. His wolf traits were almost gone.

I gingerly closed the passenger door and set my hand in my lap. "Under control?" I asked just as evenly.

He leaned his forehead down on the steering wheel. "Might never be under control again."

I looked out the windshield and gave thanks to whatever gods would choose to listen. I'd barely escaped death-by-raging-werewolf tonight, without balancing his emotional grid. Dumb luck alone wouldn't help for long, though.

five

WEISS SCRATCHED his nape. "We gotta go to Downtown. Morris James needs to get on this."

I frowned. "Wouldn't have pegged you for the delegating type."

He smiled, staring through the windshield. "I'm not. In case I don't make it past the couple of days we've agreed to try this balancing thing, the investigation needs to go on without me. Best way to get that done is to involve other agents right now."

"Making preparations in case you get executed?" I asked, looking away.

"I've spent about ten years of my life building and strengthening the PBI, Sands. I'm not taking it down with me if I fail."

I gripped my knee, cracked my neck. "Giving up?"

"Never. Just doing what needs to be done while I'm still sane enough to make the decisions." I watched out of the corner of my eye as he took his phone out and hit some buttons. "Jackson, get Rick Barton on scene to take any scent tracks he can. Morris James will be in contact too, full cooperation."

He put the phone in the cup holder between our seats and started up the engine. "On the upside, now you've got another solid reason to work with me on this. Five dead bodies, that symbol drawn in blood—whatever the fuck it's supposed to mean—makes sense to have a shrink work on it too."

I swallowed thickly. "I don't think this will end well."

"Whatever the fuck does?" he whispered and backed out of the Silverline forest road until we hit asphalt.

The drive downtown was silent. His gaze stayed glued to the road, and for a while I thought he actually forgot I was even there. The fishing-and-hunting shopping center up ahead was the front of the Bureau's Downtown branch. It looked weird, a hulking shape in the night. The actual storefront wasn't lined by lights, only the parking lot enjoyed the perk. It made it easier to move a lot in and out of the place without drawing too much attention. The "official" way in wasn't up here anyway, but underground from the parking lot's lower level. Weiss's Beamer slid in the underground level of the parking lot after the gate security lifted the barrier. Security Guy flashed us a smile and nodded as we passed him by. Traveling with the PBI director did come with some obvious perks. Weiss parked and got out of the car in silence. I followed him to the large double doors and stuck my hands in my pockets as we got through them just as easily as we had the parking lot security.

One of the agents standing there zeroed in on Weiss and walked right up. "Evening, Director. Anything I can help with?"

"James in?" Weiss asked.

The guy nodded. "In his office. You might wanna knock, though. Might not be alone," he added, barely containing a sly grin.

Weiss snorted and walked by him.

I rushed to catch up. "Why do I get the feeling you won't knock?"

He looked at me over his shoulder. "Do I look like the knocking type, Edel?"

"Glad to see you're back to your regular asshole-ish self."

"Oh yeah, I'm a fucking ray of sunshine."

We reached Morris James's office. Weiss simply opened the door and stormed inside without a care. I looked around for a moment, stepping inside carefully. If they wanted me out, I was sure Weiss would have no issue with barking the order at me.

James sat there, feet propped up on the desk and leaning back in his chair. "Director," he said, nodding.

Weiss glared at me. "Close that door 'n' sit down." He leaned against the wall and fixed James with his gaze. "We've got a shitstorm brewing, Chief."

I couldn't tell if they were pulling each other's chain or being serious, but then again, I was tired and unaccustomed to so much leader testosterone floating in a room.

James got his feet down and stood up. He walked around the desk, leaned against its edge on our side of the room, and looked at Weiss, frowning. "What's up?"

"Five dead bodies," I said when I saw Weiss wouldn't reply.

James looked between me and the werewolf standing there. "Must be some fucked-up shit if he got you on it," he said, frowning.

I forced myself to smile. "Thanks."

"Didn't mean you're a bad guy, Sands. You're cool, but if your expertise is needed, then shit is serious."

"It is," Weiss finally said. "Two of the five dead bodies are leaders. James, I want you to join the investigation."

Downtown Chief Morris James frowned so hard, I thought he'd pull some brow muscles. "Five bodies is an easy investigation for you, Weiss. What's the catch?"

Weiss smiled grimly. "Amanda's execution happens this week. I might be... indisposed for a few days 'cause of that. So I want this to keep going with or without me."

James nodded. "Got it. What can I do?"

"Stay in touch with Barton and Jackson for now. And if I make the call, you're taking over, and jumping in like we both know you can."

James widened his eyes. "Taking over? You dying or something, man? No way you'd give up being in charge of an investigation, or anything else for that matter, otherwise."

I gulped and looked at my knees while I crossed my legs. Weiss didn't say anything for a while, and James didn't move or speak either. In the silence of that office, I saw clearly that Weiss had lost hope for the night. Somewhere in that car, probably after he'd come out of the red by some miracle, he'd lost hope. Maybe tomorrow morning he'd find it again, but right now he looked close enough to hopeless to send chills down my spine.

"Mate execution takes a big toll on alphas," I cut in. "He's going to be just fine a few days after Amanda's gone," I told a suspicious James.

He looked between the two of us. "I take it the rumor is true? You two hooking up?"

"We're a couple, yeah," said Weiss. "Not mates," he added when James regarded him strangely.

"But you will be after her execution?" James asked with a frown he obviously tried to tamp down.

"Our private lives are less interesting than the five dead bodies," I replied. "Why don't we focus on them for now?"

"Curiosity is in a detective's nature," he said. "Right, so the dead bodies. I'll get in on the investigation so I can take over if I have to. But I'm sure I won't, not if you two are teaming up."

I smiled. "Thanks, I think."

Weiss stood there, his hands in his pockets and looking at me. I couldn't read his expression well, and I didn't have the energy to read his emotional grid again tonight. Whatever he was thinking about, it almost took my breath away to look at him.

"We'll talk in the morning," my so-called lover told James. "Just wanted to touch base tonight, be sure we're on the same page."

"Right," James replied. "Talk tomorrow, then. I'll get in touch with Jackson tonight to get up to speed. And Weiss?"

"Yeah," the werewolf said, finally looking slightly more like his regular annoyed self.

"Thanks for the vote of confidence," James said, smiling.

Weiss nodded, then looked back at me. "Let's go."

I got up, waved at James, and went out. Weiss walked beside me, hands still firmly stuck in his pockets. We got to his car, got in, and as he drove us out of the parking lot and back into the streets, I finally broke.

"Weiss?"

He looked over for a second. "What?"

"You need to act like yourself around everyone."

"And how's that?"

"You know," I said and cleared my throat. "Bossy, pushy, barking, and growling high and low."

He smiled. "James knows losing a mate hurts even if the only thing between those mates is hate. Thanks for keeping an eye out, though."

"He lost a mate?"

"His brother did. James got to see it all firsthand. I think it was seven years ago. Mitchell James had just been promoted to Downtown

Chief. He didn't get along with his consort, not really; they used to argue and even fight it out in public. But when the poor bastard got hit by a truck, Mitchell was a ghost for a few days."

"He quit, I'm guessing? Which is why his brother got the job?"

He slid past a car, barely avoiding scratching it. "Mitchell killed himself, even though he used to say he hated the guy. Sire hormones get to your head, you know?"

"James's brother killed himself?" I asked in a small voice.

"Yes. Surprised you didn't know. But then again, it was before your time and people don't really talk about it."

"Why don't they?"

He shrugged. "I threw one agent who did through a window. Nothing major, but it got the message across."

I gulped. "I take it you and Mitchell used to be close?"

"I'd stop asking about it, if I were you," he said in that lethally calm voice that usually announced someone was about to get their ass whooped.

"Right. So, considering I'm pretty much burned out for the night, how about I sleep at home instead of going back to your house?"

He tapped his fingers on the steering wheel. "You helped me out of the red without using the fey shit tonight."

"Effort you're obviously appreciating, judging by the way you choose to word it," I said dryly.

"I do appreciate it. You probably saved us both. I was wondering how it is you did it, though."

"Not sure. I just sat there, made some lame jokes, and you snapped out of it. It's your merit, pretty much."

"Seriously doubt that. However it is that it happened, it means you can help me out of the red even without the magic tricks. That means you're not going anywhere, Edel. I need you now even more than I did before."

I looked out the passenger's window. "If you do lose it, I'm gonna be the first casualty."

"All the more reason to try your best, huh?" he asked as we reached the front gates of his home.

Security Guy nodded and gave me a look again. Wonderful, I'd probably get to see that sweetheart Tricia too.

"Know what?" I asked, tapping my fingertips on my knee. "Considering I'm risking not only my career and the Council's wrath, but also my life, you need to sweeten the deal."

He parked but kept the car doors closed. "How so?" he asked, finally looking at me.

It was dark on his driveway. Some light made it out of the house, but not enough to pierce the darkness. Inside the car it was even darker, a strange kind of thick darkness that seemed impenetrable no matter what kind of light might be around. His eyes glinted strangely, more white than light blue, and I could hear his breathing was weirdly loud.

I cleared my throat. "Since we don't know how the days ahead will go, I want you to stop by Travis and Rick's office tomorrow morning and sign in support of our draft."

"Your draft?"

"The Anti-Abuse Act draft," I corrected him.

"You want me to sign in support of a draft Amanda tried to pass by Council years ago," he said flatly.

I swallowed. "Not her version of it. We're working on one abiding by basic human rights, pretty much, and human anti-abuse legislation."

He smiled strangely. "Everyone will think I'm doing that because we're fucking."

I frowned. "It couldn't be because you might think the draft is the right thing to do?"

"Definitely not. My position on that hasn't wavered over the years, Edel. Leaders and their mates define their own rules naturally."

I gritted my teeth at the nickname. "And when leaders cross those 'natural lines'?"

He reached out and wrapped his fingers around my throat without squeezing. The touch felt intimate—menacing but intimate. It made my stomach quiver, though I tried to ignore it.

"Growing pains," he said in a low, thick voice that made me gulp. "Leaders and their mates find their balance through trial and error. And that bumpy road is part of the process. Sterile rules won't help the matings. They'll take out a part of the real bonding and replace it with cold contract terms. I don't think it's for the better of the community." His fingertips massaged my flesh, his fingernails brushing my skin.

"Shared pain, like shared pleasure, tightens the bonds in a couple," he whispered. "Don't you think so?"

I bit the inside of my cheek. "I don't see why that should condone abuse."

"Don't you?" he asked in that strange, low voice.

I felt his fingers tighten slightly around my throat.

He grinned and leaned in closer, running his nose through the hair at my temple. "I might help you understand sometime."

"We agreed on some rules," I said as calmly as I could. "You're breaking them."

He snorted. "That's exactly how your precious draft will work. Cold rules that will prevent us all from being who we are with each other. And how will that help our inner monsters connect?"

"Inner monsters shouldn't connect. They should be buried deep down inside, kept away from the ones we care about."

His fingertips danced over my throat, pressing down slightly, but still in the caress territory. "Of course you'd think so, fey prince. You don't have a wild soul like we do."

I blinked slowly, trying to push out the excitement from my thoughts. "Because I'm not a shifter, huh? But Amanda's a werewolf like you, and she thought the same way I do. Isn't it possible that you're choosing to overlook things just to keep that philosophy of yours?"

He growled low. "Don't mention that traitorous bitch. And justifying your views by citing her judgment isn't smart since she's a deranged criminal."

"A feral monster, isn't she? I would've thought you'd be proud of her 'wild soul.'"

He pulled away and chuckled. "Travis did say you love to mindfuck."

I exhaled slowly. "And you don't? What were you doing just now, Weiss? What the hell were you doing?"

He looked out the windshield. "You know how he killed himself?"

I frowned, for a minute not getting what the hell he meant. "James's brother?"

"Hung himself. He could have picked a faster way to go, like a gunshot to the head. He chose hanging, one of the most painful and slow deaths. His body kept trying to heal the damage until it was overcome by it. I spent a lot of time pondering how long it must have taken to actually die, and wondering what he was thinking about as it happened. When his brother found him, he was a mess. Shit happens to a body when it's hanged, you know?"

"I know. I'm sorry for his loss."

It wasn't a pretty mental picture. For all our "paranormal" qualities, none of us were infallible or immortal. Our bodies healed faster than humans, yes. Some healed faster than others, depending on the species. But we all suffered, and we all died.

"Aren't we all? Doesn't do anyone any good, though," Weiss murmured.

I turned to look at him. "Why would you think that?"

"It changes nothing, helps with nothing. Feeling sorry is useless."

I frowned, totally lost. "You're saying regrets are useless?"

"Pretty much. And your rules will be just as useless. If leaders are abusive, then they'll keep being so. If their mates report it or not remains to be seen. If Mitchell would've allowed it—and being the sire, he had to allow us interfering—we would've nailed that motherfucker's ass to a wall five ways to Sunday. But he didn't, because he took the abuse as part of their intimacy. And when his abuser was killed, supposedly he couldn't conceive of a life without him. So he killed himself shortly thereafter. Anti-abuse rules would've made dicksquat difference."

"It's not that simple, obviously," I said. "Mitchell could have walked away easily. He was the other one's sire. He was the one in a position of authority, yet he chose not to use it. Suppose tables would have been turned, though. That the other one, the leader's mate, would have wanted to walk out—it wouldn't have been possible, not without the sire's accord. Would an abusive sire give accord for their consort to leave them? Of course not. Abusive relationships are very hard to get out of, but if people decide to, they should be able to do it. They should be able to walk away from their leaders, with or without the leader's consent, if there's abuse there."

He snorted. "What if it's going to be used as an excuse to dump a figure of authority instead? No matter the rule, it gets perverted and used against the very principles it stood for. And what will it have changed?"

"I refuse to accept you're so blind as not to see. Victims of abuse will have a way out. True, it might be abused by some. But to deny victims the right to walk away from their leader abusers just so the walking away won't be abused by some is simply ignorant."

"Maybe. But all forms of authority rely on the idea that there's at least one level of it you can't appeal against. I don't think the community is ready to live by these rules of yours. They'd need the education geared toward lack of abuse so they'd have half a chance to follow the rule."

I raised an eyebrow. "You're saying leaders are educated toward abusing?"

"They know there's no way to appeal their decisions. Their mates know that when they become their mates. My pack knows there's no way to appeal my decisions. It's what keeps order in the ranks."

"The draft refers to abuse in matings, not in your pack."

"Really? And how do you imagine authority works in the pack, huh? I have direct power over some, who in turn have power over their mates or former mates, and so on. It's a pyramid of authority, and it works."

I cracked my neck. "Right. Except for the Amanda thing."

He clenched his jaws, then said, "Every rule has its exceptions."

"So after the new rules are in place, the community will adapt. There will be some exceptions, but I believe it will help those who need help and have no way to get it."

"You remind me of Mitchell so much," he said softly.

Exactly what I wanted to hear—again. "Do I?"

"He was an idealist too. Look where it got him," he added bitterly.

"You were close?"

"Close, yeah. You sound so much like him. You even move like he did. I don't know how to explain it. It's not a physical likeness, but it's striking...."

He drifted off there. Mitchell James was the one I reminded him of? Was he the one Weiss had been with and left in order to pursue his political career beside Amanda? It did explain why James looked at me weird now. So I had to thank Mitchell for Weiss saving me five years ago. I was alive because Mitchell wasn't, in a twisted way. Life worked in some pretty fucked-up ways sometimes. And I so didn't want to dwell on that now.

"The draft will prevent abuse, Weiss. It'll help mates be together and respect each other, regardless of their leader or nonleader status. Why are you so against that?"

"It's gonna open a can of worms we'll regret having opened lower down the line. But I'll sign it if it's what you want. Happy?"

"Ecstatic," I whispered. "Now open these doors and let me out. I'm dead on my feet."

I heard a muffled click, and then I could open the door. I got out of the car, walked into the house, and got up the stairs without looking back or waiting for him. I went straight for my bedroom, threw off my clothes, got his T-shirt on with a pair of sweats from my gym bag, and got under the covers. Singledom did have one advantage: there was always a lot of room to turn in bed. I fell asleep pretty much instantly.

six

I WOKE up to a strange noise and the distinct sensation my covers were sliding off. I looked at the foot of the bed—blinked, frowned, looked again—a tiny gray ball of fur stood there, growling as he pulled at my covers. ·

"Let go," I mumbled and held the covers tight.

The tiny thing growled again, this time clearly, though in a funny high pitch like a squeaky toy. He shook his head with his teeth still gripping my covers.

"Let go," I said in a sterner tone.

He squinted those almost-white eyes at me and stepped back, his tail held high and proud. I suddenly let go of the covers and grinned as he fell down on his ass with the covers falling over him. The little furry guy needed some manners. Clearly he hadn't gotten any, not that I was entirely surprised. Alf didn't strike me as the type of kid who'd let anyone get a word in. Maybe his dad, but then again, Weiss didn't actually shine in the manners category either.

Furry got out from under the covers and sat down on top of them, looking pretty happy with his new nest.

"Go get your dad," I said.

His tongue lolled out, and he cocked his head to the side. I snorted and smiled; the little guy was too cute to resist. Of course, that thought only lasted about a minute—until I got out of bed and saw my shoes: chewed on, totally destroyed.

"Did you do that?"

He got up and pranced out, the proudest little thing in existence. For a second there I was slightly tempted to catch and throttle him.

Weiss burst in through the connecting door between our rooms and sat at the foot of my bed. "He likes you," he said, nodding at my ruined shoes.

I snorted. "What would he have done if he didn't, chew my jugular out?"

"He could try, you know. Certainly did with Amanda."

"What?"

"Tried to attack her a few times. Obviously my little monster has better instincts than me."

"So him trying to kill me is a sign of affection or not?"

He grinned. "Depends."

"On?"

"Whether he manages it or not. If he doesn't, then he likes you. You'd be surprised how strong he is already."

"Wow. Just, wow. One, I don't intend to find out. Two, you're buying me new shoes."

"Lucky you didn't have more pairs here. He would've gotten to them all in one go."

"You sound terribly proud," I replied, exasperated.

He smiled. "He's my boy. Of course I'm proud."

I could only guess how proud he was of his son's first pee on the carpet. I winced at the thought, realizing I did kind of make the dog parallel there. Terrible thing I'd witnessed my father do countless times while I was growing up. Shifters were as good as barn animals to him. But then again, we were all as good as barn animals to him.

"You need to train him or whatever it is you call it. This isn't acceptable."

He snorted. "Not his fault you didn't put your shoes away."

"Right, like hang them from the freaking ceiling?"

He waved off my comment. "Get a move on. Breakfast in ten minutes, and then we're off to the office."

"Excuse me," I called after him as he walked out. "What am I going to do, go barefoot?"

"Relax, Edel. I'll get you some flip-flops."

I ran both hands over my face and took another glance at my ruined shoes. The soft Italian leather was completely peeled off of the tips, and bite marks and claw marks rained down all over whatever else was left. I shuddered to think what might await me inside the shoes. Might've even peed in them for all I knew. The little beast had done a good number on them, had to give him that. Next time, my shoes would go on the top shelf of the closet, and a lock and key would go on that closet door, or I wouldn't spend another night in this place.

A short shower later, I got last night's clothes on and went downstairs in my workout sneakers. Weiss was eating something and glancing over a paper, Tricia was glaring at me over a cup of coffee, and her brother was fussing over a laptop.

"Morning," I muttered.

Bert looked up and smiled, Tricia squinted at me and looked away, and Weiss ignored me. Right. I sat before the plate of scrambled eggs and ate some, had coffee from the pot in the middle of the table, then cleared my throat. "Solved the shoes thing. I'll just wear my sneakers."

Weiss looked up. "I'll have someone go over to your apartment and bring some of your things over."

"I can go and take what—"

"Wasn't a question," Weiss stated.

Damn it. "I'm going," I said firmly.

Either I'd stand my ground or get swept under his alpha bullshit for good. Presuming we wouldn't both end up dead in a few days, it was important to stand up to him while I could.

Weiss set the paper down, and without taking his eyes off of me, he barked, "Leave us."

I made to get up.

"Sit your ass down, Edel," he gritted out.

His two pack mates got up and made themselves scarce.

Weiss leaned in closer over the table. "When it's time for you to have an opinion different than mine in public, I'll let you know," he said in a steely tone. "You won't question my word again while you're in my house. Got it?"

"You seem to forget I'm not part of your pack, Weiss. You have nothing to lord over me, and I won't pretend you do either."

"Oh really?"

My heartbeat sped up, but I wasn't giving in. "Really."

In five seconds flat the chair had gone down, and I was pressed against a wall with Weiss's hand closed over my throat. He wasn't actually squeezing, just holding me in place and keeping his hand there. Obviously the man had a neck fetish. As I'd noticed before, when really pissed, Weiss didn't growl. He just stared with those almost-white eyes, sheer doom and destruction radiating from him.

"Say that again," he said in that deadly cold voice.

I gulped. "This isn't the best time for a power play."

"Always a good time for a power play, Edel. Except I'm not playing."

Of course I was getting turned on, because that was how fucked up my wiring was around him. "I don't like to be served. Get it through that thick skull of yours."

"Do fey go through a daredevil stage in the morning? Like a boner for getting killed?"

"You do have a way with words. That's all you've got going for you to try and intimidate me. Might work with some Shakespearean insults."

"I've broken limbs for less attitude than you're giving me right now."

"I've given more attitude to crazier, nastier figures of authority than you."

He smiled. "I'm not your father."

"I'm not your pack. Your alpha thing doesn't work on me."

"And yet you're afraid."

"You're huge, usually mean, and able to do serious damage—of course I'm afraid."

"Not enough to do as I say, though."

"Exactly. Just pretend I'm a person, and that you're a person too and ask me about things that involve me. Then you won't have to bark orders at me that I won't follow. And let's be clear here, I won't follow your orders outside of strict PBI business."

"I could rip your head off," he said calmly.

"I could report your situation," I shot back.

He smiled. "Not if I rip your head off first."

We glared at each other for a while. Either I was becoming delusional, or I was starting to read him without reading his emotional grid. While he might've been tempted to follow through with the threat, he couldn't. Because he needed me, true, that was part of it. The other part? I was the ghost of Mitchell, if what I thought was true. I'd have to look into it as soon as we got to the office. I possibly had even more room to maneuver if that were true, and I did like to have a clear image of just how much room I had.

"We cool?"

He snorted. "Dunno about you, but I'm anything but cool. I'm not going to kill you yet, if that's what you're asking. Might change my mind by lunch, though."

"There's that to look forward to, then," I commented.

"You look like a tiny, breakable thing, but you're a pretty resilient bastard, aren't you?"

I smiled. "I did fight my way out of Fey Court, Weiss. And it wasn't a poetry competition."

He smiled. "Good. I don't like pussies."

Was that in the literal sense, or more of a metaphor? "Right. Now can we go to work?"

He stepped back and stuck a hand in his pants pocket, taking out some cash. "For the shoes," he said reaching out.

"That's more than one G."

"Too little?" he asked.

"Are you out of your mind? They were good shoes but not plated in gold."

"Don't know, don't care. Let's call this an advance on all I'll owe you. Alf is going to raid your room for shoes to destroy for a while, I have a feeling."

I shook my head, horrified. "Why would you think that?"

"I used to chew on my mom's shoes when I was a kid."

"I'm not his mom."

"The main thing is, you're not his alpha, though. Everyone's shoes are fair game except for mine."

I snorted. "Then I'll just leave my shoes in your room."

"No, you won't. You'll solve it on your own or not at all."

I massaged my temples. "This some sort of fucked-up pack power play again?"

He grinned slowly.

Sweet dangling lobes, how I hated the hotness of him right now. "For how long did you chew your mom's shoes?" I asked in a defeated tone.

"It went on for a while."

"How long a while, exactly?"

He looked away. "Not too long, but not because I stopped trying to find her shoes and chew them out. Just take the damn money."

I did, though I didn't feel good about it. We went out to the cars, and I headed for mine while Weiss headed for his.

"Where the hell are you going?" he called out.

I looked between my car and him in a general "duuh!" way. "My car."

"You're my partner, you ride with me."

I crossed my arms over my chest. "Fine. But we'll do it in my car."

He furrowed his brows and looked it over, then snorted. "Don't think so."

I cocked an eyebrow. "What, is my royal chariot not worthy of you?"

His icy blue eyes focused on me, and he grinned. "I see you're coming around. Good for you. But we're taking my car."

"Then I want to drive," I shot back.

"Like that's ever going to happen. Get in the fucking car, Edel. I don't have time for your princely airs. We'll go places. My car has clearance like I do. Get your ass in," he barked and got in himself.

The clearance thing did make sense. I didn't actually want to take my car or drive. I did want to make our boundaries clear, though. Leaders, especially pack alphas like Weiss was—and with a big pack to boot—tended to take their own authority for granted. I wasn't a subject of that pack authority, and the sooner he accepted it, the better off we'd be. I suspected that being able to essentially laugh him down from a rage hinged on our differences. Best way to lean on them was to actively emphasize them. By instinct, Weiss's animal knew it could take out any pack member of his and suffer no repercussions. Alphas could do that now, which was part of the reason Travis, Rick, myself, and Naty Stein were working on anti-abuse rules, for mates primarily, but we hoped to develop them toward leader interactions by and large, to establish where severe leader action was called for and sanctioned and where it was abusive. The more aware Weiss was he wasn't my alpha, the better chance we had to make this insane experiment work.

I walked to his Beamer and got in.

He was tapping his fingers against the wheel, looking out the windshield. "I know what you're doing."

I turned to look at him. "Sitting in your car. Hardly tough to figure out."

"I mean challenging me. You're getting revenge on a figure of authority."

I sighed. "Am I? Suppose this will circle back to my father, won't it?"

"Everything does, fey prince. That's what being the son of Matthew Sands, King of Fey, means—everything about any fey circles back to him."

"I'm an outcast, Weiss."

"He's the one who cast you out after trying to off you. Like I said, circles back to him."

"Was there a point to this line of discussion, or were you just flexing your psychoanalytic muscles?"

"You should be very aware of the difference between me and your daddy."

I clacked my tongue. "Let me guess, you'd never be as much of an asshole? Because you often are, just less evil."

"You're making me want to meet the guy." He shook his head. "That's not it, though. Guess again."

"You wouldn't try to kill me?"

"I won't fail if I try. Don't push me, Sands."

"I don't push, I just push back. Stop pushing, and I'll have nothing to react to. It's only going to be a few days before we know for sure where you stand. Let's just get through them with as little damage as possible, good deal?"

He sighed. "Fine."

He drove us to PBI headquarters. When we got out of the car and were walking toward the building, he glanced over at me. "Oh, and Sands?"

"Yeah."

"You're doing my paperwork while we're partners."

I rolled my eyes. "What about confidential stuff, the for-your-eyes-only kind of paperwork?"

He snorted. "I'll just postpone working on it. I always do."

"What is it with you and paperwork?"

"Fucking hate it," he spat. "I'm anything but a paper pusher."

"Fine. I'm going in for a meeting with Travis, Rick, and Naty. Have someone bring the paperwork over to my office, and I'll work on it."

"Fine," he grumbled and walked on faster.

I could feel almost every pack member's gaze on me as soon as I set foot in the lobby—many, many glares, some curious glances. Perfect, the news was out that I was Weiss's new squeaky toy. I walked holding my head up high, pretending not to notice all the attention I was getting. Pretending to not notice death glares got impossible when I reached Travis and Rick's office, though.

In fact, Rick was glaring at me with so much passion I could almost feel layers of my skin melting off. "You horny son of a bitch," he spat as soon as I closed the door of their office. "You couldn't even wait for Amanda to be properly dead before jumping Weiss's bones?"

Travis cleared his throat. "Rick...."

Rick held a hand up and kept glaring at me. "What is it, tell me. The monumental asshole aura, the heartless bastard manipulator air? What?"

I smiled. "If that's what I find attractive, you should be worried. I found your mate attractive too."

"Shut the fuck up," that mate barked at me. "Now if you ladies are done catfighting, could we focus on the draft?"

I shrugged. "Naty in yet?"

"She can't come in, some freak thing going on at the Medical Care Unit. She'll go over our work and send in hers during the day. Got your proposals?" Travis added.

I nodded and reached out with my keys. "Here."

The thumb drive on my keychain contained all of my research and draft proposals. After putting it all together, the four of us would come up with a final draft to show the Council by Monday. We pretty much had to have it done by the weekend, so a day or two after Amanda's execution, the Anti-Abuse Act draft would actually become public. She'd tried hard to get this done, years ago. Ironically, it was she who had gotten it to happen now, even if via murders rather than diplomatic channels.

"Weiss will sign it too," I mentioned casually.

Rick gaped at me. "You're shitting me. How good a head do you give?"

I grinned. "We both know who you can ask. But if you think Weiss is as easy as that, you're out of your mind. I just reasoned with him and—"

"Mindfucked him, somehow," Travis gritted out. "That's what you do."

"Ye of little faith!" I recited. "Why are you so bent on thinking he can't just agree to something that's going to be useful?"

"You insane?" Rick screamed. "This will work toward limiting his authority, one way or the other. Who do you know that's in a position of power and wants to give away some of that power?"

Someone who has no other choice was my honest answer. But I went with "Someone reasonable."

Rick threw his hands up and stomped out of the office. Travis and I watched him go.

"What's wrong with him?"

"I think he's got this freak affection for Amanda," he said softly.

I frowned and looked at him. "He waived counseling after she shot him. Do I have to enforce him taking it after all?"

Travis made a face. "I think it's more about Rick's abusive little shit ex than Amanda herself. Can't decide if that's better or worse."

"Neither would be good. If you think he needs the counseling, tell me. He won't find out we talked. I'll be the bad guy who's forcing him into it."

Travis sighed. "He hates you already."

I smiled, a fake little smile I'd practiced in years of Fey Court. "Perfect, there's nothing to lose, then. I'll be in my office if you want to discuss the draft."

Travis grinned. "Got any paperwork to do?"

"How'd you know?"

He snorted. "Weiss used to dump it on Amanda back in the day. Can't decide if it's a good or a bad sign that he's doing the same with you now."

I blinked. "Right. You guys heard about last night?"

All cheer escaped Travis's face. "Probably part of why Rick's so tense today. That pentagram case is fucked up, even by my lax standards."

"Did Rick catch anything useful?"

"Nothing. Part of why he's so pissed. He could smell nothing on-site except the victims themselves, investigators involved, us, the guy who found them, and the passersby."

I widened my eyes. "Wait, like nothing-nothing else?"

"No scent trace to follow up on. Not good."

"Does Weiss know?"

A loud crash sounded from the director's office. He shot out of there cursing and growling, everyone getting out of his way.

"I think he just found out," Travis mumbled.

I rushed behind him, reading his emotional grid. It came easier than it had yesterday, so at least there was that going for us. His turmoil was obvious, anger, disgust, faint traces of fear—no rage, though, at least not yet.

I finally fell in step with him—or more like in jog while he stepped. "Take it easier," I whispered as low as I could.

He growled but grabbed my arm and dragged me into the elevator. "No fucking traces?" he ground out as the elevator doors slid closed. "The poor bastards didn't crawl there by themselves, did they?" he spat.

Just perfect. If he worked himself into a rage, I'd be closed in an elevator with a crazy, violent werewolf alpha. How could a guy's morning get any better?

I winced. "Did you figure out all of their identities?"

He nodded tightly. "All leaders. It's definitely going into the Leader Murders file."

I frowned. "Just because they're leaders doesn't necessarily mean they're connected to Amanda's victims."

"Two of them were part of the samples kit we got from Black's ex-lab assistant. Some of them are connected to the case, they're leaders, and they're dead. Does that big brain of yours picture that as coincidence?"

"Guess not. But you need to calm down."

The elevator stopped, and the doors binged open. The stench of the morgue slapped me in the face as soon as I stepped outside of the elevator. It wasn't Lora's fault, but she was a troll and smelled five kinds of nasty from afar, and that was on her good days. We both walked to the "courtesy cabinet" where the anti-scent ointment was and smeared generous amounts of it under our noses. Sweet flapping wings, the smell was bad today. That usually meant she was in a bad mood, oozing out more Eau de Troll.

Weiss strode in, me tailing him. He opened the door of the actual morgue and barked out, "What have we got?"

I took a deep breath through my mouth and stepped in too. "Morning, Lora."

She looked between the five dead bodies. "Not a good morning. Not good at all."

SEVEN

PBI'S TROLL pathologist shook her head. "They were all killed execution style."

Weiss frowned. "Execution style? Does that make sense to you?" he asked me.

I scratched my chin. "The way we found the bodies arranged and execution style… no mutilation?"

"Aside from being shot in the back of their heads, and then having their blood collected, nothing done to them that I can find traces of: no signs of struggle, no ligature marks," Lora informed us.

I frowned. "The first victims had been mutilated. They were personal kills, there were personal connections involved. Execution could suggest the actual kill wasn't the goal, or that the way we found the bodies arranged wasn't the goal."

"What was the fucking goal?" Weiss asked, looking at each of the bodies.

"Can't tell yet. Drugs or any incapacitating substances in their blood, Lora?"

She shook her head.

"More than one perp," Weiss said. "How else would someone get two lycans, two vampires, and a werewolf—all leaders—under control and execute them?"

"What about the shots?" I asked Lora.

"Close range," she said, looking over her reports. "All of them close range. Time of death coincides for all of them, sometime between eight and ten a.m. yesterday."

"Monday morning, someone arranged five dead bodies near the Silverline jogging route, but nobody left any traces, nobody saw it, and it took us almost twelve hours to find them?"

Weiss frowned. "They seemed riper than that."

She nodded. "There were some solvents poured over the bodies. Maybe to extract more… liquids for the pentagram?"

I stuck my hands in my pockets. "Could it be why Rick didn't find any scent traces? The solvents erased traces of their killers from the bodies?"

"I'm still working on that theory. But the traces of their killers wouldn't have just vanished. They would've been integrated into the remains of the victims. They'd show in DNA analysis. Might take me a while to look into it, but I'll let you know as soon as I find out."

I sighed. "You're right. Even so, it wouldn't explain why there were no scent traces around the bodies either."

Weiss ran a hand through his hair. "Team of five to hit them each separately, or a team large enough to keep them under control and off them all together. Lora, please text me the moment you find out anything, will you?"

"Sure, Director," she said, nodding.

"Thanks," he replied and walked out.

"One more thing, Lora," I said, crossing my arms. "Was their blood extracted?"

"Collected as it drained from the wounds—along with the rest of the organic materials, I'd say. Aside from the gunshot, I didn't find any signs on the bodies to suggest the blood was extracted in any way. I think someone stood by and waited for the blood and other dissolved remains to seep out, then collected it," she whispered, shaking her head.

I shuddered. "Right. So we can assume one of the killers stood by after the actual kills were done?"

"Probably."

"Thanks," I said as I walked out.

When I reached the elevator doors, I found Weiss leaning against the wall and staring up at the ceiling. "You okay?"

"Execution-style gunshots in the back of their heads, then the bodies arranged in that freaky way, and the pentagram drawn in blood. One of these is a red herring?"

"Might be. But why go through the trouble? If it's Amanda's network like we suspect, why go through the trouble of the special effects? A pile of dead bodies would have worked just as well."

"Maybe the sick fuck who replaced her in the bunch is more artistic," he stated flatly.

I crossed my hands at my back. "The question is, how did they manage to leave no trace behind at the crime scene? I mean, if even Rick couldn't catch a scent of someone…."

He hit the back of his head against the wall. "Fuck me if I know."

Again, I wished I could. I didn't let the thought flutter through my mind, though. There was no time to fantasize now. Maybe later in the day, surely tonight….

"Maybe I should try talking to Amanda?" I wondered aloud. "She's being executed Friday, after all. I might catch her in a… talkative mood?"

He snorted. "While smelling of me? Good luck with that."

"Maybe Travis and Rick, then? They could go in. Rick and Amanda formed some kind of connection, I think. Maybe he'll get her talking."

"She's a stubborn bitch, but we'll have a go at it. What's to lose, anyway?"

I didn't think he actually wanted me to answer that, so I didn't. He looked older for a moment, his hair grayer than this morning, the lines around his eyes and mouth deeper.

"How could they have erased even the scent traces?" he muttered. "I don't think I've even heard of that kind of shit before. We didn't always have a tracker on the field, sure, but when we did they always found traces—even if faint. How the fuck could someone leave no scent traces?"

"There's no way, unless we're not talking of creatures made of anything organic. And I doubt robots arranged the bodies."

He turned to look at me. "Maybe Rick has some issue, and his scent isn't working right?"

"We can have Dr. Black test him, but I doubt it. He would've noticed the change happening. Let's take Travis and Rick in with us today when we visit Dr. Black for your blood work."

"Blood work? For the… temper, right. Yeah, we'll do that." He pushed away from the wall and called the elevator down. As we waited, he turned to look at me. "I always wondered, can you do any more magic tricks aside from that emotional balancing thing?"

I worked my jaws. "I'm not a pony, I don't do tricks."

"Right. You know what I mean."

I sighed. "I'm not that skilled as fey, but then again I'm only part fey. I can do some basic earth magic, but nothing impressive."

He stepped closer. "But other fey can do impressive stuff?"

"They call it 'magic' because it's impressive, right?"

"A simple 'yes' or 'no' would've been better."

"I'm not a simple 'yes' or 'no' guy," I said and walked into the elevator as it opened its doors. "So, what now? Except doing your paperwork."

He grinned and got in too. "It's already waiting for you in your office, by the way. You go handle that while I supervise Travis and Rick's try at talking to Amanda. We'll go to the victims' homes after that."

"All five of them?"

"I've already got investigators on scene everywhere. When they're done processing the homes, we'll take a look too."

"So two lycans, two vampires, and a werewolf. Except the two who'd been reported or suspected of abuse, do we know anything about the others? Anything that would make them targets for Amanda's network?"

He walked out of the elevator after the doors binged open, and I followed him, no clue as to where we were going. "The vampires— Gene Connelly and Donna Tempe—were part of the same S&M club. The one Travis and Rick busted that hormones-trafficking little shit in."

"Right. Any connection between that club and the rest of the vics?"

He shook his head.

"And the werewolf? Was he part of your pack?"

"Christian Woods wasn't one of mine, but he was alpha material. Not mated as far as we know, at least nothing on record. Then again, if he was rogue he wouldn't have made it official with us."

"I would've thought they'd go after one of your pack. I mean, what better way to piss you off?"

"Would've made it easier on me. I would've known a whole shitload more on one of my own. This guy, I don't know what the fuck he was about or what he was doing and for whom. No affiliation with the community as far as we can tell."

I hummed. "What does that leave? I mean, if the Council wasn't his authority, can we assume he answered to another?"

"He sure as hell didn't get discovered, and he made a living obviously. If the Council wasn't his protection, then he had some other form. Only one that comes to mind," he muttered darkly.

I swallowed thickly. "The Fey Court. No other faction has enough influence in this area to keep someone under protection. We sure he lived here, though?"

Weiss snorted. "Of course we're fucking sure. Don't tell me you're looking for excuses for your daddy, Edel," he spat.

"Of course not. But in case you didn't consider it, having anything to do with the Court is a horror. Just wishful thinking that we wouldn't have to, I guess."

"Go take care of the paperwork," he said, waving me off.

I wanted to do just that, so I turned around with the intention of walking to my office. But I didn't walk, just froze there. Coming toward me in what looked to me like slow motion was a group of seven fey: six of them walked in rows of twos, with the seventh one striding in the middle of their little formation. It was this middle one who drew my complete attention. His long, blond hair streamed behind him. The waist-long, tiny braid that signaled his status was sprinkled with gray here and there. His bronze-like skin seemed to glow despite the wrinkles and expression lines digging sternly into his face's hairless flesh. The straight line of his lips matched the straight line of his light brows, making the stormy gold eyes shine out like jewels of fire. I gasped, and my heart exploded in a crazy rhythm I didn't think it could hold for long before bursting. He wore a simple suit, nothing fancy or extravagant, which only drew more attention to him. The wide expanse of his shoulders looked more impressive than his guards', matching lean but strong muscles—I knew from personal experience—and the sheer image of fey strength had the whole lobby stand still. We didn't get to see them around the Bureau too often, after all.

The group stopped walking when they got close enough to me. I looked around slowly, making an inventory of my options. No way to avoid this, no way to run if they decided to get funny. I wouldn't manage to fight six of them, not even in my wildest dreams. None of the Bureau would intervene if they attacked me. The Council and the Fey Court had signed bilateral pacts of noninterference with each other's official business. And I was, without a doubt, official Fey Court business—they had a hit on me for five years now. The protection I was granted by Weiss made it impossible for my father to send assassins out to get me, but if he could claim I'd triggered a conflict, he was within his rights to respond to the threats. And if he'd go that route, he'd speak Fey, a language only he, his escorts, and the fey advisors he'd sent here spoke. There'd be nobody to translate. He could claim anything—including direct threats against his person. This was why I avoided fey almost as much as everyone else in the Bureau did. They were wily bastards.

The guy in the middle grinned crookedly, the same cruel, panic-inducing kind of grin I remembered from childhood. "*Ad no abba er*," my father crooned.

"*My traitor son*" was as nice a greeting as I could expect. "I bow to you, my father and king," I said through clenched teeth.

If possible, even more attention zoomed in on us. Anything deviating from fey protocol could be claimed as an insult to the King. Anything I'd speak in Fey could be claimed to mean something else. By speaking in the language everyone understood, everyone knew what I did and did not say. Even if the fey claimed differently, I'd have witnesses—and there was no shortage of those. Of course my father must've thought about it, which had to be why he approached me instead of ignoring me. Making sure I'd acknowledge he's my father before the whole Bureau instead of just the Council. The bastard wanted to hurt me as much as he could, of course. As if everyone here didn't mistrust me anyway thanks to my genes, to be the "fey prince" now would make me even more of an outcast.

"*Var na lit u naum*," he said, still grinning.

"*Forgot your mother tongue*"—classy. I smiled coldly. "My mother spoke Elvish."

His grin disappeared. "*Mau dna no ban, abba*," he sneered and walked away, followed by his guards.

"You'll die soon, traitor." Pffft, typical of my father. Though the "soon" bit worried me. He didn't make empty threats, not ever. That could only mean my father was planning something, and whatever it was, it wouldn't be good. With him, it never was.

I didn't look after them as they left, though I was dying to find out what was going on. The Fey King didn't go out of the realm for just any reason, and to come here, to the Council's seat of power—there had to be a really good reason. I made a mental note to try and find out later, but right now the buzzing in my ears and the feeling my nape was on fire screamed I needed to run for cover. Everyone was still staring at me, and I didn't want to look around and see what kind of expressions they wore. Shock, distaste, mistrust—that much I could feel pulsing through the entire room. Freaking brilliant, just what I needed.

I walked to my office with as much calm as I could force into every step, closed the door behind me, and leaned against it for a moment. I was pretty confident I'd escaped any possible offense-to-the-king framing, so I was probably in the clear for now. But I wouldn't be for long. Thoughts began to rush and screech through my mind, a subtle thread of panic slowly weaving itself into a net. My gaze drifted over my office, not quite settling on anything. I couldn't shake the feeling this was just the beginning of something I wouldn't like at all. Weiss's paperwork gripped my attention, and I breathed a sigh of relief. What better way to go into mindless bliss if not filling out paperwork? I sat at my desk and got to it.

What felt like an eternity later, my office door opened and closed. Weiss's electric presence filled the room, and my gaze shot up to his on instinct.

He watched me for a while, sticking a hand in his pocket. "Heard you ran into Daddy dearest."

I looked down at the page I was working on. "Bet you got colorful descriptions of the moment."

He snorted. "A fucking rainbow of descriptions, but that's not my point. I watched the security footage of it, heard the discussion. What did he say to you?"

"Oh, you know—that I'm a traitor, and that I'll die soon—same old."

"Obvious where you get your mindfuck skills from," he said.

I cracked my neck, still looking down. "Thanks. Was there anything else?"

"Don't get snappy with me, Edel. I might not be as cruel as your father, but I'm no lamb either."

I sighed. "I'm sorry. I'd just like some time to calm down."

"Do you hate him?" he asked, walking over to the chair in front of my desk.

"Yes."

He sat down, the lines of his body drawing my gaze. "He's still your father. No love there at all?"

I worked my jaws. "None whatsoever."

He leaned forward in the chair, setting his elbows on the edge of my desk. "I find that hard to believe. Either you're as heartless as he is, or you're lying. Whichever it is, I don't like it."

I sighed, rubbed both hands over my face, and leaned back in my chair, stretching my legs out under the desk. "It's personal, okay?"

"Might be, but I want to know."

"Because you've been a stellar example of sharing personal information so far?" I asked flatly.

"This isn't about you, me, and feelings, Edel."

I lifted an eyebrow. "Really? What is it about, then?"

He sighed. "Your father just threatened the Council with becoming the community's protector."

I blanched. "He what?"

"Got the signatures for it too. Apparently the stream of leader murders has caused more unease in the community than the Council was willing to admit to. The Abuse team and the leader abuse prevention act don't seem assertive enough measures. The Fey King wants to declare the Council incompetent and be the protector of the community until a new Council is assembled."

I stared, horrified. "He can't do that."

Weiss's eyes went icy white, though his face didn't become wolfish. "Yes, he can. There's a bilateral treaty signed between the Council and the Fey Court. In case either one of the two is deemed incompetent by their people via 250,000 signatures, the other will assume the protector role until a new Council or Court is put in charge. Your father has the signatures. We have a few days to verify them, but I have a feeling that won't help us much."

My hands were shaking, I realized. "You can't let that happen. He's going to destroy everything you've worked for. Then he's going to kill me."

He gritted his teeth. "That's what I think. He stated he's willing to lose those signatures on one condition. Care to guess what the condition is?"

My blood went ice-cold. The shivering traveled up my bones from my hands to the tips of my hairs, then slid down to my toes. "That you turn me over to the Court and retract the Council's protection."

"Yes," he nodded tightly. "Now, I have to wonder why your death is on par with staging a coup. Thoughts?"

"I can't imagine…," I murmured.

Weiss reached over the desk, then slapped my cheek. "Snap the fuck out of it. I need you to think."

I gulped and put a hand over the cheek he slapped. My face throbbed there, the sting going through my system. I frowned. "That was uncalled for, asshole."

"The fuck it was," he snarled. "You were going panicky on me. I can't afford the luxury of a fuckup right now. Think. Why would your death be as valuable as a coup?"

I worked my jaw, balancing my own emotional grid. "He's a power-hungry heartless monster. Nothing is worth more to him than that, not even getting even with me for disobeying him."

"So this isn't about you?"

"I don't think so. He'd love to squish me like a bug, sure, but not as much as he'd like to take over the Council's community. And I wouldn't trust him to keep his word. He's going to kill me, then use the signatures anyway."

"The Council's thinking exactly. That's one of two reasons you're here instead of in the Court's custody."

"And the second?" I wondered, peering into his eyes.

He looked away. "If you're killed now, I'm dead too. No Council, no PBI Director, and a fey protectorate—that's the fucking Armageddon."

I smiled. "So you told the Council about your… bouts of temper?"

He snorted. "You soft in the head? Of course I fucking didn't. I told them I'm mating you first thing after Amanda's execution. They could choose to waive your protection, but it would mean they'd lose my allegiance. Not something they can afford right now. So you're safe."

"As long as I'm useful to you," I added.

"And I'm safe as long as I'm useful to the Council. Going into rages won't be it. All the more incentive for you to keep me in fucking balance, Edel."

I shook my head and looked up at the ceiling. "Dear waving wands, what did I do so wrong to deserve all of this?" I inhaled and exhaled slowly, then looked back at him. "Won't the Council be pissed when they see you don't mate me Friday?"

He grinned ominously. "Oh, but I am going to, Edel."

eight

"HAVE YOU lost your mind?" I screeched.

"Call that doctor friend of yours. We need to have my blood tested ASAP, just to clear the rages theory. Once that's settled, we'll know better where we stand."

I lifted my eyebrows. "You can't possibly mean to mate me on Friday."

"Why not?" he asked, shrugging. "You're working on the Act to allow our mating's dissolving with or without my accord, right? So you know you won't be trapped. It's gonna change nothing, Edel. Relax, the deal will still be the same."

"No, it fucking won't!" I snapped. "Not if we get mated for real."

"Would you rather go into Fey Court custody?" he asked tersely.

I cracked my neck. "Of course not."

"Those are your rosy alternatives. If it's any consolation, I'm stuck between a rock and a hard place too. Either I get put down for rages I'm sure I don't have, or mate a guy who's obviously repulsed by the idea of mating me."

"I'm not repulsed," I screamed, throwing my hands up.

His gaze zeroed in on me. "You look like I'm forcing you to eat shit with a spoon."

"Because of the situation, not the mating tangent. I'm not happy to be fake-mated after I'm fake-dating someone, but that's far from being repulsed."

"Would you feel better if we dated for real and got mated for real?" he asked in a perfectly neutral tone.

I got up, then walked toward the window, though all I could see from it was his parking spot. "That's obviously not an option. It can't be for real as long as there's no interest, can it?"

He got up and walked toward me, stopping a couple steps behind me. "Because you're not interested."

It was a cross between a statement and a question, though I wanted it to be more of a question. I wasn't sure which one it was, and I rubbed a hand over my brows trying to decide. "Because *you're* not interested," I finally said.

He took another step closer, making the old hardwood floors of the office creak slightly. "Are you?"

"You know, I can't decide if you're oblivious or simply sadistic. Which one is it, Weiss? Are you truly not aware, or do you enjoy playing with me like this because you *are* aware? I'm dying to know," I whispered faintly.

"Turn around," he commanded.

"Just answer the question, please."

"Turn the fuck around," he snapped.

I flinched but remained frozen to the spot. He reached out and grabbed my shoulder, turned me around and pushed me against the wall. My back hit the window with a thump, though considerably less loud than the thumps of my heart. I couldn't look at him, I didn't dare to. It would crush me to see rejection in his gaze. I could at least save myself that pain.

"Look at me," he commanded.

"I don't want to."

"The fuck you don't," he said and fixed a hand under my chin.

Before I could retort, his lips hit mine in a painful, bruising kiss that was really more like a punch. I gasped at the force of it, and he took the chance to deepen the contact. His tongue lashed into my mouth, hot and cruel, and seemingly famished for something. He pushed me hard against the wall, his body pressing into mine mercilessly. I whimpered and sagged against him, all traces of rationality disappearing. If he wanted to play me like a silly puppet, then so be it, I decided. I'd be happy even with that cruel contact, with the knowledge it was nothing but a game and politics for him. Because

I was that desperate and weak, I realized. I was that painfully lonely, the promise of his touch felt like salvation regardless of the reasons or end games. I gripped the shirt on his arms and bunched the fabric in my fists, pulling him even closer. It would hurt—somewhere down the road, this moment of mindless need would gut me. But at least I'd have the glorious memory of how all-consuming it was, for that one stupid second.

He pulled back from my lips but kept pressing against me. "This isn't just about needing your talents or wanting you as a bargaining chip to keep myself alive. I do need your talents and I will use you to get things done. It's who and what I am. But this is not all about that," he whispered.

I gulped. "Why would I believe you? Making me fall for your lies right now would make things easy for you. And you're the kind of man who'd use my feelings like that."

He grinned. "I am. But I'm not faking, Edel. The hard-on is real, and the interest behind it is real too."

"The interest to fuck?"

"To fuck, to plan, to deal with this whole lot of shit together. What more could there ever be?"

"Feelings," I whispered.

"Feelings," he repeated, rubbing his lips against mine. "Never been good with those."

"Don't string me on just to use me, Weiss. I'll do whatever it is you want me to do, play whatever game we have to play to survive this shitstorm. I'm grateful to you for saving my life five years ago and trying to help me now—for whatever reasons of your own."

He stepped back, rearranged his hard-on, and rubbed a hand over his brow. "This isn't fifth grade, Sands. I've gotten well fucking beyond the love notes stage of my life. What are you looking for, sappy declarations of everlasting love?"

"I'm looking for a real connection. For an open, honest, heartfelt connection."

He frowned. "And you think I'm not capable of one, is that it? Because I'm such a power-hungry monster? Like your father, maybe," he gritted out.

"Sweet flapping wings, no! You could never be anything like him. I don't question the fact you have feelings, Weiss. I'm just sure you don't have any for me. And unless you think there's a faint possibility of them ever developing, then let's not do this. Let's just do what we've agreed to do until we ride this storm out, no hard feelings."

"Wrap up whatever it was you were doing and get your ass downstairs. I'll be waiting in the car."

I frowned. "Where are we going?"

"Christian Woods's house, Edel. The world doesn't stop revolving because of my feelings or lack thereof," he barked out and stormed out the door.

I stood there, totally dumbstruck for a while. What the flipping wing had just happened? I tried to make some sense of it all. All confusion aside, I had to call Dr. Black and set that appointment for Weiss's blood work. Rick had to come in and have his scent tested too—better to use his test as an excuse to have Weiss there. I texted him to let him know we'd be going there later on. Rick replied he was okay with it. After making the call and scheduling the scent tests for an hour later, I texted Rick the time and closed my office door. Weiss must've been fuming already and keeping him waiting might get me killed via raging werewolf asshole.

To my surprise, when I got into his Beamer, he was the picture of calm. After I closed the door, he revved up the engine and burst out of the parking lot, the speed pushing me into the seat. I gulped but kept my mouth shut, set on doing so at least until I was back on solid ground. The man was out of his freaking mind, driving like a lunatic and barely missing impact with a truck and two other cars. I gripped my thighs so hard, my knuckles were white, but I didn't say a word. I also prayed the seat belt I fastened religiously would save me, should anything occur. Weiss's driving made surviving the ride a miracle, in my opinion.

The car stopped in front of a shabby two-story building in the less glamorous part of the city. Weiss got out of the car, slapped the door shut, and went around the front of the car to stand by the door of the building. I did my breathing exercise as I got out too and closed the passenger's side door gingerly. Weiss's Beamer chirped as he set the alarm on.

"Get a move on, princess," he barked and took the front stairs two at a time.

Ugh, right. I braced myself and followed. What I really wanted to do was scream my damn lungs out at him and give him a sturdy piece of my mind right about now. But pissing him off wasn't the wisest thing I could do, not with a potential rage coming and still so much of the day to get through—besides, it was only Tuesday. So I just focused on relaxing and trying to go for as close to non-hissy-pissy-fit as I could. I walked up the front stairs and pushed through the dirty front door. The hallway of this place smelled like a mix of piss, days-old barf, and a sprinkling of shit—foul was a severe understatement. I tried my best to push down my gag reflex and rushed in the direction of the open door I could see ahead. Weiss stood there, hands in his pockets, looking around.

"This is where Christian Woods lived?"

He nodded. "And there," he said, pointing to the outline of a body, "is where his accomplice, mate, or whatever was killed. Agents found the body earlier when they checked his residence."

"How'd we know where he lived?"

He sighed. "Got lucky. He had a subpoena delivered here. Whoever was protecting him had him under human cover. Someone tipped us off when we started researching the name."

I looked around. "So his DNA was in the batch of leader samples we got from the hormones traffickers. His accomplice or mate was killed, and he was killed in the pentagram batch. I don't see many connections here, do you?"

"I went in to see the accomplice's body before I came to see you. I know that face."

I frowned and looked toward him, though he wasn't making eye contact. "Personally? You knew Christian's accomplice personally?"

"Yeah. Bobby Springs—he was someone's squeeze. I saw him by accident, but it stuck to mind since I thought I recognized his scent yet didn't know his face. These things stand out to an alpha, you know?"

"Whose squeeze was he?"

"Tricia's," he said through clenched teeth.

"Why would she go out with a rogue?" I wondered aloud.

"Exactly what I'm gonna ask her," he growled. "Let's go."

I rushed behind him. "I set up Rick's scent test with Dr. Black. I'm thinking we should drop by, see how that's going."

He glanced at me for a moment. "Why the fuck would I hold his hand? Got a mate for that, doesn't he?"

Pffft. "Because we'd stop by Dr. Black's office?" I asked in a "duuh!" tone.

"Right," he muttered. "Fine, I'll have Tricia taken to Downtown, then, since Dr. Black's place is closer to it than HQ. When we're done with that, we go straight there."

I watched him get into the car and read his emotional grid. He was pissed and outraged in faint amounts, even disappointed. Not raging, though, and not even remotely in love. Of course not—not that I was allowing myself to hope for it. But if he'd been interested in me at all, even faintly, some of that desire would've shown even now. There was sexual desire, his hard-on had spelled that out. But no romantic feelings I could see, and I should have seen them if they were there. I'd been right—he wasn't really interested in me. Not much of a surprise there, after all. Now all I had to do was decide if sleeping with him would make things better or worse for me in the current situation. On the other hand, at least he wasn't going into a rage either, so there was that going for us. He honked the horn, of course, so I hurried to get in the car too.

Fifteen minutes later I was close to heart palpitations and trying very hard not to throw up as I stood in Dr. Black's parking lot. "You'll get us killed, crazyass," I gritted out.

He looked at anything but me. "Get a move on, fey prince. We're wasting time already."

True to his bastardly ways, he went into the clinic and left me there. That cocky, presumptuous, heartless bastard wouldn't get away with it, I promised myself that. My revenge would be swift and merciless, but it had to wait for now. All the better, I could plot it out rationally, after the rage went away. I shivered as I recognized my father's approach in my words. That froze me up good enough to solve all my nausea and heartbeat irregularities. I walked inside too. Weiss sat in a chair in front of Dr. Black's office, legs crossed and his frosty disposition obvious by his whitish eyes. I knocked on Dr. Black's door and walked in.

"Ah, Mr. Sands!" he said, beaming from inside. "Please come in."

I gestured for Weiss to come with. He got up silently and walked inside, stuffing his hands in his pockets.

"This is the friend I was telling you about," I told the good doc. "We need his blood tested for incipient rage," I added.

Dr. Black nodded. "Sure, sure. Name?"

"White," Weiss said without blinking. "Henry White."

Dr. Black frowned. "You look like…."

"Henry White," I cut him off.

Dr. Black hummed, looked between the two of us, and then smiled. "Henry White it is, then. Let's just hope Mr. White doesn't have incipient rages, or the PBI will have to take him into custody. I'll have to call it in, you understand."

Weiss growled viciously.

Dr. Black gulped but held a hand up. "I'll have to report *Henry White*'s incipient rages situation. Agents will realize, after he'll be long gone, that the address he's given me is sadly a fake one, and his blood workup will be mysteriously gone—perhaps due to the new lab technician."

"Thank you," I replied, still reading Weiss's emotional grid for signs of a rage.

The blood collecting went quickly.

"When will Sands hear from you?" Weiss asked.

"First thing tomorrow morning," Dr. Black replied. "Now, if you'd like to see your friends? They're still in, getting the results of the test explained."

"We'll catch them later," Weiss snapped. "Thank you for your help, Dr. Black."

He nodded. "All right. For what it's worth, Mr. White, while you display a dizzying array of characteristics I could sink my psychoanalytic teeth into, you don't present as a case of rages—even incipient."

"Thanks, I think. And thanks for helping out," Weiss added.

The doc smiled. "You've got Mr. Sands here to thank for that. He called in some favors. I just couldn't refuse his request."

Weiss frowned as we walked out of the clinic and headed for the car. "What the fuck was that supposed to mean?" he barked.

I looked at him sideways. "Dr. Black has a unique sense of humor. Don't worry, I didn't do anything that would trace back to you to get this favor."

"So what, it was a blowjob or something like that, that wouldn't leave a paper trail?" he growled.

I checked his emotional grid—jealousy. Huh. "Of course not. How would it look for your boyfriend to offer blowjobs at the corner of the street like that?"

He squinted. "That supposed to be funny?"

"Not really. By the time I called him, rumor had already gotten around that I was your new boyfriend. Don't worry, I just offered help with some research he's been having difficulties with."

"What kind of research?"

"Behavioral patterns of—"

He held a hand up. "Forget I asked."

I grinned as we got into the car. "Weiss?"

He sighed, his hands on the wheel but the engine still off. "What?"

"I'm sorry about earlier, in my office. I was a mess after seeing my father, and with all the cheery news of his plans too… I'm sorry, I didn't react well to our discussion."

He leaned back in the seat and slid his hands down the wheel until they rested on his thighs. "What do you want, Sands?"

"Like what, from life?"

"From this," he said, gesturing between us. "I like things clear and simple."

"And feelings are messy," I added softly.

"Talking about them is," he grumbled, looking straight out the windshield. "Give me a game plan. That's what I'm good with."

I inhaled deeply, braced myself. "I'd like us to go wherever you'd be willing to take us."

"Because you're into me?" he asked, still looking away.

"I thought you didn't like to talk about feelings."

He peeked at me sideways. "Only about mine. Yours are fair game."

I smiled. "I'm into exploring this, yes."

"I can't tell if you're lying or not. Your heart's beating fast, but it could be for any number of reasons. So I can't tell."

"Why would I lie, and what about?" I asked, frowning.

He turned to look at me, finally. His eyes were a darker shade than their usual icy blue, his pupils blowing out. The intensity of his gaze took my breath away.

"You could be trying to get under my skin. One reason might be that you're a dormant agent of your father's, waiting for the best moment to strike and take over."

I gaped at him. "You can't possibly think that after I've worked five years at the PBI!"

He snorted. "Time is no issue for a well-trained agent, Sands. We both know that. You've been waiting because the right circumstances hadn't presented themselves. Now maybe they have. Your daddy dearest works us from the outside, you from the inside. And what better position than from under my skin?"

"Paranoia is a new symptom, or was it always there?" I asked snidely.

"All clever plans sound half-nuts, until they're carried out. I know you're hiding something. You have been for years. No one is as private as you've been. You don't really mix with PBI agents. You went out with Travis and dumped him supposedly for someone else, but nobody showed up beside you. You go to a human gym, have more human friends than from our community. PBI protocol is to withdraw our new community members from their former human lives, Sands. Whose protocol is it to keep their people under human cover?"

"Fey Court's," I muttered, realizing how it could look.

The question was, if he thought I really was a fey spy, why hadn't he simply interrogated it out of me? My resemblance to his dead lover had kept me safe? Maybe he had hopes of turning me into a double agent of sorts? Did he think he'd turned me into his spy, maybe? And as that thought popped into my head, another, even darker, one appeared. What if I was still alive because he thought of me as an asset via that double agent possibility? What would happen when he found out I wasn't such an asset after all? At this point, I thought I might as well go for the truth. After all, either he'd believe it, or take it as me trying to not blow my cover. Both options seemed to semiwork for me right now. Far as I could see it, my life hung by a thin thread, and whichever way I looked at it, the thread was tightly tied to Weiss.

"I have been hiding something, Weiss. But it's not what you think."

He cocked an eyebrow. "Oh really? What is it, then?"

Deep breath in, slow breath out. "I've been head over heels in love with you for about five long, lonely years."

nine

WEISS TURNED to look back out the windshield. He started the car and drove us downtown. Silence rode with us the whole way there. We passed through the security checkpoint in the underground parking. Weiss pulled into the big D-marked parking spot.

"Say something," I whispered as he turned the engine off.

He tapped his fingertips against the wheel. "Why mingle with humans?"

"I feel less like the odd duckling with them. I've never fit in, you know? I wasn't elf enough for my mother's side of the fence, not fey enough for my father. After my mom left, the more I grew up, the clearer it was for my father that I wouldn't be the asset he'd planned me to be. I didn't agree with his politics, despised them in fact, and didn't take orders well. In the end I defied him, and you know how that ended. At the PBI everyone seemed to mistrust me. I guess I was too fey for their comfort. Humans don't see any of that when they look at me. They just see a guy. I can be one of many when I'm with them."

"Because you're pretending to be something you're not," he said. "How's that any good?"

I shrugged. "Better than nothing."

"You go out with humans too?"

I nodded. "Never more than the one date, though. I can't pretend well enough I'm a human, not in a romantic relationship. Human friends are great, as long as I'm careful about the lines. With friends I see occasionally, I can pretend to be what they have to believe I am. I don't sleep with them in my bed. Not that I've been doing much of that, either," I added, smiling bitterly.

He hummed. "You're either trying to reinforce your cover or being honest."

"Question is, on which of the two will you decide?"

He smiled. "Neither for now. We'll talk about this later, when we get home. Right now, I have to ask one of my betas why she's involved in this huge-ass shit."

James was waiting for us by Investigations Room 4. "This right here is some grade-A clusterfuck," he muttered, looking between us.

Weiss shrugged. "Shit happens. Has anyone talked to her?"

"Just as instructed, nobody was in. Weiss, are you sure…?"

The werewolf alpha growled. "Questioning me, James?"

"No, sir."

"Good," Weiss nearly spat out. "How long has she been in there?"

"Hour and a half," James said.

"Right. Showtime. I need you to look on from the observation room and report to me if there's anything weird about her body language," Weiss said, staring at me.

I lifted an eyebrow. "By telepathy?"

They both rolled their eyes. "Earpiece and mike."

Right. Read Tricia, someone I didn't like to begin with. How hard could it be? I knew nothing about her and her body language, and the bare minimum I might get could be tainted by my personal opinion of her. Pffft, piece of cake.

James and I entered the observation room as Weiss went into the interrogation one. I noticed the speakers and mike setup.

"Guess this is where the magic will happen?" I asked, gesturing between the techy stuff.

"You press that button there and talk into the mike. Be gentle with his ear, don't shout into it." He smiled as he looked through the one-way glass. "That's where the magic happens, though," he said, pointing at the interrogation room. "We're just a pair of eyes."

"Right. And Weiss has some earpiece?"

He nodded. "I was surprised to see Tricia brought in."

"He was surprised to make the connection, I think. Supposedly she used to go out with one of the nonleader victims."

"What's the toll up to?"

"Five leaders, six vics," I said, mentally adding, *and counting.*

"This is one fucked-up case."

It was. I kept my eyes on Tricia through the glass. Her hands were crossed, her stance was defensive. She tended to avoid eye contact, seemed to remember it was a bad idea, and then made too much of it.

"She's hiding something," I spoke into the mike.

Weiss didn't say or do anything to acknowledge he'd heard, but I had to operate on the assumption he did. I couldn't see him, only his back. He started pressing her about information on Bobby, now and then throwing a curveball in—enough to help me decide on a baseline.

"He's done this before, worked with someone like me," I said.

James smiled. "Used to work that way with my brother."

My heart thumped. "Oh? Didn't know you had a brother."

He crossed his arms over his chest. "Nobody talks about it. I can see how you wouldn't have known."

"Were they partners in Weiss's earlier days or something?"

I knew I was pushing, but I had to find out more about Mitchell. Who better to impart that knowledge than his brother?

"She's nervous, press on that topic," I said into the mike, then stepped back. My eyes stayed on Tricia now, and I kept reading her emotional grid in short flashes.

"They used to work together before Amanda showed up," James finally said. "'Course, when she strode in, she grabbed the entire spotlight beside Weiss."

I peeked at him sideways. "Forced your bother into retirement or something?"

"Spite mating, then suicide. Weiss will tell you that my brother killed himself over his consort's death, but that's a lie."

"Really? Why would he lie?"

James smiled. "Tends to, when he feels guilty about something. My brother was crazy in love with Weiss. From bro's side, it looked like Weiss felt the same. Of course, he needed a Weiss heir to the pack crown. That's where Amanda came in."

I sighed. "He dumped someone he loved to get an heir? From Amanda?"

James smiled. "Karma is a bitch, huh? Though Alf seems decent enough so far. Of course, he's only seven. No good figure in his family to emulate."

"Keep pressing, she's close to breaking," I said into the mike and stepped back again. "You think Weiss is responsible for your brother's suicide?"

"My brother was insanely lost in him. You might not understand just how much, nobody did except for me. I knew my brother, and what loving Weiss made him into... the bastard became the sun of his galaxy, the air, the water, the food, the thoughts—everything. Weiss was his everything. Then the bastard just left him, cut all ties. Amanda was all that mattered: researching her, turning her, getting her to fall for our dear werewolf alpha."

I knew profiling and research preceded the recruiting and turning part, but still, thinking about Weiss looking up prospective mates that way sent chills down my spine. Like he was looking for an apartment or a car, looking up specifics to determine if it would fit his list of needs. Amanda was a chess piece on Weiss's board game, and I realized more than ever that the rest of us were all the same. Even his son, whom I did think he loved, was a chess piece on that board. As long as we were useful in his game, he'd fight tooth and nail to keep us within reach. Traditional pack alphas, coming from families of pack alphas like Weiss did, were political monsters. The scheming and dealing was drilled into them since they were kids, and I could tell from my brief time around Alf that he already was an astute politician and strategist at age seven. He figured out my place in his pack's rank pretty much instantly, decided on the best way to approach me that wouldn't piss off his alpha but put him in a position of power over me—chewing my shoes, however funny to contemplate, was his way of asserting his authority over me. I could only imagine how those instincts would evolve in say ten years, or twenty.

That aura of raw power was part of what attracted me to Weiss. I couldn't blame him for being who he was, especially when who he was turned me the hell on. But it was scary at times to contemplate it, more so now that I was actually involved with him in a way. Having a crush on him from afar had been easy, I realized. It was living inside of his games and having a crush on him that really got my adrenaline pumping.

All so scary, all so exciting, and that was without even considering making out with him or anything remotely in that area.

"He dumped my brother and forgot he ever existed," James said, bringing me back into the discussion.

"Maybe he thought it would be the best way for both of them to move on," I offered in a small voice.

"You don't understand. When he started dating Mitch, Weiss knew he'd mate a female. He fucking knew it all along. It was all part of his grand plan."

"And he told your brother that? From the beginning?"

He sighed. "No, he didn't. But his pack knew. Of course, since my brother wasn't pack, he glossed over the rumors as just that— rumors. I'm told you need to be pack to understand their politics. For vampires like us, it's more of an effort to get the whole shitty thing. Our politics run more in the swift demise direction, rather than long-run tactical maneuvering. You know how sometimes you tend to see other's actions mirroring your own motivations and thought processes? Mitch did that, I think. He thought that since he wouldn't have done what Weiss was doing, that it meant Weiss wasn't doing it either. I kept trying to tell Mitch that Weiss's pack wouldn't just spread rumors, not about the future of their pack. He wouldn't listen, of course. Why would he, when the light of his eyes kept shining down on him so sweetly?"

I frowned. "So Weiss was already alpha when he was dating your brother?"

"Not yet, no. But he was scheming to become the alpha, planning to murder his father. Can't say I blame him for it. I would've caved and murdered the bastard years sooner, if I'd been Weiss."

"How did that happen, his father's murder?"

"Well," James said, leaning against the window and looking at me. "The new Council didn't like old Weiss. He was too wild, too erratically violent to fit into the new world order scheme the new Council was planning. See, our territory's dirty little secret is it looks all legalized and properly regulated, but it was built on blood, all of it. Vampires, werewolves, elves, and fey even, all of them fought, murdered, blackmailed their way into today's relative appearance of peace."

I looked at him sideways. "I know that. My father was part of the… founding fathers of this so-called peace."

"Right. So you know they replaced the ones who'd fought with new, cleaner figures of authority where they could."

"Meaning anywhere but in the Fey Court and Elf Lord's Guard," I replied.

"Right. The Council's new face had to match the diverse, properly regulated frame they were working on. Weiss's dad was one of the bloody fighters, the kind of face that wouldn't fit into this new picture of civility. So the Council made its support clear for Herman to replace his father, provided that he'd make some agreements with them. Becoming the officially sanctioned pack's alpha was penciled in as supporting a dynasty."

"And you can't have a dynasty without heirs, I get it," I said, shaking my head.

"So there you go, Amanda was in, my brother was out. Weiss did a terrible job at making the change too."

Maybe because his heart was broken too, I thought. He'd cared about Mitchell James enough to still feel guilty about him and miss him now, years later. But of course James didn't know that, and I wasn't going to blab Weiss's secrets to anyone.

"It's why Weiss is responsible, as far as I'm concerned," James went on. "He threw my brother off of a cliff, built him wings of wax and allowed him to glide for a while. Made him think he could actually fly, that the wings would hold—that they existed in the first place. Then he melted them off and left Mitch to fall, to crash to the ground. And he did crash. He was broken in a way nothing could mend. He acted like he was okay for as long he could, and then, when he had no more good reason to pretend, he just… let go."

I swallowed thickly. "I'm so sorry for your loss."

"Don't be. Not while you're taking the place my brother would've killed for. Just know this: Herman Weiss is incapable of thinking about anyone but himself and his agenda. He's a ruthless, heartless, evil motherfucker."

"Yet you seem to respect him," I observed.

He smiled sadly. "I respect everything deadly. And he is deadly. Look at his history. Who do you know that got close and didn't end up paying for it with their lives?"

My heart constricted. "Just because of your brother's unfortunate and regrettable situation—"

He held a hand up. "He helped his father tear his mother apart because she was supposedly cheating on him. He killed his father to become the pack's next alpha, with the Council's approval. He killed my brother in all ways that mattered even before he killed himself, and he's getting Amanda killed too in a way. Love him, if you must. Just be aware it's an extreme sport few end up surviving," James whispered sadly.

Weiss's thick growl exploded in the interrogation room. "Tell me the fucking truth!" he snarled, his face morphing into wolfish traits.

Tricia jumped out of the chair, her face morphing into wolf traits too. "You're dead, you son of a miserable bitch!" she screeched like a banshee.

James and I both stepped closer to the glass.

"Her body language is changed. She's aggressive now. Doesn't fit the image of a pack beta toward her alpha," I muttered into the mike, though I wasn't sure he was listening anymore.

"Huh," James said and clacked his tongue. "If she's not acting like his beta, she's one of the traitors?"

I contemplated it. "She's on Amanda's side? How could she…?"

"Hormones," James spat. "If Amanda got her on hormones, then her real alpha isn't Weiss. Question is, who is it?"

Tricia jumped at Weiss, clearly intent on going for a kill. He threw her against a wall, a sickening crack accompanying the impact. Her body slid to the ground as blood splattered out of her mouth.

"What are you after?" Weiss snarled.

She smiled. "Amanda will be free. You'll have to set her free. She'll take you out, you heartless monster. You and your whore fairy," she said and spat blood on the floor.

I swallowed thickly. "Shouldn't someone go in there?"

"And get killed too?" James said. "He's her alpha officially. He has right of life or death over her."

I crossed my arms around myself, shaking my head. "That's just wrong."

"Maybe," James commented. "But then again, what the fuck is right?"

"Your favorite bitch is in custody," Weiss said with a lisp. "Who's calling the shots now?"

"Wouldn't you like to know," Tricia said, coughing out more blood.

Weiss chuckled eerily. "You might think you're going to die today, but you won't. I won't let the Council take you into custody, you little bitch. I'm going to take you into my custody as your alpha. And I assure you, you'll pray for death each and every moment for the rest of your long, miserably painful life. Tell me what I want to know now, and I'll spare you the torture. I'll let you die today."

I shivered. He'd lost the lisp, and he was in fully human form now. He was thinking rationally, and planning, or threatening at least, to torture her for a long time. A sick part of me couldn't help but admire his viciousness. My monster liked his monster, and no matter how scared I was of both of them, they seemed to click in frightening, visceral ways. My father would've approved of Weiss's tactic. He would have taken it further. If I'd let my father's rigor take over, I'd take it further right now. I'd suggest taking it further, whisper it sweetly into that mike before me. I wrapped my hands around myself tighter, and I stepped forward. "She's not afraid of pain. You have to crack her some other way. Offer her something she'd want. Something she'll be compelled to say yes to. Offer her her alpha," I whispered into the mike.

Weiss stepped back from Tricia's broken body and leaned against the glass divider. "Locking you up in solitary would help clear your head. How would you feel about not seeing Bert?"

Tricia was unperturbed.

"It's not him," I whispered into the mike. "Who could her alpha be, if she's so dedicated to Amanda? Mention Amanda herself. We need to see the reaction."

Weiss sighed. "Or I could have you locked up with your precious Amanda."

Tricia's eyes snapped up, her pupils blowing wide enough to darken her eyes.

"That's it, she recognizes Amanda as her alpha," I said into the mike.

"Fucking hormone trafficking," James muttered beside me. "Like regular pack dynamics weren't fucked up enough on their own, now we have free radicals as pseudo-alphas too?"

Weiss walked calmly out of the interrogation room and moments later came to join us. He stood there, hands stuck in his pockets. "What do you make of that, Sands?"

"It's those marking hormones, it must be. But if she recognizes Amanda as her alpha, who is she obeying now that Amanda is in custody?"

"Someone who'd be Amanda's pseudo-beta," James chimed in.

Weiss ran a hand through his hair, disheveling the neat comb-back. "Fucking Christ, another snake in my own house, and I had no idea. She could've killed Alf at any moment just to get back at me."

I wrapped my arms around myself tighter. "True, but she didn't. Either Amanda herself asked for his protection, or this pseudo-beta running the show now."

"Could it be Bert?" Weiss asked in a small voice.

"Don't think so," I replied. "She didn't have enough of a reaction to his name. He might not even be in on it, as far as we know. Tricia was belligerent toward me as usurper of Amanda's rank, but Bert was friendly. I don't think both of them are in on it. We need to talk to him, though. If she's not talking, then the next best source of information would be someone close to her."

Weiss sighed. "That's Bert all right. They pretty much spend all their time together. Except when they're out on dates and shit. Do you think we can get any more information out of her, James?"

James puffed his cheeks. "Threat of pain didn't make her talk, and she won't believe any promise of pleasure. I don't think there's much to gain here. But we will try, if you want us to," he said, looking at Weiss.

"Do that," he said and walked out. "Come on, Sands. We have another beta to talk to."

"Bye, James," I called out behind me as I went for the door.

He didn't reply, or maybe I didn't hear it. The conversation we'd had stuck in my mind, parts of it turning round and round in my thoughts. Every story had as many sides as participants, of course, but could James be right? Was Weiss lying to himself about Mitchell's suicide? He did feel guilty about something. It was what gave me more space to maneuver around the prickly werewolf alpha. If he felt guilty, and I did remind him of Mitchell, then I had a lot of room to wiggle in. I could work the situation to be sure he wouldn't give me off to the Fey

Court, like my father had asked. But why would he ask, now that I thought about it? He'd been living just fine for these past five years, knowing I had a life on the Council territories. Why go through the trouble of personally requesting me now, at threat of protectorate for the territories?

We walked out of the building and got into the car. Once we were seated, Weiss leaned back in the seat instead of turning on the engine. "Right under my nose. She was right under my nose, and I had no clue. I should just give myself into the Council for terminal rages and be done with it. Might actually do the pack a service."

"Don't be an idiot. You're their alpha because you're the strongest, and they recognize that. Do your best for them and yourself, don't throw the fight."

He snorted. "This from a fey prince who chose to run screaming rather than become his daddy's heir?"

"You don't pull any punches, do you?" I asked, squinting at him sideways.

"Since we're on the topic, though, why Daddy would want you dead so bad? Why right now?"

I tapped my fingertips against my knees. "I was just thinking about that, actually. The only thing I could think of is the lineage issue. If he knows his reign is coming to an end shortly, there's no way he can cut me out of the position of king unless I'm dead. But that would mean he knows he's going to die soon, and he has chosen his successor, one he wants to assure as next in line."

Weiss snorted. "Well, if the Fey King is going to die, then today had at least some good news. Seriously, though, if you're outcast, how could you inherit the throne?"

"I simply would, as soon as he died," I said, shrugging. "It's the one piece of legislation the Court refused to let him change while I was there. Pretty sure they stuck to their guns since too. It's the basis of the whole fey-elves peace treaty: the treaty child—meaning me—would be next in line after my father, whatever happened in the meantime. That way, someone part elf would be in charge. My father's sister married my mother's brother, an Elf Lord, to mirror the treaty-child policy. Unless I'm no longer fey, or my cousin is no longer elf, we're heirs."

"And you think pack politics are fucked up?"

"All kinds of politics are fucked up," I snapped. "But why would my father be so sure he's dying? Why come after me now, unless it's a sure death sentence?"

"Do fey get cancer or something?"

"No. The only thing that would get him killed for sure this fast is spending too much of his magic on something. But why would he do that?"

He tapped his fingers against the wheel. "Maybe we have to find out who's supposed to be his successor, once you're out of the picture. Might give us a lead."

"But how would we do that?"

Weiss grinned. "We need to talk to Bert."

"How would that help?"

"Let's just say he has a source in the Fey Court."

Weiss started the engine and drove home like a maniac. I was starting to get used to it. In fact, my life didn't even flash before my eyes when we nearly ran into another car at a stop sign. When we got to Weiss's home, we found Bert sitting in the living room with a whiskey bottle half-empty beside him.

ten

"SO SORRY, boss," Bert slurred. "Traitor bitch sister...."

Weiss walked right up to him and slapped him twice, good and hard. The smack resonated through the room. "Snap the fuck out of it. I need you now more than ever," Weiss growled.

Bert shook his head. "Sorry, boss. What can I do?"

He did manage to say it with less of a slur, but he was still hammered. News circulated freakishly fast through the pack, obviously.

"Who has your sister been spending time with lately?" I asked.

Bert frowned. "Well... had that boyfriend. Bobby, or Billy?" he wondered aloud. "Smelled funny, but I can't remember his name."

"Bobby," Weiss spat. "Who else?"

"Dunno of anyone else, boss. Not after Amanda was taken into custody," Bert added.

Weiss stepped closer to him, leaned down a little to look him straight in the eye. "Can I trust you, Bert?"

"Yes, boss."

"Prove it to me," Weiss demanded.

"Whatever you want me to do, I'll do it," Bert stated solemnly.

"Still have that fey contact?" his alpha asked.

Bert nodded.

"You go out there and find out who the Fey King wants to designate as successor to the throne. Don't come back here until you have a clear and sure answer."

"Yes, boss," Bert muttered and got up. "Shower first," he said and walked out of sight.

"And just like that, you'll trust him?" I asked incredulously.

Weiss flopped down in a chair, resting his head against the soft padding. "If he's still my beta, he'll go in there and try to find out. Either he comes back with information we can use, or he gets killed in the process. Either way, we find out the results. If he simply goes away and doesn't come back, then he's a traitor too and trying to make a run for it. In which case I'll hunt him down myself," he added tiredly.

"And how will we know if his info is good or not? He could come back with any kind of shitty name."

"Well, if it makes sense to you once you hear the name, then it's not entirely made up. So he'll either have figured it out by being loyal to me, or he'll be feeding us fey-dictated info to throw us off track—in which case we'll know he's on that side, and it'll get him killed too."

Never mind that I'd been away from Court so long new names could very well be at play there. Then again, my father didn't trust new faces, so it would probably be someone he knew he owned and had been testing for a while that he'd designate his successor. Someone who was helping him right now, to prove their loyalty to his politics. There were only a handful of names that came to mind.

I pinched the bridge of my nose. "Right. And how will we know if he's with the fey or with us, if I'm iffy on whatever name he comes back with?"

Weiss snorted. "Fucking Christ, what kind of prince are you? I have my own source in the Court, one I do trust."

"Seriously? And you couldn't just ask them and be done with all of this?"

"I need to know where Bert's loyalties are. And I'll be sure about yours too after today."

I bit the inside of my cheek and watched him dubiously. "What makes you so sure about this source of yours? What if they lie and feed you false info?"

"It's someone I own. I trust their sense of survival will keep them on my side."

I frowned. "Someone you own? Like you think you could've owned me?"

"Trust me, Edel, if I say I own someone, then I do. Now sit your ass down and let me relax for a second. It's been a hell of a day."

I flopped down on the couch and stared blankly ahead. After a while, Bert went out. Neither of us said a thing, we just sat there in Weiss's living room and stared. At some point I felt his eyes on me, the focus making my ears buzz.

I looked at him. "What?"

"By tomorrow morning I'll decide if you're on my side or on your father's."

"Will Bert be back by then?"

"Maybe not. But I'll be pretty sure about your loyalties anyway. If you are on Daddy's side, Sands, you're going to regret ever trying to play me."

I smiled. "Unfortunately for everyone, my father included it seems, I'm not playing at all."

"Maybe," he said, still searching my gaze for something. "Maybe."

My heart thumped, my muscles burning up with energy. "And how will you decide tonight?"

He grinned slowly. "You're about to find out."

My heart thumped harder, and I swallowed. "How about giving me a clue?"

"No need for clues. It's gonna be real easy to figure out," he said calmly as he took his phone out of his pocket. He hit some buttons, then put the phone to his ear. "I want five agents to guard my home tonight. And send Naty Stein to pick my son up from school. She's taking him for a sleepover. Of course she doesn't know, but she'll find out when you call and tell her so. Say I'm asking for a special favor. She'll get it. Oh, and don't bother me tonight unless there's another vic found." He looked at me as he said those last words, slowly took the phone away from his ear, and shut it off. Then he threw it on the chair and got up.

I gulped, my heart beating faster. "Why send Alf away? What are you planning to do?"

"Investigate," he murmured in a thick voice. "On your feet, walk up the stairs and into my bedroom."

"Why?"

"Because I said so," he growled.

I jumped a little when I heard the growl, and got to my feet. With as much calm as I could fake having, I took each step slowly, torturously so as I walked up those stairs. I knew he was watching me, walking after me, allowing some distance there. I felt his gaze on my back, making my ears buzz steadily. Blood pumped through my veins at an insane pace, making my whole body throb. I paused for a moment when I reached his bedroom door, looked behind me. He signed for me to go in, so I turned the knob and did so. I walked up to the window and crossed my arms around my body, trying to hold myself together for fear of exploding. I heard the door close behind me, and silence fell over the room.

He was here with me. I could hear his deep breathing. I could feel his scent crawling up the floors and walls, slipping inside my lungs and slowly building a hard-on.

"What are we doing?" I asked, my voice catching.

"Take your clothes off," he commanded in a stern, deep voice.

I shivered and turned around. "What?"

My breath hitched as I watched him. His pupils were blown wide, that raw power vibe of his radiating off him. His pants were tenting a little, and there was a visceral kind of hunger in his gaze that gave me a long, body-wide shiver.

"You say you've had a thing for me for years," he muttered. "Tonight you'll prove that."

I gulped. "By sleeping with you?"

He grinned crookedly. "By submitting to me."

I shivered again. "What do you mean?"

"Take. The. Clothes. Off."

I took in a deep breath, exhaled slowly. If this ended up being some cruel way of mocking me, then at least he'd know by the end of it that I was sincere. That I did want him in ways even I was terrified of. I'd take whatever cruelty he'd dish out, because even cruelty coming from him would feed a starving part of my soul. So I slowly lifted my hands and brought them to the edges of my jacket. I slid it off, letting it fall to the floor. Then I unbuttoned my shirt slowly, to be sure the shaking of my hands wouldn't put me in the lame position of missing one. I swallowed nervously as I took the shirt off and let it slide to the floor.

His gaze roamed over my naked chest, my shoulders, my arms. "Keep going," he whispered in that deep voice that made my heart flutter.

I opened the button of my pants, slid the fly down. The growing bulge of my groin appreciated the extra room as I slid the pants down and stepped out of them. My skin prickled up in goose bumps when I stood just in my briefs.

"These?" I asked in a shaky voice.

He nodded, his gaze still roaming over me. I took in a deep breath, stuck my fingertips inside the waistband of my briefs, and pushed them down. The hard-on sprang up proud and free as I stepped out of the briefs too. And there I was, naked, hard, barely standing in one place in front of him.

He leaned back against the door as his gaze zeroed in on my hard-on. "You shave all the hair off?"

I swallowed hard. "Fey have no body hair."

"None?" he asked stepping closer.

I stepped back on instinct. "None," I whispered.

"Are you trying to run away from me, Edel?" he asked in a deep amused voice.

"N-No," I stuttered.

"Then why are you stepping back?"

"I don't know," I whispered breathlessly as he reached me.

His palms rested on my shoulders for a moment. His flesh was burning hot, so hot that I thought I might explode in flames just from feeling it. He breathed out slowly, a gust of hot air falling over my face as his hands traveled down my back. When they reached my ass, I shivered and stepped closer to him, pushing my naked skin against his clothed body. My hard-on rubbed against his thigh through the pants, and I groaned at the contact.

He chuckled. "Cold?"

"No."

"And yet you're shivering," he said, nuzzling my hair. "Because you're afraid?" he whispered right into my ear.

My heart skipped a beat. "Because you're touching me," I whispered back.

"And you've wanted me to touch you?"

"Yes," I said, exhaling sharply as his hands gripped my asscheeks.

"Tonight should be a very happy night for you, then. I'm going to touch you for a good long while," he muttered and bit the shell of my ear hard.

I twitched and pushed myself harder into him. Sweet flapping wings, if he was for real, then tonight I'd finally have everything I'd been fantasizing about for years. His breath fell on the sensitive skin behind my ear, and I shuddered, feeling my hard-on swell almost painfully.

"You should take your pants off," I mumbled into the crook of his neck. "I might be... overcome with excitement and ruin them."

He chuckled, the vibration traveling through my ear cartilage. "I can afford a new pair of pants, Edel," he whispered thickly.

"Don't call me that, please."

"How should I call you, then? Hmmm, fey prince?" he whispered huskily as his fingers slipped between my cheeks and probed the sensitive flesh.

I twitched and rubbed my forehead against his chest, my heart working overtime. I could hear my eardrums click with all the tension in my body. "Don't be cruel, please, not now."

"Oh, but I am cruel," he whispered as his hands gripped my flesh almost painfully. "I'm very, very cruel. Haven't you heard? I'm the big, bad wolf."

Gods, I was going to die. If he planned to just play around and throw me away before actually being with me tonight, I was going to implode.

He leaned his head down and angled it so our lips touched. I leaned up a little, drawing in a sharp breath as his burning lips pushed harshly against mine. He stabbed his tongue into my mouth, pushing against mine with punishing hunger. I whimpered and opened my mouth wide for him, giving myself over to him entirely. His hands shot up from manhandling my ass, one of them gripping my head while the other wrapped around my back and held me tightly against him. The way his hand held the back of my head, so proprietary and warm, had my heart doing somersaults inside my chest. The kiss turned sloppier, slippery as night finally fell over the world. Sweat popped up on my chest, the heat of his body, of his embrace, of him holding me like this making my skin moist all over.

By the time he pulled back, I was breathing so heavily I started thinking I might have a panic attack coming. His gaze shone in the night light streaming through the windows from outside. I swallowed thickly and slowly got down to my knees in front of him, my hands trembling as I reached up to his fly. He stared down at me, his face a study of composure as I slid his zipper down. The big bulge in his boxers called to me like a siren, and I desperately wanted to introduce myself. I pulled his pants down, all the way to his ankles, and after he stepped out of them, threw them in the pile of my clothes. His boxers came next, and I swallowed thickly as they slid down his muscular thighs, following their way down until they met his ankles. He stepped out of them too, and I threw them away. I just took a moment to sit on my knees in front of him and admire his incredible, muscular, hairy body from down here. Seeming to understand my fascination, he took off his shirt. And then all of his exquisite body was exposed, all the hard ridges of his muscles softened by the dusting of dark hair. My throat got impossibly dry, and I swallowed a couple of times as I stared at his hard-on. He looked down at me, his gaze burning hot as I licked my lips, slowly opened my mouth, and finally wrapped my lips around the head of him. Dear magic wands, he tasted better than I could've imagined. The soft, velvety skin tasted like heaven, so good that I wanted more. I slid his hard dick down my throat, humming in delight as the taste and scent of him got me almost drunk.

He wrapped a hand around the back of my head and started moving, fucking my mouth with deep strokes, pushing down my throat like he owned it—like he owned me. I swallowed around him, pushing down the gag reflex each time it tried to ruin my joy. I moaned around him, felt his body tense each time I did. I wrapped my hands around his hips, holding on to his asscheeks as he fucked my mouth. His motions got harder, brusquer as I stuck my nails into his ass and grabbed at him harder. I just couldn't have enough of him. I wanted more. I wanted him deeper, harder. He growled deeply as hot streams of cum shot down my throat, and I swallowed with delight, enjoying the way he shuddered while I did. Then when he pulled out of my mouth, I licked him clean until my tongue got dry.

He massaged my scalp with the hand he kept fastened to the back of my head, keeping me close to his dick. "Get on the bed for me," he muttered in a rich, deep voice.

I reveled in his "I just came" voice, and my heart swelled at the idea I'd given him that voice now. I'd made him cum. I'd enjoyed the taste of him in my mouth. I'd imagined this so many times, hoped, dreamed, wanked to the idea of it, but none of my fantasies compared to actually having him inside my mouth.

I climbed on his bed, faceup, and propped myself up on my elbows so I could watch him move. He walked to his nightstand, got some condoms, and I thought lube, out of the drawer, then looked down at me and grinned in his gloriously naked state. "Top or bottom?"

I swallowed. "Whichever. You're a top, I'd imagine," I said, grinning.

He snorted. "I'd be a top even if I was bottoming. A top bottom." He climbed onto the bed. "That was good, Tim," he said as he settled over me. "Lemme show you my appreciation." He moved down my body.

I inhaled sharply as he fastened his lips around a nipple and sucked it hard into his mouth. My hard-on started weeping precum, my hips pushing up against anything within their reach. He chuckled and bit on my flesh, making me scream out.

"Risks of taking a wolf into your bed, my prince. We tend to like biting," he whispered as he moved to my other nipple.

I gripped the sheets and pulled hard as he bit my other nipple, this time harder and pulling at the flesh while still keeping it between his teeth. I heard a subtle ripping sound as I pulled harder and harder at the sheets.

His hand slid down between us and grabbed my throbbing dick. "Good to know you'll enjoy it too," he muttered, grinning, then bit the soft skin at the side of my tummy.

I jumped a little and shivered, the bite punishing enough to send pain signals through my system but still pleasurable enough to keep me hard. "Just don't bite off anything major," I whimpered as he nuzzled against my hipbone.

He chuckled. "Major? What's major? This?" he asked, blowing out air over my dick.

I flexed my ass, pushing up a little. "Definitely."

"What about these?" he asked as his other hand gripped my balls and rubbed them snuggly into his fist.

I shuddered. "Also major," I groaned between panting breaths.

He hummed and leaned down, sucking one of my balls into his mouth and pulling on it as he had with my nipple. I pushed my legs as widely open as I could and wiggled my hips around, the sensation close to blowing my mind. "Careful," I gritted out. "Overexcited… might…." I trailed off as he closed the hand wrapped around my dick more tightly. Then he hummed, still holding my ball in his mouth and sucking it.

My hips twitched, and I groaned openmouthed as his fist began to work my dick. I squeezed my eyes shut, trying to hold off the impending climax. Not yet. I wanted to have him touch me more. Who knew if he'd go there again? I tightened all my muscles, desperate to hold off.

He let my ball out of his mouth with a wet popping sound. "You're shivering again. Cumming?"

I swallowed thickly, my eyes still firmly closed. "Not yet, please," I gritted out as he pumped his hand on my dick faster.

He wrapped his lips around the weeping head of my dick and sucked hard. I screamed and arched off the bed, my spine coiling and cracking softly as I pushed it to its limits. Heat exploded through my extremities, the blast gathering in the lower area of my stomach and shooting out of my dick in burning hot spurts. He pulled away, letting the streams of cum land on my stomach, my hip, everywhere on the bed as he kept pumping his hand on me and milking me dry. I shivered, and my body twitched all over, entirely out of my control. He finally stopped moving his hand but kept holding my dick in a tight squeeze. My body still throbbed, the afterglow of that glorious orgasm keeping me somewhere up in the sky, floating on puffy clouds of bliss. I felt weightless, the sensation going on for much longer than it ever had. I didn't move, barely dared to breathe as the sensation of floating kept going.

He moved up on my body and kissed me, this time with no urgency and no punishing force. Just a sweet, almost tender kiss that made me swallow thickly.

"Thank you," I whispered breathlessly.

He chuckled. "My pleasure."

"Was that the test of my loyalty?" I asked, smiling goofily.

He snorted. "'Course not. But I'd been wanting to do that for a while, and what better time than the present?"

I opened my eyes and looked up at him as he still held my body down. "What's the test, then?"

"Not done doing things I've been wanting to do to you."

My heart jumped in my chest. "Really?"

"Oh, yeah. I've been carrying a pair of very blue balls ever since I first saw you, Timothy Sands. I've been wondering for quite a while how your throat would feel around my dick and how your skin would taste. I'm going to have my fill now, before we do anything else."

Cold realization settled into my stomach. "Because if you don't decide I'm loyal to you, then you'll kill me."

"Exactly," he replied, rubbing his nose against my temple. "It would be a shame, since I'm enjoying you so very much," he whispered. "But if you're a traitor, I can't give you the chance to ruin me. Not when we both know you can."

I shivered and closed my eyes, trying to focus on the heat of his body wrapping around mine instead of the cold fear in my stomach. "What do you want me to do to prove myself?"

"Not yet, Tim. Let me enjoy you some more."

eleven

A GOOD couple of hours later, I came to realize Weiss had been starved for physical contact with someone. There was simply no other way to make sense of the need for constant touching, the borderline tenderness of his version of "enjoying me." He did enjoy me into five more orgasms, which I couldn't complain about—at least not now. I might tomorrow, when my body would be drained of energy, but there'd be the "blissed out of my mind" spark making up for it. He'd been careful to always make me cum before he did, though I would've stolen at least two advances there anyway.

Relaxed and entirely exhausted, I lay there beside him in his bed. "Wow."

He grinned. "You do know how to keep a wolf entertained."

"I sincerely hope not. I was trying to keep the man entertained. Wolves, I'm not sure I would want to entertain."

His beautiful bright blue eyes focused on me. "I assure you, my wolf will find you very entertaining once you meet. He'll probably try to sniff out your groin and hump your leg."

"That's… disturbing."

"We're a package deal, you know."

"Might take me some time to get my mind around it. In the meantime, I hope to not have your wolf form humping my leg, though."

He snorted. "You afraid of meeting my wolf form, Sands?"

"Ah, so it's back to 'Sands' now that you've had your way with me."

He got up from the bed, still buck naked, and walked over to a side table where he had a bottle of water. "I didn't have my way with you," he said and winked at me.

Wow. Weiss winked? Disturbing. "I kind of think you did, unless the last hours have been a very vivid figment of my imagination."

He drained half the bottle and put the lid on it. "You know what I mean."

I got up into a sitting position and leaned against the headboard. "Yeah, I do. Why didn't you have your way with me that way, then?"

He grinned. "What, you want more already? Shameless little fey prince."

I pursed my lips. "I'm not little."

He leaned against the side table. "Yeah you are, compared to me."

I snorted. "Honey, everyone is little compared to you."

He cocked his head to the side. "Might have a point there."

"Still haven't answered my question. Why didn't we have intercourse?"

He crossed his arms over his chest and looked out the window. "That's a mating thing, for me."

I cocked one eyebrow. "You saying you won't have sex with someone you're not mated to? I'm pretty sure you weren't a virgin when you mated Amanda."

He sighed. "No, I wasn't. But I'm not going there with you until Friday, when I will mate you."

The way he said it, the daring look on his face, and the way his gaze met mine were all a big "dare you to challenge me on that" festival.

I ran a hand through my messy hair. "Is that supposed to be some kind of incentive program or something?"

"Maybe. Would it work that way? Would wanting to have me inside you make you more into the idea of mating?"

"Look, I'm very much into any idea concerning you. I hope you're clear on that by now. It's not my motivation I'm worried about, it's yours. Still haven't told me how I'm going to prove my loyalty to you."

He flexed his knee, my focus zooming in on how his thigh muscles moved. Gods, he was one gorgeous monster of a man.

"What do you know about shifter fey?"

I widened my eyes. "You mean bitten or born?"

"Bitten," he said in a slightly gravelly voice.

"I know they often die during the transformation process or the first time they shift."

"Pure fey don't take shifter bites well, I've heard that. What about mixed ones?"

"Don't know much about that. Why are you asking?"

"I want to bite you, Sands."

I swallowed thickly, fear congealing in my stomach. "You can't be serious. You want to do an experiment on me?"

"Not an experiment, a proper turn. I want you to be turned by me, make you part of my pack."

I pulled my knees closer to my body, feeling too vulnerable all of a sudden. "That's crazy. Your pack won't welcome a fey prince into their ranks, you damn well know it. That's if I survive the process at all, which I don't quite think I would."

"Let me worry about the pack's reaction."

"These are my options? Have a go at a foolish, very likely deadly change, or become a traitor in your eyes?"

He didn't even blink. For a moment there, all I saw was the heartless monster James had been talking about. I hadn't been fooling myself into thinking that he was feeling anything for me, but from that to so easily playing with my life, there was still quite a way to go.

"I do know a couple of half fey who've changed well. In fact, they became stronger as fey once they did change. Their magic became much more powerful," he said as calmly as if we were discussing sliced bread.

"Those are my options?" I asked again. "Go for the bite, or become your enemy?"

"In case you haven't noticed, Sands, I'm fighting for my life and my pack's future here. I can't afford another traitor in my ranks."

I looked up into the ceiling. "Amanda and Tricia were part of your pack, weren't they? Didn't seem to keep them from doing what they did."

"True," he growled. "But I didn't bite Tricia, and Amanda took the hormone therapy to kill my effect on her. You won't do that."

"Which means you'll be able to control me, as my alpha."

"Which means I'll know for sure which side you're on, fey prince," he said coldly.

I got up and walked closer to him, my fists clenched. "We met when my father's assassins were trying to kill me. You've had me in your Bureau for five years, during which you fucking know I never once met the Court members or had any contact with any fey until yesterday in the Bureau's lobby. My father has publicly admitted to wanting me dead, for flap's sake. I've known about your issue since Monday and haven't turned you in to the Council. How could there be any doubt about my loyalties?"

"My beta turned against me overnight, and I trusted her to begin with. Why would I think you wouldn't? For all I know, you're just waiting for the right time to take me down."

I shook my head, exasperated. "You're crossing the line into paranoia, Weiss."

"Maybe," he stated coldly. "But it would make you a shifter, not fey. I think there's a law which automatically declares you dead before the Fey Court once you become a shifter or a vampire, am I right?"

I nodded, still frowning. "How long have you been thinking about this?"

"Before coming into your office on Monday. I might seem like a moron to you right now, Sands, but I assure you I'm not. Morons and pussies don't survive in a pack, let alone become alphas."

I blinked a couple of times, turned to look out the window. "It would clearly take me out of the running for my father's throne."

"Yeah," he muttered. "Convenient for him, you, and me. Well, at least it would be, if you're not undercover here."

I wrapped my arms around myself. "But I could die."

"Or you could become stronger," he added after a while. "Your magic would become more powerful, you'd be free of the Fey Court's influence once and for all—and you'd be safe from your father," he whispered sweetly.

I smiled. "But who would keep me safe from you?"

He stepped closer, his heat starting to warm my back. "Nobody. That's the whole point. You'd be mine in ways nobody could ever undo, Anti-Abuse Act or not. The mating that will take place on Friday could be undone at any time once the Act comes into effect, so you wouldn't have to worry about being trapped in my bed."

I chuckled. "Right. I'd only be stuck with you as my alpha."

He stepped closer still, his chest touching my back now. "You'd have proven complete loyalty to me, Tim," he purred right against the shell of my ear. "And to the pack and Council," he added sweetly.

"And you could use me and discard me in any way and at any time, no questions asked," I added tersely.

"Well, you're coming up with an Anti-Abuse Act, aren't you? So you'd be protected."

"In a mating, not in pack dynamics," I snapped.

The very fact he was ridiculing Travis's, Rick's, Naty's, and my work was annoying in and of itself. But asking me to risk my life was the cherry on top of it all. "You fooled around with me tonight to sweeten the deal, didn't you?"

He sighed. "I took you into my bed tonight because I wanted you there. I still do. But I can't pretend the rest of the world doesn't exist anymore just because I got a taste of you."

He wrapped his arms around me. I flinched but didn't pull away.

"Think about it from my perspective," he whispered, tightening the noose of his arms around me. "I've been betrayed by close to everyone I trusted in the last couple of weeks. All that's left is for the Council to turn against me, and for my pack to launch a coup. I want to trust you completely, Tim. I need to have someone beside me who I know I can trust fully. I think you could be that person. I want you to be that person."

I swallowed thickly. "But I have to risk my life in order to become that."

"Yes," he whispered, nuzzling my messy hair. "Think of it as a proposition you can't refuse. If I don't mate you, if I take my protection away, the Council might turn you over to your father just to buy some time."

"You're actually threatening me, while you have me wrapped in your arms?" I asked, flabbergasted.

"I can't mate another traitor," he stated simply. "It's not threatening. It's simply laying it all down in clear terms. Don't think I'm doing it for chuckles either."

I froze midbreath. "Mating me?"

He sighed. "Pushing you to make this call. I want you to be on my side, for both our sakes, now more than yesterday. I love having you in my bed, Tim. I love the way your skin feels to the touch, how you shiver when I run my hands down your body. I love how you taste, how you go limp in my arms when we're kissing, how you submit to me in subtle, delicious ways I'm not even sure you're aware of. I love the way you turn your face into my chest when I hold you," he whispered, running his nose through my hair. "I want to feel I can connect with you without the risk of you getting me killed for my weakness," he whispered, barely audible.

I swallowed thickly, trying to not let him influence me. This was, after all, one of the biggest decisions of my life. I shouldn't let him charm me into making the choice he wanted, instead of the one I should be making for my future.

"Tell me about Mitchell James," I said in my most pretty-please-like tone.

He stepped away and sat on the bed, leaning against the headboard. "Fair enough. You tell me about Travis, and I'll tell you about Mitch."

I glared at him. "Can't you just do something for once without trying to work your own angle through it?"

He grinned. "Of course not. Do we have a deal?"

"Fine," I said, throwing my hands up. "But you go first."

He snorted. "No, I don't. I like to watch you go first," he said, grinning.

My face and chest heated up as I remembered blowing him, then him watching me cum with so much hunger each and every time.

"Fine," I muttered, glaring.

He patted the bed beside him, so I walked over and settled in close to him, my head on his stomach, facing him. "I got together with Travis because I... liked the type," I started.

"The lycan type?"

I bit my lower lip. "The snarling, growling, wiseass alpha type."

He grinned. "My type, then."

"After a while, I realized it wasn't working because I was always thinking about... someone else."

"The mystery guy you left him for," he added.

"You," I whispered. "I left him because I was always thinking about you."

His gaze turned searching, and we looked into each other's eyes for a while. Was he even able to believe me at this point? Believe anyone, about anything? I sure wished he could.

After a while he smiled. "I always wondered if your gaze did linger on me or not every time we met. I thought it did, way back when. But it could have been you being grateful, nothing more."

"So you suspected I was into you?"

"I wondered, not suspected. And I never really allowed myself to ponder it too long, not with Amanda in the picture."

"Tell me about Mitchell," I prompted.

"Mitchell," he whispered in a strange, hollow voice. "We had a deal, you know? That after Amanda delivered me an heir, I'd end the mating. Then Mitch and I would be together. That was the deal."

"What went wrong?"

He looked away. "Amanda was a lot more perceptive than I gave her credit for. Maybe she found out, maybe it was just instinct. She was very into me back then," he said, snorting. "Wanted to be my only thought all day, every day, and fought with me like a hellhound when it was obvious it wouldn't go that way. I don't blame her," he added. "She never knew that to me she was more of a tool than a person. I pretended to be into her when I wasn't. I lied to get that heir, planning to get rid of her as soon as my child was delivered."

"Cruel," I said before I could stop myself.

He ran a hand through my hair, playfully pulling on it. "Yeah. I could be a cruel asshole back then. It's always at a price, though, that much I've learned."

"What happened?"

"By the time she became pregnant, Mitch was already convinced I'd been stringing him along. That I didn't plan to leave Amanda for him at all. He consorted with that asshole just to spite me," he said, shaking his head.

I swallowed thickly. "Do you really think he killed himself because of his consort's death?"

"Who could possibly know what was going through his head by then? The Mitch I'd known and cared for wouldn't have done any of it, getting together with the guy, fighting with him in public and throwing punches like they did. James blamed me for the change, of course. I blamed me as well," he added.

"Do you blame yourself for his suicide too?"

He ran his hand through my hair again, seeming to think it over. I started to think he wouldn't answer, but then he drew in a big breath and whispered, "Yes." He didn't sound broken about it, rather bitterly resigned.

"I'm sorry for your loss," I whispered, not sure what else to say.

He smiled. "First time anyone said that to me about Mitch's death."

"Threatened everyone with evisceration if they said it?" I asked, trying for a joke, lame as it was.

"Maybe," he said, pulling playfully on my hair again. "Be my safe bet, Tim," he said out of the blue. "Be the one I know I can trust to stick around for me."

I nibbled on the inside of my lower lip. "Are you messing with my head, Weiss?"

"I thought you were the one famous for mindfucking," he said, smiling lazily.

"Imagine the pair we'd make," I shot back.

"I do imagine it. Question is, do you?"

I worked my jaws. "Risking my life is a bit of an expensive price to pay for it, though."

"Is that a 'no'?" he asked, wrapping his hand lazily around my throat.

"Will you kill me if I say no? Throttle me, maybe?" I dared ask.

The parallel wasn't lost on me. He'd choke me to death, in a way similar to how Mitch had killed himself. Could I take that to mean I could matter nearly as much to him in the future? Or was it all manipulation, all with the ultimate goal of deciding if I was with or against him?

He blinked slowly, then fixed his gaze on mine. "We'll both end up dead if you don't say yes. Why do anyone the favor of either of us dying earlier?"

"You honestly think me not becoming part of your pack could get us killed?"

"The Council might decide to screw over an outcast fey. They can't screw over the pack alpha's mate when the mate is pack too, not as easily. That is, if I don't go raving mad in the meantime."

I sighed. "I don't think you will. Whatever causes your rages, it's not hormones, and it's not some psychological problem either. I would've picked up on one by now."

"What is it, then?"

"Maybe some drugs? Dr. Black will be able to tell us more when he gets the results. I'll talk to him about turned fey too. If anyone knows something about that, it would be him."

"Fair enough," Weiss said, nodding. "After all this soul-searching, I'm hungry."

"So it was the soul-searching, not the fooling around?"

He pulled on my hair again. "I never fool around. Now get your ass up, and let's raid the kitchen. Wear something, in case someone's home."

"Scared I'd offend their sensibilities?"

"Scared I'll have to twist their necks for ogling my mate-to-be," he said, pushing my head off of him and getting up. He pulled on a pair of boxers and threw me some sweats, then marched out of the room.

I got the sweats on and followed, realizing I was kind of famished. By the clanking and grumbling coming from the kitchen, I guessed Bert hadn't left him anything cooked. I went into the kitchen and found Weiss munching with abandon on some pastrami. Couldn't help grinning. "So this is a wolf out on the hunt?"

He made a face at me. "Raid the fridge. It's my best offer. Finders keepers," he added, rummaging through some casseroles.

"You're kind of scary sometimes."

He turned around, a couple fries hanging from his lips. "Me?" he asked, getting his brows up in a funny face.

My heart thumped hard. I reached out, plucked a fry from his stash, and ate it. He studied me and grinned before loading his mouth with a new batch of fries. The man ate like a caveman, but there was something terribly endearing about watching him pig out on whatever he found "raiding the fridge." It was the first time I actually felt like I was enjoying eating with someone, and I'd had the dubious pleasure of many meals with company since I'd been a kid. But eating with Weiss like this, no shows of protocol, felt raw and intimate. I enjoyed every morsel I got, regardless of what it was, of how it tasted. I could've eaten straw, and it would have tasted spectacular right now.

And as we kept eating like that, a thought started making rounds through my head: I might not be so averse to going through the bite if Dr. Black had some good things to say about it. If it wasn't certain death, I realized I might actually want to go ahead with it, insane as it was. I consoled myself with the thought that everything outside of singledom was a kind of insanity anyway.

twelve

WE WENT to bed in separate rooms again that night, though the communicating door remained open. I took the time to contemplate the why while I couldn't fall asleep. I could have taken Weiss's policy to not go forward in bed—to behave like a real couple—as a sort of traditionalist approach to mating, maybe even him being gallant. Of course, it could also be that he was waving something he knew I wanted in front of my nose, putting the price of biting me between me and that prize. Knowing Weiss, I suspected it was a bit of both, if not more of the second. As he'd said himself, he could be a cruel asshole. It was part of his nature, part of something I'd been more or less pining after for about five years. The asinine, bossy, commanding alpha attitude was part of the package, and I was into the whole package, not just parts of it. That's the thought I drifted asleep on. I had terrible nightmares that night, saw myself die in agonizing pain after his bite. Each time I woke from sleep and managed to go back to it, a new nightmare came to me, showing a slightly different version of that terrible death of mine.

When I woke up the nth time, I decided it was time to give up on trying to sleep. Much of it was the fear every fey had ingrained into their minds since they were babies. Mixed fey blood was bad, which meant I was bad in a way—even if I was mixed by political design and the King's pet project too. But as bad as mixed blood was, further "muddying it up" with vampire, wolf, or lycan bites made that fey into a monster. We were regaled with endless stories of stolen fey kids, bitten by some of the transforming species, then dying in horrifying ways as a result of the bites. Saying a transforming bite was a taboo was too little. And Weiss was right, as soon as it happened, even if the fey died as a result, they were officially expelled from the fey population. Rumor had it there was a "list of shame" somewhere, kept under lock and key by the Fey Court, which spelled out each of the names of the transformation-wanna-be ex-fey.

So here I was, considering making it onto that list. It would divest me entirely of my father's legacy, of any claim to the throne, to any of the privileges I could theoretically stake a claim to even as outcast fey. Outcasts were still fey, that was the key thing. Bitten fey weren't fey anymore. So taking the bite would clear up my father's desire to kill me. If it were all politics, throne successor issues, then me being bitten would make killing me useless. Unless it was a personal thing, him just wanting to punish me for the terrible crime of not playing by his rules. Weiss did have a point about the Council's protection. As his pack member and mate, I'd be as safe as I might hope to.

I thought about what it would mean to me to lose the fey status. I didn't really identify myself as fey, not since I was a kid, and it was made clear to me that I wasn't really fey enough to think of myself as one. So what would I really lose? I knew I was oversimplifying things because Weiss was a factor here. Not being fey would now help me become part of his pack, his mate. After knowing him for five years and lusting after him for the same duration, there wasn't really much left to discover, I reasoned. Either I wanted this thing, or I didn't. And as he'd so clearly put it, I was working on a protective Act for the status of a leader's mate. I was going to build an Act to defend my rights; what better position could I ask for under these conditions?

Of course, all of that was useless to me if I was going to die trying. So the real question here was, could I really survive the bite? I called Dr. Black as soon as it was a reasonable hour for it. The conversation left me with two distinctly interesting facts: one, that Weiss was not suffering from any stage of the rages, that his hormone screening came up perfectly normal, and that he didn't have suspicious substances in his blood either—Dr. Black had thought to check—and two, the doctor knew of several not only nondeadly, but highly successful transformations of mixed fey. He'd done a research paper on it, in fact. The science of it said bitten fey had no actual reason to take bites any more badly than any other species, mixed or not.

That was shocking for a moment or two, before I realized that thinking about it rationally would bring anyone to the same conclusion. If there was no metabolic, scientific reason to think a bite would affect fey in any way differently from others, then why would they die from it?

Which meant the Fey Court had been enthusiastically and profusely lying about that for a really long time. That didn't strike me as shocking, I was sad to say. The one noticeable effect bites had was to upgrade the magic of the bitten fey, Dr. Black said. And why would the Court want powerful fey outside of its sphere of influence? It all made perfect sense, in fact. While the bite was potentially deadly, as it was for anyone getting it, it wasn't particularly dangerous to fey—mixed or not.

I went downstairs and found Weiss and Bert at the breakfast table, discussing something in hushed tones.

Bert looked up and smiled, sniffed a couple of times in my direction, and smiled a bit wider. "Morning," he said.

Had he just smelled Weiss on me? I felt my face heat a bit. "Morning. Back already?"

He grinned wider. "My source comes up with what I want really quickly."

Weiss pointed toward the chair beside him. "Hurry up, have your breakfast. I wanna head into the office as early as we can."

I sat down beside him, and got something to eat. Then I glanced between Weiss and Bert. "Could I ask who your source is?"

Weiss snorted. "You have a 'yes' or 'no' answer to give before being privy to that kind of information."

I took a deep breath, released it slowly. "Yes."

Weiss snorted. "Yes, you know you have to give me that answer?"

"No, I meant my answer is yes."

They both stared for a few moments, and then Bert got up and left the room.

Weiss looked at me curiously, cocked his head to the side. "Just like that, yes? Last night you were having a hissy fit over it, but now it's yes, just like that?"

"I talked to Dr. Black this morning. For starters, you're not going through rages, you have no strange hormones in your blood, and no other suspicious substances either."

"Right. I'm not sure if that's good news, though. Means me going ballistic on things out of the blue is a problem that's all up here," he said, pointing toward his head.

I sighed. "We can do some tests for that too. I'll examine you, but I'm telling you now, as a trained specialist, that you don't show any signs of violence-inducing mental illness."

"So, the sudden yes was caused by...," he prompted.

"By what Dr. Black had to say. Apparently, the Fey Court has been bullshitting everyone for a long time."

He snorted. "I'm shocked. So the bite isn't as deadly as you thought?"

"Not any more than it is to any other species out there, no."

"You're sure about this, Sands? About that yes?"

I nibbled on the inside of my lower lip. "As things stand, it's the best option I have. That *we* have."

He rapped his fingertips against the table. "I'm annulling my mating with Amanda as soon as we get into the office, and announcing that we're doing the bite and mating ceremony tonight."

My stomach tightened. "You don't waste any time, do you?"

"The sooner it's done, the better it serves us." He leaned over the table slightly and squinted. "You doing the nervous bride gig, man? Pussying up on me?"

I frowned. "Don't be an ass."

He growled. "Don't try that kind of attitude with me, Sands. It won't go over well."

"So I need an attitude adjustment?" I asked, batting my eyelashes.

He snorted. "You're gonna get one, that's for sure."

I cocked an eyebrow. "You'll scare it into me?"

"I'll thrust it into you," he said, grinning crookedly.

Of course it had the desired effect, making me immediately visualize him fucking me. I was entirely derailed from whatever sass I was or wasn't about to give him.

He chuckled. "That's more like it. The blushing bride gig is a much better way to go."

I shook my head. "I'm not a goddamn bride!"

"Of course you're not. You're gonna be my mate."

The way he said it sounded very unlike the regular Weiss. He seemed to be almost dreamy, mildly excited, even—dare I contemplate it?—touched. It could all be an act, of course. Whatever magic I'd display after the shift, it would benefit me, of course, but it would sure benefit him too. The rages scenario would disappear entirely once he had a fey mate beside him, and for right now, that would make his position with the Council as secure as it might get. Benefits all around, wasn't that why we were really doing this? The fact that I wanted him, and that he seemed to want me too, was a mere detail. And if that wasn't the basis for a solid future, then I didn't know what might be.

"Come on, Sands, get a move on," he muttered as he got up from the table. "We've got shit to do, murderers to catch, matings to plan."

"Quite the day, huh?" I commented as I followed him out to the car.

He shrugged as he got into the driver's seat. "Just another day at the office, more or less."

I sat quietly in the car while he drove us to HQ. When he parked his car in his usual spot, my gaze found the tiny window of my office. I'd stared at him from that spot every morning, every goddamn morning for the last five years. Now I'd get to have him, as much as Weiss could be had. Sure, the circumstances weren't exactly ideal, but then again, when were they, and for whom?

I got a couple of stares as I walked to the elevator, and I was pretty sure they weren't due to me accompanying Weiss—at least not all of them.

"Looks like you got pretty famous," Weiss said when we got into the elevator.

"Yeah. Dear old Daddy took care of that."

"Just wait till they hear about the mating," he quipped.

I sighed. "Are you sure you want to do this now? I mean, the pack might not take it too well, considering...."

He pushed his body into mine.

My back hit the elevator's wall, and I gasped. "What are you...?" I muttered.

"Whatever else kind of shit is going on, you should know I want to do this. That I want to have you by my side, as long as I know I can trust you."

My heart beat wildly. "But you can't know, can you? You won't ever be able to really know, will you?"

He snorted. "I will know as soon as we're mated and I've bitten you. That's the most I could ask for, and you're giving it to me. It doesn't go unappreciated, Tim."

Shivers traveled down my spine at how he said my name. I tried to shake off the effect. "How will you show your appreciation?"

He chuckled. "Oh, you'll see."

The elevator doors binged open. He stepped away from me and strode out as if nothing had happened. Me? I was hard, my heart was pumping like crazy, and I kept thinking about Weiss naked. Because that was the effect he had on me, and he knew and used it as he wanted. For the hell of it, because he could. Because that was the kind of man he was. And it turned me the hell on.

I adjusted my stiffy and walked over to my office to pick up some papers. Today I had to see Travis and Rick, hopefully Naty too, to discuss the draft for the Act. I was certainly looking forward to Rick's reaction to the news of me and Weiss mating, not to mention the biting thing.

I knocked on Travis and Rick's office door.

"Yeah," Travis called out from inside.

I stepped in.

Rick's nostrils flared, and his face darkened. "What. The. Fuck. Have you been doing?" he gritted out.

I sighed. "It's touching that you care so much."

Travis reached a hand out and massaged Rick's nape. "Chill out," he whispered.

Rick shook his head. "Just come out and say it."

I stuck my hands in my pockets. "Okay, as you wish. I'm mating Weiss before Amanda's execution."

Travis's eyes widened. "You're what?"

Rick squinted at him sideways but said nothing.

"Look," I said, staring out the window, "there's a lot going on that you might not know."

"Aside from the fact your father came in here yesterday and said some fey shit to you?" Travis asked tersely.

"Okay, so you might know *some* of what's going on. The point is we can use this in our favor."

Rick snorted. "Thinking of benefits other than fucking Weiss? 'Cause none of us, except you, is interested in that."

I smacked my lips. "You can be an asshole all you like, but this might help us. One of us will have direct experience with being the mate of a high profile leader. I can't be the only one seeing the potential in that."

Travis snorted. "Oh, we're all seeing the potential. I'm not sure if you're seeing the shitload of trouble coming your way along with those benefits."

I smiled. "Travis, I appreciate your concern, but I'm a big boy. I can take care of myself."

"And yet he wants to protect you," Rick observed.

"Honey, are you jealous?" I quipped and turned around.

Rick threw me a death glare. "You're a fucking moron, Sands. He's using you for some reason. That's what he does. That's all he does," he added.

I gritted my teeth. "Because you know him so well after, what, a month here?"

His gaze hardened. "I know the asshole type, Sands. I know the type real well."

"I'm not saying you don't, but Herman Weiss is a person, not a type. So is everyone else," I added as kindly as I could.

Rick turned away from me, faced the wall.

Travis looked in his direction, and then found my gaze with his. "Look, I'm not saying you don't think you know what you're doing. I'm saying you should be very careful here. I'm sure it's what Rick is trying to say as well. I don't think Weiss is a bad guy, but he is the alpha of the werewolf pack. You'll agree his motives won't be separate from the pack's politics, yes?"

"My father told me he wants to kill me yesterday. He delivered on the threat, pushing the Council to leave me without its protection. He's determined to get me killed. Now, you tell me if Weiss's motives can be any worse than that."

Rick turned around. "Your father is threatening the Council?"

I nodded.

"What with?" he asked, wide-eyed.

Travis sighed. "There's an accord of protectorate between the Fey Court and the Council. That's the only thing they could really leverage."

Rick shook his head. "What?"

I cleared my throat. "The Fey King got the necessary signatures to declare the Council incompetent if he so chooses. If he goes ahead with it, the Council will be dissolved, and until a new one is appointed, the Fey Court will be the protector of the community and territories."

Rick massaged his temples. "You're talking about a fucking takeover here!"

"Pretty much," Travis replied.

"And getting together with Weiss helps how, exactly?" Rick asked, looking less pissed.

"Well," I said, "as his mate, the Council can't revoke its protection of me. Not without breaking ties with the werewolf pack, which we all know they won't do. I don't think they'd go against Weiss. There's no other likely alpha in sight, so I'm pretty sure they won't go there. Being Weiss's mate will keep me as safe as I can be."

"And that works for him how, exactly?" Rick countered.

I sighed. "There are things I can't tell you, you have to understand. But be sure it's not entirely selfless, on either side. Okay?"

Travis cracked his neck. "I trust your reasoning, as long as I feel I can trust you. As long as you don't go love-struck on us," he added.

"Fair enough," I said. "Now, is Naty coming to this meeting? Are we finally discussing the draft?"

She did come a couple minutes later. After a few hours of discussing options and directions, sound exploded from the hall. It was clearly a werewolf conflict, as in turned wolves. The growling, snapping, and the whine of furniture as it got destroyed couldn't be confused with anything else. I walked out into the lobby to find two werewolves going at each other's throats, just as expected.

I sidled closer to one of the bystanders. "What's going on?"

He shrugged. "Weiss just dissolved his mating with that bitch Amanda. These two are trying to go for the open position."

I gulped. Wasn't he supposed to announce our mating too?

Weiss ran in, in his huge-ass, scary wolf form. He growled and went for their throats one at a time, settling the conflict real soon. Once that was done, he growled again so hard the fucking walls shuddered, and then he went into his office. In a minute or so, he came out dressed in different clothes than this morning. "Let's settle this. There's no opening for the mate position, are we all clear? I'm having a bite and mating ceremony tonight at my house. The matter is settled already."

"Who's the future mate?" one of the wolf fighters asked after she'd shifted back into human form.

She stood there totally relaxed and entirely naked, slightly pissed off.

Weiss grinned. "Timothy Sands is going to be my mate. If anyone has an issue with that, speak of it now so I can beat your ass and get it out of your systems."

He looked around calmly, his icy stare hard and oh-so-fucking hot. Nobody else spoke up. True, not the whole pack was there, but it seemed to me that the way he put it made it impossible for anyone to say a thing.

And just like that, I was officially scheduled for a bite and mating ceremony for tonight.

thirteen

WEISS FOUND my gaze with his and cocked his head to his office. Every pair of eyes in the room settled on me as I walked over to him and went inside as requested. He glared at everyone out there once again and then came in, closing the door behind him.

My heart was beating wildly. "Well, that was...."

He grinned. "Sweet, right?"

I frowned. "You get off on pack members fighting among themselves?"

"When it's for the chance of getting in my bed, yeah. I'd be worried if none of them did."

"How... egomaniacal of you," I muttered.

He growled. "Any alpha worth his salt has pack members vying for his attention. You're going to be pack from tonight on, Sands, get with the program."

"I can't be down with violence just because it's what you're used to."

He walked closer to me: slow, measured, scary-ass steps. "Pack politics are the politics of the most powerful. If you can't deal with that, everyone will walk all over you. Just to make it clear, I won't come to the rescue where I feel you should handle shit yourself."

I swallowed hard. "I'm not a wuss, Weiss."

He grinned. "Perfect. You'll have the chance to prove it."

I knew he was right. I knew what pack politics were. I knew it all, and I understood becoming pack meant dealing with it all... but it all seemed too savage when I was witnessing it. What would it feel like while being in the middle of it?

Weiss's phone rang. "What?" he barked.

I watched his expression as it morphed into a proud grin.

"Fine, get him home," he said and closed the conversation.

"What?" I asked anxiously.

"Alf got into a fight at school. Almost broke a kid's arm."

"Why the hell do you sound so proud?"

He snorted instead of an answer. I could guess his thought process. His son had gotten into a fight and had won it, brutally, as it seemed. The stuff of an alpha daddy's dream. This was how werewolves were. This was what I was getting into.

"Got any problem?" he asked, as if guessing my thoughts.

I leaned back against the wall. "We haven't discussed Alf."

He frowned. "What's that supposed to mean?"

"It means, as your mate, I'll be the boy's stepdad. I want to discuss my involvement in… our family life."

He cocked up an eyebrow. "Go on."

"Will I have a real involvement in his education, in his life?"

"Do you want to?"

I snorted. "Of course. But I want to know where you stand."

He smiled oddly. "You'll be as involved as you want to be. But your word won't go over mine."

"How about we discuss options instead of racing to the finish line?"

"Have you met me yet?"

"Right. We need to be able to make compromises if we're going ahead with this mating thing."

He stepped closer. "You wouldn't dare go back on your decision. Or make me go back on my word before my pack," he added in a dangerously calm tone.

I gave him a level stare. "That's not what I'm trying to do. Simply trying to draw some lines here, reasonable ones."

He stepped closer again. "And if I don't confine myself within your neat little lines?"

My skin prickled at his nearness. "Then I'll try to persuade you."

A playful grin appeared on his lips. "Oh really? And how would you do that?"

My pulse spiking up, I walked the remaining distance between us and nudged his chest with my forehead. "I'll find a way," I whispered.

He chuckled and ran a warm hand up and down my back. The caress sent a rush up my spine.

"Our people went over the pentagram crime scene again," he said after a while. "No matter how many times Rick checked it out, he still found no traces of any suspects. I don't get how someone can go all artist with someone's guts and leave no trace behind."

I inhaled his scent. "It's some kind of magic."

He stepped back and grabbed my arms with both hands, his gaze inspecting my face. "What?"

I sighed. "If it is, then it's high-level magic. The kind only a handful of people might be able to pull off."

"You're shitting me," he said coldly. "You've had this on your mind all this time and didn't fucking mention it?"

The tone felt like a slap over my face. I winced mentally. "It's not the kind of option I would've even considered normally. But after investigating the area twice already, I don't see what other options might still be on the table. While hiding someone's presence might be chemical, leaving no traces behind just doesn't seem plausible. Not when we're talking about five bodies. Either the placing and... drawing... were done by magic, or the covering of the tracks was."

His hands dropped from my arms and went into his pockets instead. "Which would be harder to pull off?"

I considered it carefully. "Either would require serious use of magic. We're talking Fey Court level here," I said carefully. "Which would make sense in light of the King's threats against the Council."

He cocked his head to the side. "That makes sense, I suppose. The outcast wolf, Bobby Springs, seems to have had some ties to the Court as well."

I frowned. "This is the first I'm hearing about that."

"Bert told me about it this morning."

I clacked my tongue. "So I take it I'm in the trust circle now?"

"Closer to it than this morning. Besides, if you are a traitor after all, you'd know that already. Why would the Fey Court go all out on scheming now? What's their endgame?"

I thought about it. My father had never expressed much of a desire to take over Council territories or meddle with their affairs. But then again, he was an unpredictable, cruel bastard.

I shook my head. "I'm not seeing anything other than wanting to have a new Council installed. Maybe one that would serve his goals better for some reason. Whatever his endgame is, I'm sure it's not really connected to me."

"Agreed. He's just trying to get to you along the way, since he can. Is there any way to know for sure the Fey Court is involved?"

"A powerful fey can detect another's magic work. But I'm not strong enough, and I don't think we'll find anyone else willing to do it either. If the King has an agenda, then all of them will rally behind him. They have no other option."

Weiss grinned. "So you're not strong enough now. What about tomorrow, though?"

"You mean after the… bite?"

He nodded.

I bit the inside of my lip. "There's no way to know. Dr. Black said all fey experience some kind of magic power spike when they're transformed, but I have no way to guess if it will be enough or not. I guess we'll just have to wait and see."

He sighed, walked over to the edge of his desk, and leaned his butt against it. "Something about this whole thing doesn't smell right. Wouldn't your father know you might detect this magic involvement?"

"I don't think he sees me as that capable," I gritted out. "And he doesn't know we're contemplating this transformation thing. Or at least he didn't know until today. If he has spies in the Bureau, he'll find out about it soon enough."

"True. He already tried to get you out of the Council's protection, to get rid of you. Just in case, maybe?"

"Maybe. But what is he after?" I wondered aloud.

Weiss breathed out hard and looked out the window. "Bert's source says there's definitely something fishy going on in the Court. For a while now the Court meetings have been happening in a very, very small circle. Most of the members attend inner-Court issue meetings. Your father and his trusted Court members have pretty much constituted a secondary one. It's called a High Court or something."

The blood froze in my veins. "That's the name Bert got from his source? A High Court?"

His light blue eyes zoomed in on me. "Does that have any kind of special meaning?"

"Bert's source didn't say?" I asked, frowning.

"If it has any special meaning, either he didn't know it, or didn't share."

"Is the source a Court member or a lesser rank?" I asked.

"Not up for discussion."

I gritted my teeth. "Well, if he is a Court member he should have known what a High Court is. So either he's not a Court member, or he's not being entirely honest with you. And if the source isn't entirely honest, I'm not sure I'd trust any of his info."

He smiled. "I like your thinking. But the suspense is killing me here. What the fuck is a High Court?"

I went to sit down in one of the chairs in front of his desk. "When the King calls a High Court, it means either the kingdom is under attack, or they're preparing to attack someone. I don't suppose there've been any attacks against the fey lately?"

"Not that I know of, no. Fuck's sake, they're preparing to attack us, aren't they? Fucking fey," Weiss said spitefully.

"Gee, thanks," I muttered right back.

"You know what I mean," he snapped. "We have to go to the Council with this. This is serious shit. You're sure about that High Court?"

"Positive," I said, nodding.

"Fuck," he said, shaking his head. "At least it's going to give them extra incentive to appreciate you as an asset. On top of becoming my mate, you know the Court and you are on our side. With what info we can get from the inside, we at least have some basic idea about what to expect."

"Well, at least you know I'm on your side," I said flatly.

His gaze found mine, the intensity of it turning my knees to jelly. Good thing I was sitting down. Weiss's eyes were the most amazing ones I'd ever seen. That clear, light blue could so easily turn from an ocean of freezing waters to something hotter than the summer sun.

"I think if you weren't, you would have bolted by now. Only an idiot traitor would stick around at this point, not to mention going forward with tonight's ceremony. I might doubt your loyalties, for no fault of your own, but I don't doubt your intelligence. You're no idiot, Sands—I trust that."

Well, I had at least that going for me, then. "If the King is going for an attack on the Council...." I trailed off there, shivering. "This is going to be really, really bad."

He pushed off the desk. "Let's not wank the time around. We'll discuss this with the Council. Let's move."

The way there was all a blur to me. I didn't really register the way up in the elevator. Wasn't even sure if we waited or not before going in. I just suddenly realized we were going into the Council's meeting room, Weiss holding my hand and guiding me inside.

"I hear congratulations are in order," one of the Council members said as soon as we got inside. "May your mating be a happy, prosperous one."

"Thanks, we appreciate it," Weiss replied. "Sadly, that's not what we're here about. Of course, you're all invited to the ceremony tonight. But we've got other issues to discuss right now."

Well, I guess protocol had been kicked out the window for this meeting. Or maybe Weiss never went with the protocol of addressing the Council, something I wouldn't find too shocking, all in all.

Naty Stein's mother leaned forward. "This sounds like bad news."

Weiss squeezed my hand. I took it as a sign to go ahead, so I jumped right in.

"From what we've learned so far, the Fey King has assembled the High Court."

"Why is that an issue for us?" another Council member asked, frowning.

I looked around the room, meeting all of their gazes. "As you know, I'm the Fey King's outcast son. And as of tonight, I'll cease to be fey altogether."

"Because of Herman's bite?" another member asked.

I nodded. "Fey law officially annuls the fey status of one who goes through any transformation from the natural fey state."

"Why don't we know about that?" snapped another member.

I sighed. "There are two sets of rules: the real ones that never go outside of the Kingdom, and the public ones, which you probably have been made privy to. The fey status, like the High Court assembly, is the kind of info available within the Kingdom only."

"How fortunate we have an outcast fey joining our ranks, then," Mrs. Stein crooned. "Weiss has always been a smart alpha, but this seems to be one of his better tactical moves."

My stomach tightened at her words. I knew Weiss didn't know about this whole situation before asking for the bite and mating thing, but still, the whole thing seemed even less personal.

"What does this High Court mean for us?" Mrs. Stein asked.

I took a deep breath. "Either the Kingdom is under attack, or they're planning to attack. That's the only reason it would be assembled. And considering what the King and Court have been up to lately...." I drifted off there, not sure how much to reveal of what Weiss had told me. "I ran into the King in the lobby yesterday. He spoke to me in Fey, assured me he will kill me. Considering I'm still under your gracious protection, this means he's planning to be hostile toward the Council."

Weiss looked at me sideways and I felt his hand squeeze mine again. Was that a sign of approval? I didn't know.

One of the Council members got up from the table and crossed his hands behind his back. "Ladies and gentlemen, it looks like we might be going to war."

My skin prickled.

"What might we expect?" he asked, looking me straight in the eye.

"Well, fey war is... dirty business. There have been a couple. The strategies and points of interest are studied in the Fey Academy. The main thing about fey war is it isn't what you would expect. There's no real confrontation, not if they can avoid it. They're more of the... inside job kind of approach. They work at weakening the leadership of their enemies until they can turn at least a few important figures against that leadership. Usually it's with promises of establishing a new leadership that would involve those traitors. So if they're assembling the High Court, either they think they're going to, or already have, found support within the Council," I added sheepishly.

Weiss turned to me, wide-eyed. "Well, you didn't tell me about *that*," he snapped.

"You didn't give me a chance," I whispered. "You said we should talk to the esteemed Council ASAP, so I thought I might as well tell you the full story here."

Everyone in the Council looked around, a strange kind of silence settling into the room.

"We all trust everyone else in this room," Mrs. Stein stated after a while. "That is, all except you, Timothy Sands. What if you're trying to work your father's angle here?"

Weiss took one step forward and crossed his arms. "His allegiance isn't up for debate any more than mine is. Either you trust us both, or neither of us. Or do you suspect I'm a traitor?"

His voice rang out clear and strong, full of authority. It made my pulse spike, but I was even more affected by his words. He was clearly taking my side in front of the Council, under no uncertain terms.

"We trust you," the man who'd spoken before stated clearly.

"Oh, Herman, of course your loyalty is never questioned!" Mrs. Stein backpedaled. "If you trust him, then we're left with no other option than trusting him too."

Pretty clear way of saying "we're going with this because we need you and you're insisting."

"Now we have to discreetly find out who else we're sure we can trust," she added calmly. "If the Fey King thinks he can turn important community members against us, then we need to know where those vulnerabilities are. And deal with them," she added, her voice ringing out like a death sentence.

"I'll work on my pack, and anything else you might want me to assist with," Weiss said.

Mrs. Stein smiled. "We know we can always depend on you, Herman. Dealing with the pack and investigating that new Leader Murders case sounds like a plateful, though. Once we have those covered, we'll see what to do next."

Weiss bowed his head, I did the same, and he led me out of the room. We walked into the elevator, and the doors binged closed.

Weiss hit the stop button. "Don't ever fucking do that again! You tell me what matters before we go in front of the motherfucking Council," he gritted out.

His body pushed mine into the cold wall, his breathing erratic and me shaking.

"Got that?" he growled again.

I swallowed thickly. "Yes."

"Did that on purpose?" he sneered, pushing his nose into my throat.

I shuddered. "No, I didn't."

I read him in a hurry. A rage was coming on; I could see the signs clearly. His pulse spiked, the emotional grid going a fiery red. Oh, sweet flapping wings! I was closed in an elevator with a borderline raging werewolf alpha.

I sent out a wave of cooling, blue energy. It hit him, the calming energy trying to cool down the burning red of his rage. They struggled, but the blue didn't win. I panicked. He was going into a rage, in a blocked elevator. I was going to die on my to-be-mated day, killed by the intended mate.

"Weiss," I whispered faintly.

His face morphed into the wolf traits. I could feel his pointy fangs slightly digging into my throat. I was fucked. I breathed out a trembling sigh and decided we all had to die at some time. This would be mine. Not a pretty death, but then again was there such a thing as a "pretty death"? They all sucked. I closed my eyes tightly and breathed out slowly.

I could feel him sniffing my throat, his chest rumbling loudly—a cross between a growl and something of a purr. He sniffed me with deep whiffs, pushing his nose harder and harder into my throat. My knees gave out. I could feel myself slide down the wall. But then the sliding stopped, with Weiss gripping me and holding me in place. His emotional grid still showed the fiery hot red of the rages.

fourteen

HE HELPED me slide down the wall gently. I sat on the floor, my legs spread out, and him crouching between them. He was growling constantly, a rumble that I was freakily starting to enjoy. I cocked my head to the side and allowed him access to my throat, hoping the submissive gesture would buy me some time. To do what, I wasn't sure. He took deeper whiffs, his emotional grid starting to waver between the red and a calmer orange, a more manageable state of rage.

"I think your pack is going to be pissed if you bite now instead of tonight," I muttered. "They expect a biting and mating ceremony. They're probably going to bring popcorn and peanuts to see you torment my ass."

He snorted, his face going back to human. "They don't see your ass until you've changed. Even then, only a select few can without me busting their balls over it."

"Are you…?"

He shook all over and leaned his nose into my exposed neck. "Second time you pull that shit off. How?" he whispered.

I gulped. "Not the vaguest idea. Seems my jokes are so bad, they snap you out of it."

He hummed. "You do have shitty jokes."

I poked his arm. "No, I don't."

He snorted, then rubbed the tip of his nose against my neck and kissed the skin there. "Let's get up."

He got up first, then pulled me to my feet too.

"What's with the mood swings?" I asked.

He ran a hand through his hair, messing it up a little. Good material for a boner, but I was still too scared about the whole "rages in the elevator" scenario to really get into it.

"Well," he said as he pushed a button and set the elevator moving again, "safe to say it's not based on being pissed. I mean, I was annoyed, but nowhere near really pissed."

"Yeah, you're not too subtle about being pissed, so I know the difference."

He glared at me sideways, then stuck his hands in his pants pockets. "Second time I've come close to losing it around you in tight spaces. First the car, now the elevator." He stared down. "Whatever the fuck this is, we need to figure it out. I don't want to not trust myself with… my moods."

I thought he might say "with you," and maybe he was thinking it. "We need to think about this for a bit. You don't seem to have a condition to cause these manifestations," I muttered as the elevator doors binged open.

We walked into his office.

He closed the door behind us. "Not hormones or other substances, no illness you can pinpoint… what's left?"

I shook my head, the very idea shocking yet perfectly rational at the same time. "Something we can't see, only see the signs of."

He cocked up an eyebrow. "Like?"

"Like magic," I whispered and looked up into his eyes.

He frowned. "You serious?"

I nodded.

"What is it with you and this boner for magic today? You going nuts on me, Sands?"

I glared. "Look, just think about it. What else would make even an iota of sense?"

He shrugged. "Some medical issue of some sort. Maybe there's something wrong with my brain or something, like a tumor."

"Dr. Black checked your records. You had a medical checkup after the glass divider incident, didn't you?"

"Yeah, I did. Went in and did it sooner than scheduled, just to make sure I didn't crack my own skull or something."

"Well, if it had been that kind of medical issue you're thinking about, it would have shown. There's no sign of anything like that."

"Maybe it's a very small thing that doesn't show up on the scan and test I did in the MCU," he replied tersely.

"You'd consider a microscopic tumor before considering magic?"

"I'd take a tumor over magic every day," he deadpanned.

I looked at his expression, the line of his eyebrows. "Weiss… are you by any chance scared?"

He growled. "Shut the fuck up! I'm not scared, I'm concerned."

Right… it's one of those "men don't faint, they lose consciousness" kinds of things, I thought. "Look, we just established that the Fey King is most likely targeting the Council. Why wouldn't he target you as well? You're the Council's strong arm, after all. Their line of defense. Just think about it. What would be the best way to create chaos in a pack?"

He sighed. "Fucking up hierarchy. And making the alpha look like a nutjob would definitely get it done."

"It would make sense."

He walked over to his chair and plopped down into it. "Fucking fey, they don't go the normal way about anything, do they? Goddamn pussies, going behind people's backs and throwing magic instead of punches."

I gritted my teeth. "We each have our ways. That's not what we should be talking about."

He looked up at me. "Really? And what should we discuss, then?"

"We have to find a way to verify this magic theory. Is there anyone the Council trusts who we might ask about it?"

He rapped his fingertips against his desk. "The Council, no. But I might know someone who could give this a try. Someone I do trust."

"Perfect, then let's go see this person."

"I go alone. When I get back we'll know if there's any magic shit tied to me. In the meantime I want you to look over the crime scene reports and Lora's autopsy reports too. I'll have them sent to your office."

The brush-off was as clear as daylight. But I didn't push. I just smiled a small smile, and then walked out of his office. By next week I'd be his mate, the draft for the Protection Act would be ready, and if I were still alive by then, we'd have more time to work through his trust issues.

Tomorrow morning was Amanda's execution, and once that was over with, any suspicions of him going through rages would be resolved. With his ex-mate dead and a new mate to replace her, there'd be no reason to equate him going into a hissy fit with rages of any kind. Not unless he got out of control and did something irreparably stupid and public. As it was now, his rages were under control, either by me balancing his emotional grid, or via my apparently lame jokes. Something about the chemistry of close skin-to-skin contact snapped him out of the red. I knew wolf psychology as well as any community counselor would. The only thing that calmed down alphas when they went into hissy fits was the proximity of their mate or desired mate. So underneath it all, there was something about us getting together that was real. I'd figured that much out the first time he neared rage territory when we were in his car. That was the only explanation I could think of for being able to joke him down from it.

And despite the Fey King possibly waging his brand of war on us, the Council maybe contemplating to sell me off to buy some more time for themselves, and getting bitten tonight to go through a transformation that could always go wrong, I smiled. I couldn't help it, not when my heart fluttered at the thought Weiss could really feel something for me, that there was a real connection we might develop. Sure, he wasn't crushing on me like I was on him—had been for years—but it was as much as I might hope for, especially under these circumstances.

I walked into my office and found the reports on my desk. Flipping through the pages of the crime scene ones didn't bring to light anything new, sadly. I had to hope there was magic involved somehow, magic we might end up detecting, because otherwise we had a lot of dead bodies and no real lead, no real suspect. Weiss had the vics' mates and loved ones interviewed, but no obvious reason had surfaced. I might have suspected contract kills, but five of them? Unlikely, unless there was some contract killer throwing out group discounts.

Maybe this was engineered to put Weiss on the spot. Coupled with the appearance of rages, and his mate being executed for treason and the murder of community members, he'd been bound to lose his leader position. And once that had happened, chaos would have taken over the pack, leaving the Council as vulnerable as it might get. Question was, how was Amanda and her rebel group, popping hormones and marking hormones, tied to any of the fey tactics? It didn't quite click in my head, and I'd studied fey tactics at the Academy.

Lora's autopsy reports showed little more than we already knew. The bodies had been drained of blood without any visible puncture wounds. Someone had killed them and waited for all that blood to seep out, collected it, and used it to draw the pentagram over the shape already built by the bodies themselves. They'd been positioned in the pentagram symbol before rigor mortis had set in, yet blood hadn't seeped too deep into the grass and ground underneath them. The only blood was in the pentagram drawing. There had to be at least another scene; the pentagram arrangement was a secondary. But there was no humanly imaginable way the bodies could have been arranged that way without the murderer or murderers leaving behind *some* traces. Not unless they'd arrived on the scene in some kind of perfectly isolated suits, and been careful enough not to leave any traces behind, not even scent traces for Rick to detect—and he was a really good tracker, that much we knew.

I got up from my desk, stuck my hands in my pants pockets, and walked around my office. Head-to-toe suits isolating the perps? Was that even realistic? Would any kind of material keep out all traces of scent, any footprints? They must've used them from the very first instant they were anywhere near the scene. But wouldn't someone notice one or more people walking around in those kinds of suits? The Silverline woods were pretty popular with everyone in the city. Lots of people jogged there, not to mention lots of pack members did their wild thing there. Someone would have noticed suited up people; they had to. Maybe assuming magic had been involved in arranging the scene was a rushed conclusion. But using it to blank anyone's minds to it... now that wasn't too far-fetched at all.

I picked up my phone and called James.

He picked up after barely one ring. "Sands," he said curtly.

I frowned. "Hey. Is this a bad time?"

"No more than usual, I guess. What's up?"

What was up with the tone? "Wanted to talk to you about a theory regarding the crime scene of the pentagram case."

"Go on."

"It might sound crazy, but after careful consideration, I thought maybe magic was involved in arranging the bodies. Does that sound too far-off to you?"

He took a moment to reply. "I think it sounds like a good theory. There's no real explanation for the way they were arranged, is there?"

I looked down at the tips of my shoes. As an experienced field investigator, Morris James should have thought about the bodysuits idea before accepting any magic theory from me. The fact he so readily embraced it didn't sit well with me. That plus the tone he was using gave me a strange, unpleasant feeling I couldn't quite figure out. My gut feeling was that something was wrong here.

"I hear congrats are in order," he said flatly.

Did he resent me for mating Weiss? Or maybe for the transformation?

"Thanks," I replied almost as flatly. "Think about that magic idea, maybe bounce it off of someone who's seen it in action before. Maybe we'll have something to go on."

He disconnected without saying good-bye. Something was definitely up with him, something weird, and that kept bugging me for some reason. I couldn't read emotional grids over the phone, so I wanted to meet him face-to-face. Not alone, though. I wanted Weiss there too, to really get a reaction. Once he came back from his mystery meeting, I'd ask him to take James out too, and the three of us, at least, would go over to the crime scene together. If James had any issue with me and Weiss, it would provoke a reaction I could read.

Weiss strode in without knocking. He looked at my desk, covered in open files as it was, then at me. "Anything interesting?" he asked, cocking his head toward the mess in front of me.

I sighed. "I'm not sure. What about you, found anything out?"

He closed the door and leaned against it. "You were right."

My heart constricted. "Magic?"

"Conditional magic, that's the verdict."

I hummed. "Interesting. What's the trigger?"

"Couldn't say. We'll have to figure it out somehow."

"Could they undo it?"

"No. Said the fact you're snapping me out of it is the weak spot. We have to press on it with enough force to break the conditional. Whatever the fuck that means," he added. "What do you know about it?"

I smiled. "Oh, so now you're trusting me, but earlier you went out without me because you didn't?"

"It's different. I don't trust anyone enough to take to this person. Get on with what you know, or just tell me you won't share," he added.

It always had to be his way or the highway, of course. It was one of those infuriating yet goddamn irresistible things about him that drew me in. And he had a lot of those, I was sad to say.

"As far as magic goes, conditional is one of the more basic. I don't know much about it. It was deemed—" I cleared my throat. "— too low-level to study for my class. But I know the basics. It involves getting a result out of physical circumstances. The subject of the spell and the object spelled to condition them have to be in close contact a lot, if not at all times."

He cocked an eyebrow. "Low-level? I thought you weren't good with the magic shit."

I tried to hold in any pain at the memories of just how bad I had been, and how my father had reacted to me being a disappointment in the Academy. "I'm not. I can't do the stuff, but I studied it in the Academy. If I was going to be the incompetent of the class, I wanted to not be the ignorant one too."

He stepped closer. "There's no record of your upbringing in the Council files."

My heart sped up. "No, there isn't."

Another step. "Why is that?"

I swallowed thickly, hoping to ease some pressure off my chest. "I didn't choose to share it. It's not mandatory. I read the regulations before being profiled and interviewed when you brought me in."

He snorted. "Who the fuck reads the regulations before the process?"

"Obviously, I did."

Another step closer. Now we were barely apart. "You'll tell me about it. Tonight, after the ceremony. You'll pony up every bit of information you know I can't access on my own. There will be no secret, not even the shadow of a doubt between us."

"Does that go both ways?" I asked slowly.

He grinned. "My fucked-up life is an open book, Tim. Peruse any of the chapters. I don't have much about me that hasn't been documented and researched. You don't make alpha of this pack unless the Council is 100 percent sure you'll deliver on their expectations."

"Not everyone has access to those files," I pointed out.

"You do, as the counselor."

"True. But not the general PBI personnel. So, you do have plenty of secrets."

"But I'm not keeping many from you," he whispered and leaned in to rub his lips against mine.

I shivered at the soft, teasing contact, but I didn't push things further. I decided to let him run things. After all, he was pretty damn good at it.

He rumbled deep in his chest as the heat coming off of him increased. "Tonight you become mine," he whispered.

My heart thumped. "We become each other's. For a while, until your rages issue is cleared. Right?"

He hummed and nudged the tip of his nose into my cheek, pushing me to face away so he could nuzzle the base of my jaw. "Maybe. Maybe for longer. Unless you're only doing this to get my protection now, and once you feel you're safe enough on your own, you plan to dump me."

I chuckled. "Dump you? Our mating won't be undone unless we both agree to it, remember?"

"Maybe you'll try to push some other rule with that Act of yours. It's due on Monday, isn't it? If approved, and I have a sinking suspicion it will be pretty soon, everything about mated life might be different."

I looked up into those blue eyes as I read his emotional grid. "Are you afraid of change, Weiss?"

He smiled. "I'm not afraid. But I do hate it. I hate shaky ground."

"The Act won't affect mated life in the way you think. It's just a collection of rights and measures to be taken when abuse is proven to exist in a leader-slash-anyone mating. I don't get why it scares you so much. Do you think mates would run out as soon as they could because of it?"

"Who'd put up with leader shit unless they had to?"

I took a step back. "You can't be that insecure."

His gaze turned cold. "I'm not. No leader is. But few can get us, Sands. Those who can't, either end up resenting us, or running away whichever way they can."

"You're implying leaders wouldn't have mates unless they were forced to stick by their sides?"

"I'm not implying shit. Who were you talking to earlier?"

Weak deflection, but I allowed it. "There's something strange about James," I said, scratching my chin. "Nothing he actually said or did, but something about him, about his attitude just bugs me. I suggested the bodies were placed by magic over the phone, earlier."

"And?"

"He just went with it, no questions asked, no alternatives, no nothing. Just said it might be a good idea."

Weiss frowned. "That is strange. Vampires don't feel as relaxed around magic as you might. They're just as reluctant as we are, in fact. As any kinds are if they don't practice it. He had voiced no doubt at all?"

I shook my head. "Even I could come up with another theory, a very down-to-earth one: bodysuits. Impractical maybe, hard to deal with without being seen, but they could have still gotten the job done. Suits would have meant witnesses, though. They would have remembered freaky suits for sure. Maybe someone rendered anyone in the area blind with magic, which would be a more reasonable use of magic. Right?"

"Maybe," he muttered. "The bodysuits is the first theory I considered, but in light of all the Fey King shit...."

"Exactly," I cut in. "About which you know. But he doesn't. He has no reasonable excuse to take the involvement of magic that easily. At least none that we know of," I added in a small voice.

He rubbed a hand over his face. "Fuck my life. We're going back there in those woods, and he's coming with us. If he doesn't come up with some nonmagic idea, if he just runs with it like we both know he shouldn't so easily, we're taking him in."

"My thoughts exactly."

fifteen

WEISS HAD James go to the scene, supposedly to give him a status report on crime scene analysis and everything else we had up to that point. I slumped in the driver's seat of Weiss's Beamer and felt dirty. James had reacted strangely to my theory, to the crime scene, to the news of Weiss and me getting mated tonight. Of course I didn't expect him to be overjoyed. The man had made his feelings about Weiss pretty damn clear. But this level of involvement seemed deeper than mere dislike, even resentment over the whole Mitch issue. I had to admit, I was possibly overreacting as well. I certainly wasn't objective about the Mitch situation. And Weiss... I couldn't tell what the hell was going on in his head. I wished I could, but he wasn't that easy to read.

A second field unit was behind us, Rick and Travis, so Rick could take some healthy sniffs of James. They hadn't met since Rick's introduction to the scents of the community, and having a tracker's nose to sniff James's reactions couldn't hurt. While some werewolves had a finer sense of smell than, say, humans, they didn't have any super smell powers—for that matter, neither did regular lycans. Some of the oldest vampires had very sensitive noses, but they were rare and tended not to get involved with PBI official business. It was why Rick was such an asset for the PBI: he was a tracker, so he possessed an extremely fine sense of smell.

Weiss's maniac driving didn't even faze me now. If it was because I was getting used to it, or because I was too preoccupied with my thoughts, I couldn't quite decide.

We made it into the forest and jumped out of the cars. James was already there, waiting by the pentagram's remains. Even after cleaning up the place, there was just a fetid reek of death and evil there. Not the kind of evil pentagrams would invoke, but the scarier, more terrifying kind: the evil done by creatures such as me or Rick or Weiss.

James was crouched near the center of the pentagram. "Evening," he said. "Going with that magic theory? 'Cause I'm not seeing any reasonable explanation for this kind of clusterfuck. Then again, I was never too imaginative."

Weiss stuck his hands in his pockets. "You can't come up with shit, true. Anyone got any input on how five bodies were arranged in a pentagram over here, with no traces, no witnesses, no fucking nothing?"

James got up and frowned. "Is this a brainstorming session? I have a department to take care of, you know? We could've done this over the phone."

Rick's nostrils flared. He stepped closer. "We need fresh ideas from someone with more field experience."

Travis looked James over and sighed. "Have you seen anything even remotely like this?"

Rick paced around, looking pretty much aimless.

James looked at anything but our tracker, so much so that I suspected he was making a point of it. The Downtown Chief stuck his hands in his pockets, looked around the scene, and then shook his head. "I haven't got the slightest idea. Sands, you were saying something about suits?"

I nodded. "Either that or magic."

Weiss huffed. "Brilliant choices: something that doesn't seem plausible, or something that we can't look into."

James frowned. "Which one is the idea we can't look into?"

Travis smacked his lips. "Take your pick."

I smiled. "Unless we find someone who saw suits or somebody comes forth and confesses they did some spell here, we're pretty much screwed."

Weiss walked around, slowly, just like Rick was. Travis's gaze jumped around the place too. I stuck my hands in my pockets and smiled. The three of them had just fallen into step, no words spoken or ideas exchanged; they were doing the same thing. One might assume they were looking around, trying to come up with some idea we could follow up on. To anyone who didn't know them, they looked like agents desperate to squeeze some idea out of who knew what broken twig or scrap of fabric on scene. But I knew them, quite intimately, I might add. I knew their profiles like the back of my hand. I was willing to bet my right arm Rick had picked up on something, something he was sniffing for. Weiss and Travis's pacing around made Rick's sniffing about seem quite random.

What was even more interesting was the unflinching dedication with which James didn't glance in any of their directions. His shoulders were tense despite his obvious efforts to look relaxed, and though he kept his hands stuck in his pockets, they tended to cover his groin. He didn't look much at me either, which in terms of body language was even more telling than constantly staring at something. It actually took more effort to not glance even once at something than it took to keep watching something of interest. James was looking around his feet now, his shoulders stiff, his breathing regular and deep, judging by how his chest moved. My stomach clenched as errant doubts congealed into a clearer idea: Morris James was hiding something that made him feel guilty.

Once the idea clarified in my thoughts, everything clicked into place for me. I broke my rule of not reading emotional grids of those around me. As soon as I focused my read on him, guilt exploded out of his grid and almost drowned me. Thick, pungent hate coated the base of his emotions. Everything he felt was infected by it. Whatever resentment he might have had toward me for mating Weiss wouldn't be this deep. No, this was something old, deeply rooted into his very soul. This kind of hatred had been cultivated. It had been nurtured, fed, given room to grow. The guilt was newer, but strong. It meant he'd done at least one thing he didn't feel fully comfortable with. Maybe something motivated by this virulent hatred—it had to have been a strong motive to propel him into action. What he'd done, I couldn't tell. But if the PBI wanted to find out, they could. There was no such thing as a secret. If more than the one person was involved in any way, it would be discovered.

I cleared my throat. "Anyone got any ideas?"

Rick's gaze found mine. "Nothing. Let's drop it for now, maybe the night will give us good counsel."

"Maybe," I replied.

That wasn't like Rick at all. His nostrils flared as his gaze remained fixed on me. He'd caught something he didn't want to talk about right now.

Weiss stomped back to us. "Joining us tonight for the ceremony, James?"

The corners of James's lips pulled down for a second, a micro-expression of disgust. "Nah, it's a pack thing, isn't it? Vampires aren't that big on ceremony."

Unless it involved a clan member, it went without saying.

Weiss turned to look at me. "Guess we're going home."

I nodded. "Oh, Rick and Travis, we want you there too. You'll be there, right?"

"We'll be there. What time, Weiss?" Rick asked.

"Eightish will work," he replied, shrugging.

We walked back to our cars. Rick didn't give away anything, but I just knew he'd have something interesting to share tonight. That, however, was the lesser of my worries. Right now, number one was the fact I was getting bitten and mated tonight. Amanda would be executed tomorrow, and for all intents and purposes, the world was almost about to tilt on its axis as far as I was concerned.

As soon as Weiss and I settled in the car, he rapped his fingers against his Beamer's wheel.

I breathed out heavily. "Rick discovered something, didn't he?"

"Caught that, did you?"

"The question is, did James? And what the hell is it?"

"He'll tell us tonight, I'm sure. The pack will be assembled by nine, hopefully we'll have some time to talk. Whatever it is he caught a trace of, it's not good, that's for fucking sure."

I braced myself to ask the question that had been nibbling at my thoughts. "How much do you trust James?"

He looked straight ahead and drove off, slightly faster than usual. "He hasn't shown any signs of being disloyal to the Council."

"Do *you* trust him?"

His hands tightened on the wheel. "I want to say no, but…."

"But you feel guilty about the Mitchell situation. So you're not voicing what your gut instinct is saying? Or is it because of the personal connection that you doubt him?"

His lips pressed together tightly. I didn't get an answer by the time we'd made it through his front gate security and parked the car.

I got out of it and walked up the stairs, reading his emotional grid just in case the simmer turned into an explosion.

He went straight into his living room and poured himself a healthy glass of whiskey. "Can I get you anything?"

I shook my head.

Then he sat in what I was starting to think of as his chair, crossed his legs, and fixed his gaze on me. "In about two hours I'm going to bite and mate you, in front of my family, pack, and Council. Take a seat, we need to discuss what's going to happen."

My heart pounded as I sat on the couch.

He took a swig of whiskey, sat back a little, and fixed those piercing icy blue eyes on me again. "As you probably know, the ceremony is pretty simple. When everyone is here, we go back into a secure room, I change, and bite you. When we get out, you're a werewolf, I'm your alpha, and we're mated. Or only one of us comes out, if things don't work out between our wolf forms, but I expect everything to run smoothly."

He was an experienced alpha and the alpha of a huge pack to boot, so I was pretty sure things would run quite smoothly. Whether that meant he'd take me out once changed, or help me join his pack as his mate, remained to be seen. I'd read enough studies to know one in every maybe a hundred freshly changed wolves turned against the pack authority, even when it was a pack of two. Realistically speaking, aside from the chances the shift itself might go sideways, if it did go well and, once changed, I rebelled against Weiss, I'd get killed. A shiver traveled through my bones.

"I know," I said.

"What you don't know is what goes on inside that room."

"I'm the PBI counselor and a therapist, give me some credit. I've read about it plenty."

He gave me a small, cruel smile. "Reading about something and experiencing it are two very different things, Sands."

I bit my tongue. Smart comebacks wouldn't work in my best interest right now. Challenging Weiss's authority just before him changing and biting me wasn't exactly smart thinking. Whatever else I might have been, an idiot wasn't one those things.

"True," I said, nodding. "Will you tell me?"

He watched me eerily. "I doubt it will prepare you for it, but yes. Once bitten, the effect will start kicking in, probably in about one hour, two tops. Tradition advises doing something that would... get the blood pumping in the meantime. Helps the venom of my bite to run through your system."

My face heated up. "Oh-kay. And once the venom kicks in?"

He leaned forward, resting his hands on his knees. "You're going to be in a fucking load of pain. I can't give you anything to take the edge off. Having any substances in your body might fuck with the process."

A drip of sweat glided down my temple. "On a scale of one to ten, how would you rate that pain?"

"Twenty."

Crap. I wasn't into pain at all. "For how long?"

"Once you've changed for the first time, the pain fades. But Tim, I'm telling you again, there will be a fucking world of pain. You have to soldier through it until you've changed. Your body will know what to do, you just have to tough it out. You're a grown man, you know what might happen if you get... stuck."

Oh, I knew: Naty Stein had gotten stuck during the first change because of the pain. As a result, she was stuck in an in-between stage, with wolf ears and tail, but mostly human. Despite her best efforts, she hadn't managed to change in either direction again due to a psychosomatic barrier.

I cleared my throat. "How many have you bitten, yourself?"

He looked into his glass. "Quite a few of my packmates. I could probably get it done with my eyes closed and three paws tied."

My heartbeat sped up. "What will we be doing to get my heart pumping?"

"Wrestling, chasing each other through the room... depends on what mood strikes me." He swirled the whiskey in the glass a few times and took a good swig, downing it. Then he looked at me, that icy gaze zapping through my system. "Are you sure you want to go through with it, Tim?"

My heart thumped. "Having second thoughts?"

He snorted. "I asked you first. Are you sure?"

I leaned back in the couch, his presence too intense suddenly. "It's the best solution to both of our issues. You're clear of any rages suspicions if you have a... fit in public, and I'm sure to have the Council behind me as your mate."

"You realize once mated, we won't be able to undo it for quite some time. For things to work out for us, we have to stick together for a while. It's not going to be a short-term gig."

My stomach tightened at the "gig" part. "I'm well aware. If you've changed your mind, though—"

"Not at all. I want you as my mate," he muttered, looking into his empty glass.

"Under these circumstances," I added just to make things clear.

"Our whole lives are an endless row of circumstances."

"Uhm... that's very deep. But I meant, you want me as your mate under these dire circumstances," I supplied as smoothly as I could.

He leaned back in the chair and crossed his legs again. "You know why I'm confident biting you and changing you will go well?"

Because you're a cocky bastard? I wanted to supply, but I just went with a shrug.

"Because I really do want you. I've had a thing for you ever since I first saw you, that night. My wolf had a thing for you, which is rare. It's why I jumped in and helped you out."

Butterflies fluttered in my stomach. "I thought it was because I reminded you of Mitchell."

"You did, after I changed from wolf to man. But the wolf met you first."

"And the wolf... liked me?"

He smiled. "Of course. Pack alphas don't jump in to help anyone outside of their packs that often, you know."

Especially not fey, of which they were instinctively weary. They usually didn't help out anyone nonpack. In fact, I knew from what studies I'd read. Why Weiss had helped me out had been bugging me for the last five years. To be entirely honest, it was the possibilities of what it might've meant that had my panties in knots. Studies had it that pack alphas, no matter the pack's size, rarely if ever showed interest in outsiders. When they did, it was most often the case of coupling or mating interest. And after seeing Weiss in his full naked glory, after having saved my life, I was all for some coupling. That hope had been lingering in the back of my mind all this time. That foolish, teenagerish hope that five years ago he'd seen something in me—something he'd wanted. Something he might possibly want again. And every time I'd tried to reason with myself that it was a hopeless crush, masochism really, and nothing else on my part to keep daydreaming about him, that pesky, tiny sliver of a hope would resurface and whisper foolish things in my ear. And even if my best hope was a casual-fuck interest five years ago, it seemed to be enough to keep me hanging on to the crush.

Bitterness washed through me at the sudden memory of all my dreams, all the lonely nights I'd spent imagining him gazing my way, seeing me, noticing me… all the times fantasies about the two of us had kept me awake, all those near-tears moments that had bitten into my very soul. Sex fantasies were easy to take and live with. I never had any qualms about those. It was the other kind of fantasy that had me sobbing silently into my pillow quite a few times—the fantasies about him smiling at me, his gaze roaming over my body, and his palm reaching out to caress my cheek; the imagined words whispered into my ear as his massive body pushed me against a wall, his warmth, the scent of his skin crawling into my system and filling a dark, desperate emptiness that pressed on my lungs and had me gasping.

A warm hand pressed down on my shoulder, and I flinched, pulled away from my thoughts.

"Are you okay?" Weiss's voice whispered from close by.

He'd gotten up and sat beside me on the couch, something I had entirely missed. His hands rested on my shoulders, the pressure and warmth more comforting than I was willing to admit.

I nodded. "Bite jitters, I guess."

He hummed, then grabbed my arm. "Come on, we need to have a little heart-to-heart."

I followed his lead, frowning. "And it has to happen somewhere specific?"

He looked back at me over his shoulder and grinned in that evil, fucking gorgeous way only he could. "Definitely."

sixteen

AS WE made our way up the stairs, my heart started pounding harder and harder. By the time we went into his bedroom, I was just about ready to pass out.

"We need to have a heart-to-heart in your bedroom?" I mumbled.

He chuckled. "Privacy and not being interrupted go well with heart-to-heart, right?"

"I guess."

He motioned me to sit on his bed, which made my stomach clench and my spine tingle. I frowned in confusion as he kneeled in front of me on the carpet, setting his hands on my thighs. My dick went ramrod hard at the thought this might go in the direction of a blowjob. Just the thought of it had me close to creaming my pants.

He looked up at me, those gorgeous eyes dark, pupils blown out. "You do know I'm into you? Realize that I've been interested since five years ago, right?"

I gulped. "I don't think I can buy that, sorry. You don't have to play to actually bag me, Weiss. I'm already bagged, willing to go the distance for you, for both of us. Don't fuck around with my feelings, even if you don't trust me that they exist."

He puffed out a lungful of hot air. "The relationship gene obviously didn't make it in my gene pool," he muttered. "I have a hard time trusting anything right now, Tim. And contemplating the fact James might be hiding something isn't helping with my trust levels by and large either. But I do get that you're into me, apart from all the convenient reasons for us to get together now. I was hoping you'd gotten the fact I'm into you too."

I swallowed. "I can't really get things you don't show or say. I can read emotional grids, not minds, you know."

"And what does my grid tell you, then?"

"It's a jumbled mess of feelings, Weiss. I can't make out much right now, anyway."

"Fair enough. I'm not feigning interest. This isn't a fucking act."

"But you did act with Amanda, when you felt you had to. And I'm betting she didn't think it was an act at the time, did she? So you're a good actor."

He shook his head. "That's different."

"Is it?" I asked, searching his eyes.

He sighed. "I won't ever admit to having said this, but there hasn't been one relationship I was involved in that I didn't severely fuck up. Maybe Alf is the one standing exception to that rule, but the jury is still out on that one until a few years from now. I'm not built for this kind of thing. I don't really handle it well, okay? And now is not my greatest moment either. I get that I'm difficult to read and put up with, I really do get it. I'm aware of it. There are things I'm just not... good with. But I try to make up for that with all the things I am good at."

"Which are?" I asked, not able to help myself.

He grinned. "Oh, you'll find out, trust me. I'm not saying I'm in love with you. I'm not even sure I can be properly in love. I don't really know when it is you can say you're in love with someone, what makes it clear that you are. But I know I want to have you by my side right now. I know I want you to stand beside me and help me sort everything out for us and our pack. I want you around my son, for fuck's sake, doesn't that tell you enough?"

My throat constricted. I reached out a hand and ran my fingertips over his brow, the line of cheekbone, down to his lips. Tingles traveled up my arm from the point of contact, a warm, electric sensation exploding through my body. I took in a rushed breath, suddenly afraid I might choke to death. "You're a remarkable man, Herman Weiss, but you're only a man after all. Those relationships that didn't go right, they weren't your doing entirely. It takes two to tango, as they say. Maybe what really screwed them up was the fact they didn't start or end for the right reasons. You tend to take the whole blame on yourself, because you're a leader, and in your mind, everything is your responsibility, your merit, your fault."

He snorted. "Thanks, that really makes me feel a whole fucking lot better."

I kept my fingertips on his jaw line. "I'm not trying to make you feel better. You're too stubborn to listen to me, even if I'd try. I'm just speaking my mind."

"Go on."

"I think what this whole thing comes down to is what really scares us. You're scared of being betrayed again," I whispered, looking at his lips.

Gods and wings, he had gorgeous lips. Full, the lower one a little pouty, and they looked so soft and inviting despite the straight line he kept them in most of the time.

"What are you afraid of, then?" he asked softly, almost in a tender tone.

I swallowed thickly. "You're in the unique position of being able to irreparably break my heart, and get me killed. I'm scared shitless that you'll do one, then the other. And I think what has me really terrified is that you'll do the first, and not the second after that. That you'll let me have you, taste you, feel you inside me all the way down to the very bottom of my soul, and then take all that away from me because it will suit your interests to get rid of me. Just like it suits your interests to have me now. I'm terrified of having to live with the memory of being like this, close enough to you that I can almost taste the air you breathe out. Living with the fantasy has been tough, but having to live with the memory and not being able to ever have it again...."

I trailed off and swallowed again, hoping to dislodge the knot in my throat. It felt like I wouldn't ever be able to breathe properly again. And he'd reduced me to this pathetic lump of longing and despair without even properly fucking me over yet—or fucking me, for that matter.

He groaned and pushed his forehead up against my cheek. "Fuck, what a boner that just gave me. I know it's not the kind of response you were hoping for, but I'd love to fuck you through the mattress right now."

I shivered, unable to articulate a thing. I could feel his rabid heartbeat, the warmth radiating off him increasing and making my chest sweat.

"I haven't fucked over anyone I was seriously involved with," he whispered, rubbing his brow against my jaw line. "I broke up with Mitch and leveled with him when I did. I didn't fuck around on Amanda, not even when we hadn't so much as touched each other by accident in years. I know I come off as a spectacular asshole, and I'm not claiming I'm not an ass. But I don't fuck people over, Tim. Not even those who fuck me over," he whispered. "You might not be able to believe I'm really into you, and you don't have to take my word for it either. I'll prove it. But believe I don't fuck people over, because at least that much I know I'm good for."

"I don't fuck people over either," I mumbled.

He chuckled. "Great, then we'll make a brilliant goddamn couple."

He pulled back a little and rubbed his lips against mine, the velvety feel of him making my dick pound. I groaned and pushed my lips into his hard as I wrapped my arms around his large shoulders. He hummed and deepened the kiss, the hot taste of him giving me an instant high. Sweet waving wands, how I wanted him. How I burned to feel his hands on my skin, his body against mine, him inside me, me inside him, anything I could get would be fucking nirvana.

He pulled back slowly and nipped my lower lip when I tried to kiss him again.

"Stop that or we won't make it to our own bite ceremony," he chastised with a growl. "Keep your clothes on. I'll take mine off and bring a robe instead. Don't go anywhere without me; our guests are already gathering downstairs. I don't want anyone fucking laying a fingertip on you, not to shake hands, not to give you a hug, not to pat your goddamn back. The only scents on you must be yours and mine, and nothing else. We clear?"

"Okay. Should I... shower or something, to smell less like anyone else we might have met today?"

"No. Showering right now will make you smell less like yourself. I want to feel the scent of you as you are now, turned on, hot for me. I want to feel the scent of your sweat running down your stomach and the slight tang of fear you're exuding."

Fuck, that turned me on even more for some reason. I watched as he took off his clothes, his hard-on waving around like a magnificent flag of pride. He put a robe on, fastened it around his middle, and reached out a hand.

"Let's go," he said, his gaze intent and his piercing eyes breathtaking.

I took his hand, ready to get this show started. Tonight would either end in me being his mate and part of his pack, or in me being dead. Somehow the clear lines of either of those endings comforted me. There was no awkward in-between, no puzzling neither-nor moment. And I was so looking forward to some clarity. Weiss needed clarity too, though. A clear mind, as much as he could have one under the circumstances. So I focused as hard as I could to bathe his emotional grid in cool, calm energy.

When we got downstairs, I let go of Weiss's hand. Him holding hands with someone just wasn't part of his persona, and I didn't want to give his pack the sense I was taking away their alpha. Alf came running at us, jumping on his dad's back like a little monkey. Weiss walked away carrying him, while Bert followed diligently and kept begging them to not mess around with his decorations. In my humble opinion, telling them not to do something was most likely the best way to make sure they would do it, but I didn't meddle.

Travis and Rick walked up to me.

"Nice audience," Travis said, cocking his head at the flock of pack members in the dining room area.

"To be expected, I guess. I'm sorry there are some PBI who didn't make it," I added, looking at Rick.

He motioned for a quieter area near the fireplace in the living room, and we walked there. Everyone was congratulating Weiss, and not giving me much attention unless it was to stare, but more often than not, to glare instead. I got their point. Many had been hoping to compete for their alpha's attention.

Rick leaned in close enough to whisper without touching. "Something about Morris James is fucked up."

"Go on," I said.

"When we were on scene, I felt the distinct scent of Weiss, you, Travis, and me. Nothing of James, though."

I pulled back a little and frowned. "That's not possible."

Travis sighed. "My thoughts exactly."

"And yet it did happen," Rick added in a flat tone.

"Have you talked to anyone about this? Maybe it's some sort of issue—"

Rick smacked his lips. "It can be done, we've talked to Lora. Apparently someone can develop a sort of scent-repellant. With repeated exposure, my nose won't pick up on the person or thing smelling that way."

"That means access and repeated exposure," Travis chimed in. "And a clear intent for misdoings, or else why bother?" Then he leaned in too. "Amanda had something like this planned too. It's why she wanted to train Rick as soon as I recruited him. My cutting in messed up her plans."

I stepped back a little, found Weiss with my gaze. He was still carrying his son on his back, talking to pack members, shaking hands— I guessed accepting congrats. His emotional grid showed excitement, anticipation, some friskiness, which I was secretly cheerleading, but also a tinge of fear, anxiousness. I didn't blame him. If he got a pseudo-rage fit tonight, we might be headed for disaster. I summoned all the calming energy I could and channeled it to him in constant waves rather than a big splash. There was no dangerous anger boiling there, but now that we knew it was magic that provoked it, it didn't really matter—it could simply show up out of the blue and explode through Weiss. If we told him now about James, we might be looking at impending doom, specifically mine. I was the one going into a secure room with him, after all. He'd rage out on me, and nobody would even know what had happened. It could just as well come off as a change gone wrong. Blood froze in my veins as I thought that over. Oh my flapping wings, it would work out perfectly. He'd kill me, possibly come out of the secure room still raging. The pack might not report it, but they didn't have to—the Council was already here, attending the bite ceremony. With all these witnesses, they'd have no choice but to put Weiss down. Chaos would break out with pack members competing for the alpha position. And in the process, the Council would be vulnerable.

My thoughts tried to rush, but I calmed myself down. I had to be clear and rational, now more than ever. Who'd have the most to gain from this going wrong? Someone who was out to get Weiss, possibly even me. James came to mind immediately. He had the most personal of motives: vendetta. He might hold Weiss accountable for Mitchell's death, and I was the usurper to his place beside the werewolf alpha. But it couldn't be only him, I realized. No, he could have tried to get even in less obvious ways. The connection I'd just made could be made by anyone else in this room. James could have gotten his revenge in ways that would cost him less. Even if he was involved, there was more to it. I was convinced he'd had something to do with the crime scene, the guilt, the hate, the fear of being discovered... it all clicked into place. Morris James, head of our Downtown department, was a traitor. But he was no fool. Getting involved in something like this with such good odds of him becoming the scapegoat meant he thought someone had him covered, despite his transparent motive.

My gaze found the Council, all of them sitting at Weiss's dinner table. Naty Stein was chatting with her mother, her ears flickering in all directions and her tail moving frantically beneath the long blazer she wore. Who was above Weiss in the hierarchy and could protect James when suspicion came his way? Someone in the Council, I realized with a chill. A traitor, working with James, with Tricia... with Amanda. Using Amanda's hatred for leaders to clean out some key positions in the community, securing a new ring of power. A Council member could easily flip on James too, not having his back, though they might have promised to. Then they'd get rid of him, frame him and Tricia, and whatever other unfortunate had gotten involved with them, for the whole thing.

I'd promised myself I wouldn't use my ability to manipulate emotions, and had become a therapist to help people deal with their feelings. I wasn't supposed to even read them by Council law. But tonight I was fighting for my life. From now on, I'd be fighting for my family and, starting tonight, for my pack. I very much doubted that anyone in the room would have any weapon in their arsenal and, when in need, refuse to use it. I had to trust myself with making the choices of how and when to use my skills. Protecting myself and those close to me was a noble enough cause to fight for. And I decided I would use all the weapons I had at my disposal when the situation called for it.

I reached out my reading power to the Council, looking for any emotion that might give me a clue. But they were many. I was tired and already pushing my meager powers to their limits with keeping Weiss balanced. I didn't have the juice to read the whole Council right now. And I couldn't talk to Weiss, not before he bit me and I changed safely. Once my first change happened, though... once we got out of that room in one piece, things would stand quite differently. And whoever planned on me not making it out of there alive would feel strongly about my being changed and a pack member—emotions I'd be able to read, hopefully. That was, if the change itself didn't go wrong, and my new wolf self didn't have some issue with Weiss's.

"Don't tell him," I whispered into Rick's ear. "Not until we come out of the secure room."

Travis's gaze fixed on mine. "What if *you* don't make it out?"

I gave him a small smile. "If I don't, he won't be around for long anyway—call it a gut feeling. Getting him pissed before we go in there won't up our chances, though."

Rick sighed. "This whole thing is such a fucking bad idea, Sands. I can't understand how you don't see it."

"Oh, I do," I replied, blinking slowly. "It's a terrible idea, you're right. But at this point, it's our only option. Unlike you, I have faith in him," I added in a tiny voice.

He snorted. "I'm sure others did too, you goddamn moron. But they're not around to tell us about it, are they?"

The venom in his voice was a clear declaration of just what he thought of Weiss. Rick's strange bond with Amanda was one of the things I'd been meaning to look into, but hadn't had the chance to yet. I just hoped I might have the chance later on. Either way, I was willing to bet the images of his abusive ex and of Weiss overlapped in his mind somewhere—an unjust association in my opinion. Not because Weiss couldn't be an ass—which he often was, in fact, with flying colors—but because the circumstances were different, and from what I knew as the Bureau's counselor, Weiss hadn't ever actually abused Amanda. He'd just refused to end their mating, which wasn't all right, but not nearly in the area of what Rick's ex had done.

I smiled at Rick. "We'll talk about that, I promise."

He snorted. "Don't make promises you can't keep. You might not make it overnight, isn't that true?"

I gulped, but didn't lose my smile. "Any of us might not make it, Rick. That's the kind of bitch life is. Trust me, I know. But I'm coming out of that room as a newly changed werewolf and Weiss's mate, mark my words," I proclaimed in my dusted-up fey prince tone.

Rick seemed to want to reply, but the words died on his lips. He looked me over, shook his head, and leaned into his mate a little. In turn, Travis wrapped his arm around him and looked at me. "Good luck," he mouthed voicelessly.

I smiled, then found Weiss with my gaze again. Right, now that it was all set, all I had to do was actually survive this shebang. Then we'd get everything sorted out.

seventeen

AFTER TALKING to Travis and Rick, I made my way to Weiss and Alf. As soon as Weiss saw I was headed in their direction, he cut off whatever discussion he was having with one of his pack members and walked over to me, holding his son by the hand.

Alf grinned up at me. "Told you that you were tailup."

"Behave, little mutt," Weiss growled.

I kneeled down to look the little alpha-to-be straight in the eye. "How about you give me a mating gift?"

He blinked those big, icy blue eyes at me. "I made you something. Is that what you mean?"

Dawww, he'd made me something? I hoped it wasn't out of a pair of my shoes. "I mean, doing something I'll ask as a present. But thank you for whatever it is you did too," I added when he looked crestfallen.

"Bert said you and Daddy would like it," he said, looking at his shoes.

"I'm sure we will, if you made it."

"Really?" he asked, grinning.

God, he looked so much like his father. The thought of parenting sort of choked me there for a minute. I hadn't planned on having kids. Certainly not starting out with a seven-year-old alpha-to-be.

"Really," I replied, smiling. "Now, about that favor...."

"Okay, what is it?" he asked, his eyes glittering with curiosity.

I crossed my fingers. "How about you don't chew on my shoes anymore?"

He giggled. "Can't promise that."

"I've given up asking," supplied Bert, shaking his head.

Marvelous. "Can't blame a guy for trying, right?"

I got up to my full height and found Weiss staring at me oddly. "What?" I asked, dusting my knee.

He shrugged and reached a hand out. "Come on, let's do this."

Bert took Alf by the hand. The kid looked nervous, fidgety.

"You okay?" I asked him.

The little guy nodded. "Weiss alphas are always fine," he said, biting his lower lip.

Bert rolled his eyes, and Weiss grinned.

I smiled at the kid. "Sure they are."

Weiss cleared his throat. "Thanks for coming, everyone. We're just about ready to go in."

The house quieted down. One of the more ancient-looking Council members got up from his chair. "May your bite be potent and your mating flourish."

Then Weiss pulled me by the hand in the direction of the kitchen.

I frowned. "*That* was the ceremony?"

He snorted. "Everybody's a critic. But no, the ceremony consists of the whole process. It ends when we get out of the secure room with you a new werewolf and my mate. That was just a good luck wish."

I cleared my throat. "Right. Remind me to tell you something when we get out. Where are we going, anyway?"

He stopped walking. "The cellar. Tell me what?"

I waved a hand. "After, okay? Trust me on this, it's not as important as what we're going to do now."

His gaze searched mine. I felt like he was sifting through my soul, as if I were an open book and he was flipping pages, looking for whatever it was that he needed. I opened myself up to the scrutiny, knowing full well what I had to say wouldn't help us now. After a while, he resumed walking. The door to the cellar was a pretty inconspicuous thing. It looked quite harmless despite what it symbolized. This could be the road with no return, literally.

Weiss pulled it open and flipped on some switches. Two rows of neon lights buzzed to life on the cellar's ceiling. I was expecting some kind of small, dark place for some reason, but it was nothing like it. After we descended a flight of stairs, Weiss punched in a code on the keypad beside a large door. With a beep, something unlocked, and he pulled open the door.

"Take your clothes off and leave them here," he told me as he disrobed.

I frowned. "At the door?"

"No cameras or audience except me," he explained, grinning.

His robe flew to a nearby chair, and he casually strolled inside, completely unfazed by being buck naked. Of course, the man's body was a goddamn work of art, so really, what was there to be shy about? I, on the other hand, was freaking out. I'd been naked with him already, true, and it hadn't felt weird then, but now I was terribly shy for some reason.

He sighed and strolled back out. "You're gonna make me work for it, aren't you?"

He grabbed my jacket and maneuvered it down my arms, then took off my shirt, unbuttoned my jeans, and pulled them down my thighs along with my briefs. I swallowed thickly and just stared at him, moving as he told me to in order to step out of my pants. And suddenly there I was, naked, with Weiss grinning at me.

"Much better," he rumbled.

Then he grabbed me by the hand and walked us into the room. I noticed after he closed that door that he punched in another code, and that ominous-sounding lock fell back into place.

"Am I a hostage?" I asked, looking around nervously.

He patted my shoulder. "Secure room, Sands. Why do you think we call it that? Nobody gets in or out of here without my accord."

"So in case something goes wrong… there would be no help coming?"

"Not unless I open the door and call for it," he said calmly. "You're freaking out, aren't you?"

I swallowed convulsively, despite my throat feeling parched. "Ugh, a little."

"Come here," he whispered, holding out his hands.

My heart pounded as I did. When our skin touched I inhaled sharply, loving the way his chest rumbled. I could feel my pounding heart hitting against him, and his thumping steadily and strongly against my neck. I inhaled deeply, willing myself to calm down. A sharp pain struck the side of my neck. I flinched and gasped, but before

I could properly scream the pain dulled, and I felt a hot tongue lapping at the place. It didn't do much to calm the actual pain, which was only worsening, but it offered me some comfort.

When he pulled back, his face had already morphed back into human.

I frowned. "You could have warned me or something."

He stroked my arm in slow, steady caresses. "You were starting to freak out, so I thought we'd just get through the easy part."

I winced. "Wings and dust, that hurt. And that was the *easy* part?"

He nodded and pulled me by the hand.

"What now, you'll throw me over a cliff to ease my nerves or something?" I muttered.

He cocked his head to the side. I followed the direction with my gaze and noticed a sort of drawer bed and nightstand that looked like they protruded from the wall.

"What the hell is that?"

He grinned. "My choice for speeding up your heartbeat."

My throat went instantly dry. "Having sex? Well, that will get my blood pumping for sure."

"You're a horny little thing, aren't you?"

I stuck my tongue out and tumbled down on the surprisingly soft bed. "So are you, wolfman."

He grinned wickedly as he crawled over me in bed. "No, I'm not. I'm a big, fucking horny bastard. Allow me to show you the difference...."

Sweet magic wands, in about ten minutes my heart was pounding insanely, and he'd already made me cum once. I was still twitchy all over from the lightning-bolt orgasm that had crashed through my system when the pain of the bite began to grow. It wasn't tormenting, just a nagging and constant burn and tearing sensation, that, despite me not moving, still continued.

"It's starting to hurt," I whispered.

"I know," he replied, his piercing gaze fixed on mine. "It's gonna hurt, but I'll take your mind off of it as much as I can," he added, going from compassionate to mischievous.

"Why does that worry me, I wonder?" I muttered, half-dazed.

He spread my thighs wide open, and ran his hands up and down the sensitive inner sides, his fingertips slightly grazing my skin. It made my balls pull up snugly and my muscles twitch all over.

"I love how lean you are," he said as his dark gaze followed the imaginary lines his fingers were leaving behind. "And how soft and sensitive your skin is," he added darkly as he leaned in and nibbled on the underside of my knee.

I twitched and nearly jumped off of the bed, my heart thumping fast. His fingers ghosted up higher on my inner thighs, reaching the apex. I lifted my hips off the bed and gave him access to my cheeks, which he grabbed in greedy handfuls. I groaned and flexed my hips, starting to grow hard again. The pain of his bite pulsed out from my neck and spread faint webs through the rest of my body, a trail that I knew in my bones would be followed by the real pain that was to come. Weiss squeezed my butt again and ripped my thoughts away from the pain. He slowly grazed his way down my thighs to the back of my knees. With one swift push, he had my legs bent, my knees pushing into my arms.

"Hold your legs out like this," he rumbled thickly.

Shit, I would have said yes to anything right about then. I grabbed the backs of my knees with my hands and pulled them apart until my muscles ached. He licked his lips slowly as he watched the whole display. Then he slowly leaned down, so slowly that I thought I'd have a heart attack before he'd reach base. When he finally got close to anything, he chose to sink his human teeth into the apex between my inner thigh and my buttock. I screamed and jumped a little, squirming until he pinched my sack. I whined but held still, getting the message. A shockwave of pain whipped through my body, and I flinched. I felt Weiss's hot mouth hovering over sensitive skin down there, and the anticipation alone had my pulse skyrocketing. I moaned openmouthed when his hot, wet tongue flicked against my sack and up to the base of my now-hard dick. Then, as it continued its way up to my tip, I flexed my hips eagerly and pulled my legs even wider, to the point of pain.

He chuckled softly and grabbed my weeping hard-on, and with one hungry, greedy motion, swallowed me down his throat.

"Holy shit," I groaned as he sucked hard and incessantly on my pounding flesh.

He felt beyond amazing as he sucked me off, with wet, sloppy sounds, his spit dribbling down my flesh. I moaned as I felt those dribbles slide down my balls and lower, to my hole. The slippery pressure and greedy pull of his mouth had me close to cumming soon, but he wouldn't allow me to cum. With his index and thumb wrapped tightly around my base, he sucked me until I thought my heart would give out. He reduced me to a squirming, sweating, quivering mess, and yet the tight ring around the base of my cock wouldn't relent.

"Please, just… please…," I whispered again and again, my voice screechy, needy, faint.

"Shhhh," he whispered evilly as his finger worked its way inside me. Oh, fucking fey dust, I was going to die. I thrashed my head against the pillow as his finger pushed in, aided by all the spit that had made its way down there. He probed around meticulously while still sucking me off, and when he found what he was looking for and pushed on it, I screamed out. The ring at the base of my dick tightened, though, and for a second there I thought I'd cum, but I didn't. The pressure was too much, pushing against the back of my eyes, pounding into my balls, tightening my stomach in something akin to cramps. Sweat ran down my face and body, a trickle of it sliding into my mouth now and then.

"Please…," I hissed, my voice leaving me.

He chuckled and pulled his finger out. I groaned, heartbroken yet relieved at the loss. But then the finger pushed back inside, and a second one joined. He hit my prostate, making me scream out again as he swallowed my pounding hard-on and hummed around it. My eyes rolled back into my head. I was one tiny step from passing out. The pressure on my prostate increased slowly but steadily, his fingers drawing tiny circles inside. *Fuck, fuck, fuck!* My heartbeat went irregular, missing a beat now and then, before beating with furious force. Pain pulsed through my body from where he'd bitten me, each pulse of it more vicious than the previous one. With a mighty suck and groan around my dick and his fingers pushing into me mercilessly, I finally came. The orgasm clawed through me, slashing through every nerve ending and muscle, slicing through my very heart and zinging through my bones like a spiderweb of explosions, each one going nearer and nearer to my stomach where they all converged into one nuclear-sized explosion that shot down my groin and through my dick, right into the back of his burning-hot throat. I cried out with each spurt, feeling the very heart of me pulsing out and getting lost into the consuming mess of him. My body slumped and shivered as he drew out his fingers and kissed the head of my softening cock.

I cracked open my eyelids just in time to see him straddle my legs and rub himself to completion, his juices spurting out hot and heavy on my stomach. I shivered again at the contact and whispered, "Sweet gods and magic," as my eyelids drooped closed.

The last thing I was really aware of was the warmth of his body wrapping around mine, the pain of his bite gaining ground over the slowly fading afterglow, and a soul-deep sense of exhaustion. Then I fell into a strange, fitful sleep, almost too tired to even breathe.

SCREAMS. I woke up to screams, piercing, slowly growing into shrill. My throat felt raw and my skin clammy. I drew in a big gulp of air, and the screams stopped. But then they started again. I felt Weiss's hands around me, trying to keep me still, his voice pouring out in a litany of words I couldn't make sense of. If he was talking and someone else was screaming, it means it was me—I was screaming. The realization jarred me as the pain kept ravaging through my system. I couldn't pull in enough air to scream again, my heart couldn't put up with the effort anymore. The screams didn't make it out of my throat anymore, but they went on in my head. Burning, festering, ripping pain exploded through my body in a million different places, the sequence too quick to keep up with. I whimpered, a seemingly endless sound that slipped out from my lips whether I inhaled or exhaled. My body went limp, even expanding my chest for breath too much of an effort to keep up with on a regular basis. I drew in air now and then, only when I felt I was choking.

Weiss cradled me, his mouth near my ear. "Shhh, you're going to be all right. I know it hurts, but you're strong. You'll make it through. Fight the exhaustion, Tim. Fight for me," he whispered.

I wanted to tell him I would, that I was trying, doing my best, but I didn't have enough energy left to talk. I simply anchored myself to his touch, the feel of his skin against mine, his voice. I allowed his icy blue eyes to guide me through the horror of the endless waves of pain, a tsunami of nausea drowning me each time the pain receded. I squeezed his hand because it was close to mine, and it was the most effort I could expend.

"You're made of tough stuff. You'll make it through just fine, I know you will," he said softly into my ear. "You were a vision that night five years ago, you know? You'll see—when you're in wolf form, everything looks different. Images are different, scents barely resemble what you've felt in human form. When something is beautiful...." He trailed off, running a hand through my sweaty hair. "It's going to be spectacular seen in your wolf form. And you were spectacular, Tim. I couldn't stay away from you, even if I was mated and I wouldn't have cheated on my mate. But I couldn't stay away. I asked the Council to get you on board, I wanted you nearby. Wanted to see you around, feel your scent every now and then. Not too often, or I might start getting ideas. But every once in a while," he told me in a soft voice, very unlike the Weiss we all knew.

My heart thumped a little faster, the irregularities slowly dissolving into a steady, albeit still faint beat.

"Didn't have to paint too convincing a picture anyway, one of the councilors was very glad to take you on board. Mrs. Stein always saw great potential in you, for some reason. She was on my side, convinced everyone else to take you in, despite your father's demands that they cast you out."

Mrs. Stein had been on my side? Naty was a really great woman, but her mother gave me the willies. Her being the most humane out of the bunch didn't really make sense.

"It was tough to have you around, to know I could have you if circumstance would've been different, but keep away."

Goddamn wolf bastard, of course he had to tell me about that now, when I could barely even breathe. I'd make it through just so I could bite his ass.

eighteen

WE STAYED that way for a good while, pain burning through me and Weiss trying to keep me distracted. Half the time I couldn't even pay attention to what he was saying. The pulsing, burning sensation, as if my muscles were being shredded from the inside out, demanded my full attention.

But then the pain started to change. Or maybe I was just getting used to it. I could inhale deeper, and my heartbeat was steady. I blinked a few times, moved my head slightly so I could look up at Weiss.

"Did you mean a word you said earlier?"

He grinned. "That's my man. You've gone through the worst of it."

"Did you mean what you said?"

He sighed. "Of course I did. Go over there, in that corner of the room."

I frowned. "Why?"

He smiled. "The pain has become bearable?"

I nodded.

"Your first change is coming up," he announced cheerfully. "Go over there. We need to have some space between us. Now just run with what your body does. Don't try to steer things in any direction. Just follow your instincts."

I frowned. "What are you going to do once I change?"

"Change too, of course."

I crossed to the other end of the room on my hands and knees. The pain had subsided considerably, but it was nowhere near over.

Once I got in my corner, the same kind of burning pain began to flutter through my muscles, from my toes and the tip of my hairs, back down my spine, coiling in my stomach. I crouched on the floor, blanking my mind out and just letting it rip through me. I could hear Weiss's change in the other part of the room, his scent growing thicker. I closed my eyes tightly as a particularly vicious wave of pain went through me. Then I slowly opened my eyes and saw fur on my paw.

I got up from the floor, shook myself sturdily. Weiss's nostrils flared from across the room, and he started walking toward me, a steady growl exploding from his chest. I sat down on my haunches, belly on the floor, and bent my head down until he reached me. When he did, I slowly turned belly up and opened up my throat to his inspection. Hot air puffed out of his flaring nostrils as he opened his mouth, his teeth over my throat—I didn't flinch. If the Weiss wolf had wanted me dead, I would have been dead five years ago. He liked me. He knew I was now this strangely blond wolf—a fur color I haven't seen in anyone, but then again I haven't seen a changed fey before. I opened my mouth and let my tongue roll out the side as I breathed. I was aware I had my regular thought processes, which wasn't common. When changed, werewolves have their animal's thought process instead. It might fall in line with their human one; it might just as well be entirely different. Lycans kept their human thought process when changed, so I thought the perk came from my fey—or fey and elf—heritage.

The room smelled good because it smelled of him. His presence coursed through my veins, his fur was a brilliant silver and white. I wanted to see his icy blue eyes, but I couldn't from this position. I knew better than to move before he allowed it, and he hadn't yet. I was submitting to him, my new alpha, my future mate.

After a while he unclenched his jaws from around my neck and licked his lips as he sat back on his haunches. I rolled over, belly against the floor again, and looked up at him while pointing my nose to the ground. Those piercing blue eyes were fixed on me, and I'd be damned if he didn't look regal and dignified as he sat there. His focus was entirely aimed at me, and I took it as a good sign. He leaned his muzzle down and gently poked at mine. I wagged my tail a little, unable to contain my excitement. He opened his mouth and gently nipped my nose, the slight sting making me snort out a breath in a mix of playfulness and joy. I slowly got up to my full height but still kept my nose pointing to the ground before him. I pushed my forehead into his chest, and he reached over to the side of my head and nipped the fur there. It was a love-bite kind of nip, playful. I sniffed his fur, took in deep whiffs of his scent, and let it comfort me. I lifted my nose and nipped slightly at his fur, not even touching skin. He growled, not scary but impressive, and got up on all fours too.

He was taller than me, bigger, certainly scarier. I found him fascinating; I was unable to look away. All I could think about was that if he wanted to mate, he'd get on top of me and bite on my nape. I was slowly turning my tail toward him, head still held lower in deference. His nostrils flared, and he smelled around my tail. I was excited and terrified. I wanted to lift my tail in a greater show of trust, but I was still afraid, so I kept it neatly tucked between my hind legs.

He growled again, pushed with his nuzzle at my tightly coiled tail. Then he suddenly moved over me, his teeth biting into my nape and pulling my skin as he arranged his body over mine. I wagged my tail, screeched, and whined as he pulled with almost punishing force at my nape. This was the sign I was waiting for. Now came the difficult part: I had to somehow turn around and pull myself free enough to nip at him hard enough to draw blood. It could get me killed, despite his first sign of being open to the idea. But unless it happened, we were not properly mated.

Mating a werewolf alpha is a hardcore sport, even if the alpha wants it. Just nipping at him hard enough to draw blood can trigger his wrath, which would get me killed. The fact I'd attempt it was terrifying, getting blood pumping through my system all over again. My muscles were still sore, my flesh tender all over from the change. But the pain was good. I used it to keep me focused on something other than how this might go wrong. His pull on my skin turned painful, he was losing patience. I inhaled sharply and turned my head around, my mouth open. Whatever I could nip would work if I drew blood. To be fair, this would be a bite rather than a nip. I reached around harder, straining my sore body to get in closer. He growled viciously and pulled hard on my skin, I felt him biting down hard enough to draw blood. Sweet fey gods, this shouldn't feel so good and have me so petrified at the same time... but it did. I bit into him where his front leg merged into his chest. Once I'd gotten him between my teeth, I bit down with all I had, unsure just how these fresh new teeth worked. He whined and bit harder into my nape as I stared awkwardly at the spot I'd bitten. Some blood trickled down and tainted his fur.

He growled louder and shook his head, still keeping my fur between his teeth. That fucking hurt, and I whined too but kept perfectly still. When he didn't let go or go in for my throat, I slowly lowered myself on my paws until my stomach touched the ground. My tail was fully up now, my ass higher than the rest of my body. We stayed that way as the seconds crawled by, my heart hammering in my chest. Hadn't he made up his mind already? Why wouldn't he do something? I felt him let go of my fur and nuzzle into the spot, lick it a little, and relief washed through me. He'd accepted me. I was officially part of his pack as his mate now.

He reached down with his nuzzle and licked around my ear too, which sent a shiver through my body. It felt intimate and spectacularly reassuring. I got up and turned around to push my head into his chest again, my muscles twitching all over. I was a little scared now because I knew what was coming next: the change back into my human form. It could still go wrong, despite the good news of our successful mating and me making it this far. Weiss's scent permeated the air, and I allowed it to permeate me. I wrapped myself in it, envisioned it as a cocoon sheltering me from pain. *I will make it through this change just as I did through the first.* I stepped back, shook myself as the pain started rolling out. I focused on inhaling and exhaling, envisioning Weiss's scent filling me up and pain puffing out of my nose with each rise and fall of my chest. Fuck, it hurt! My head spun, and for a second there I feared I'd failed, that things went terribly wrong.

"Well done," Weiss's deep voice rang out from nearby.

I opened my eyes and stared at my hand—regular skin. I'd made it back, at least partly. The pain was still burning through me, but I slowly moved to check myself over. I ran my hands over my face as Weiss grinned down at me. I was fully human again. It was done. I was a werewolf. My energy pulsed through my veins, the sense of all the emotional grids in the house exploding into my awareness without my trying. I looked around the room. Weiss's emotions ran through me in a whirlwind, almost dizzying. I breathed through it. It took a moment or so for my senses to readjust.

Weiss walked closer. "Tim? You okay?"

I nodded slowly. "Something's different."

He snorted. "I sure fucking hope so. You didn't hold back any on the bite, did you?" he muttered as blood seeped down his shoulder.

"Sorry about that. I wasn't sure about the force of my jaws," I confessed, still looking around. "Something's really different," I said again.

He frowned. "What do you mean?"

I probed through his emotional grid. The source of his rages was right there, transparently hooked into him in an unnatural way. I could sense it, almost as if it were a living, breathing thing. I wondered if I could pull at it, shake it loose?

"I think my abilities have pushed up a notch," I said calmly as I pulled on that hook.

He gasped, his gorgeous eyes widening. "What the fuck was that?"

I gazed into those icy blue eyes. "The conditional magic leaving your emotional grid. It's gone. I plucked it out as if it were a thorn."

"Did you expect a change?"

"It was a possibility. There might be more changes. My reading abilities have evolved too. I can tell how many people are upstairs, what they each feel."

His eyebrows shot up. "You couldn't before and now you can?"

"Yeah," I said, not quite comfortable admitting just how limited I had been until now, and not quite comfortable with the change either. It was a strange in-between moment, and it felt like it might take me a while to get my bearings.

"I wonder what else has changed," he muttered.

I swallowed. "At least three people upstairs feel more anxious than curious or excited. And there's one grid I can pick out from a thousand that has joined the crowd: James."

"He finally decided to show, then. I'm not sure if it's a good or a fucking bad sign."

"Bad," I replied, shaking my head. "Rick picked up on something weird when we were at the crime scene. He could smell all of us there, but not James. It was as if he weren't there at all."

Weiss crossed his arms over his chest. "How's that even fucking possible?"

"There are pills he could've taken to annihilate his body scent. But if he took them, then it's clear he has something to hide. And if he took one now, it means he has access to them. That he could have taken some earlier too."

"That he could have given others those pills too. Are you sure about them?"

"Yes. I read a research paper on it. They're specifically tailored to each person's hormones, so if others have them too, then someone made them. Someone planned for the lack of scent," I added, frowning.

"Premeditated, of course. Could we track the substance in those people's blood?"

I nodded.

"We need to get out of here. Someone has to take Tricia's blood and screen for it. She's the only one I can get my claws into right now."

I knew what he meant. I crossed my arms over my chest too, knowing this wouldn't go over well. "Weiss, I think whoever put that conditional magic on you meant to bury you with it. I'm not entirely sure, but I think it was meant to trigger a temper explosion at Amanda's execution tomorrow, if not sooner. All I could make out was it was tied to her physical presence or the strong memory of it."

He ran a hand through his hair. "That would've meant my sure death tomorrow."

"Exactly. And most certainly mine tonight, if I hadn't been pouring calm into your grid since we came down those stairs and into your living room."

His gaze fixed on me, razor sharp. "Why the fuck am I just hearing about this?"

My heart thumped. "Telling you about it would have gotten you more pissed. That wouldn't have helped."

He began to pace around. "So I would have killed you tonight."

"Yes. And I think there are a few guests upstairs still waiting to hear that you've done just that."

"Your father was openly invested in seeing you dead."

I nodded.

"That rogue wolf we found dead was tied to him, so we can assume the Fey King was somehow involved in the pentagram murders, even if we can't prove it. Can we assume whoever has been working us is also in cahoots with him?"

I nibbled on my lower lip. "I think so. I know if I would've been my father, I would have, say, funded whatever rebel movement Amanda had started. And if my knowledge about fey war tactics is any good at all, then at least one person on the Council is also involved."

"If that's true, we're as good as fucked. The Council is an unbreakable circle of trust."

"What if it's breached? What if there is a traitor among them?"

He stomped back to the bed we'd fooled around in and plopped down on it. "We'd need solid, and I mean solid, proof. I doubt we'd find any. Though one of the Council members might be rotten, none of them is a fool."

I went to sit beside him. "Then let's not mention this until we do have solid evidence."

"Right now we need to figure out who's trying to get us killed. Are you thinking James is involved? Can you read that about him or something?"

I sighed. "My gut feeling is he's involved for sure. He might have been involved with Amanda's stunt. Think about it. He certainly does have motive."

"Right. Opportunity as well, obviously. Expertise, considering his position within the PBI. He's not part of a clan, so that might tell us how he feels about leaders," he said, looking at me.

"Maybe it does. The kind of hatred he has seeded inside him would push anyone into doing really stupid things. If there were some other benefits to gain, that only sweetened the deal. But we have to gather proof of his treason or get a confession out of him."

"God-mother-fucking shit," Weiss hissed. "He knows all the tricks in the book. Why would he confess? He knows as well as we do that without concrete proof it's in his best interest to keep fucking silent."

I scratched my chin. "True. But he can't keep his emotions silent too."

His thigh touched mine, and my heart thumped hard.

"What do you have in mind?"

"James and the traitors—if any—expect only you to get out of this room, I think. And they expect you to have a fit tomorrow after Amanda's execution."

His clear gaze searched my face. "And?"

I smiled. "I think we should give them what they want."

nineteen

WEISS GRABBED my arm and turned me around so we faced each other. "You want me to pretend I killed you in here?"

"Yes. Can anyone except you open the door?"

"Only I have the code."

"Then lock me in here. Tell everyone I didn't make it, don't go into details. I'll pick up on the ones who feel happy about it. Then tomorrow you go to the execution and fake a fit at some point. I'll be somewhere in there if we can make it happen, hidden from sight. Whoever feels happy about your fit will be clearly intent on getting you killed. I'll expand their feelings, give them an emotional high. I don't like the idea, but we're fighting for our lives here, for the pack."

"For our family," he added and took my hand in his.

I swallowed thickly. "Okay. If we're likely to get confessions, it's going to be on that wave of excitement over two apparent wins. At least we might get James, because he's very emotionally involved, considering his hate for you, and now me. I doubt the Council members, if involved, have such emotional motivation, so they're not likely to spit out the truth. But let's worry about that later."

His fingertips rubbed softly against mine. "If they don't want to blow their cover, and I doubt they want to, then they won't take any drastic steps against us immediately, to avoid being mixed in with James's actions. And if we uncover another traitor in our ranks, they'll have even less chance of turning the whole Council against us... I hope. We'll be safer if this mindfuck plan works, or as safe as we might hope to be."

I squeezed his hand. "Who do you trust right now?"

"Outside of this room, Bert. Anyone else I'm not that sure about, but I trust Bert."

"He's very loyal. I think he's a safe bet, his profile suggests it, and so does his emotional grid. He'd die protecting you and Alf."

"Here's the deal, then: I lock you up in here and pretty much pronounce you dead. Once everyone is gone, I come back for you."

I bit my lip. "What if someone hacks into your security system and sees me get out?"

"Fuck. Fine, you stay here. I'll come back either way. If you're supposed to be dead, I'd have to clean up. We find some way of getting you out of here for tomorrow. Our best chance is to sneak you into HQ tonight at some point, so you'll be there tomorrow for the execution. I'd want Bert at home with Alf, in case... our plan doesn't work out, but Alf has to be there too," he finished in a chillingly calm voice.

"If I'm dead, then the best way to get rid of me is to carry my dead body to the morgue at PBI HQ for cremation. No evidence of my death, easy-to-use service. That's how we'll get me inside. But I don't know how I'll make it into that room for the execution."

He smiled. "Let me worry about that. I'm the director after all. I do have some aces up my sleeve."

"Fair enough. Now go out there and let them know I didn't make it. Look annoyed, not pained. Many of them think this is a mating of convenience, which it is after all."

He squeezed my hand. "That's not all it is."

I swallowed thickly. "Right. But appearances work for us this time. You wouldn't be upset, just annoyed that the chance was wasted."

He got up to his impressive height, pulling me up with him. We walked hand in hand to the door, where he suddenly faced me and kissed the living daylights out of me. "I'm coming back for you, Tim," he whispered. "I'll always come back for you, no matter what happens. You know that, right? We belong to each other now, whatever the reasons for getting in this situation in the first place."

"I trust you. I'll be waiting... bare-assed, I guess," I added and snorted.

He grinned. "I'm getting such a hard-on at the thought."

I punched his shoulder lightly. "Oh, shut up."

He tapped the code into the keyboard by the door, and I heard the locking mechanism open. Then he opened the door and just as he was walking out, he whispered without looking back: "I meant every word I said tonight. Every fucking word."

Then the door locked, and I heard the mechanism set back in place, securing me inside. I was either safe or a sitting target. If something went sideways tomorrow, we were royally fucked and as good as dead already.

I felt my energy pulsing, an expanding field of awareness that slowly encompassed the whole building. I didn't have to make an effort to read emotional grids now. Rather, I had to make an effort to ignore them. I made out Weiss's grid easily, the already familiar mix drawing me in like a beacon. Alf was easy to spot too, the most anxious and scared one of the bunch. He gravitated toward his father for security, though I could guess that he put up a brave front. Travis was the next one I clearly recognized, followed by Rick since they gravitated one toward the other. Bert pinged up next. There were a lot of them I could never recognize, I thought bitterly. But James was as easy to spot, the pungent hatred singling him out. It spiked as I was focusing on it, so I guessed Weiss had just delivered the news. Little Alf was sad—not heartbroken, but sad—an emotion my energy immediately reached out to alleviate. Joy shot up in a few spots in the room, but too little of it to be significant. I guessed they were pack members hoping to become Weiss's mate now that the position seemed to open up again. I picked up a few strange mixes of emotion too, anxiousness, fear, a few spots of relief. Hmm… relief. Little of it, two main spots. Why would anyone be relieved I was dead? I wasn't a real threat to anyone but those who were my father's allies. I committed to memory those two emotional grids, determined to look into who they belonged to. Travis's grid screamed out at me, sadness and regret, while Rick was utterly furious. He might lash out at Weiss for it. Gods knew he was itching for a reason to jump at his neck. I rolled out waves of cooling energy in his and Travis's direction.

Right now, I'd done my part. It was all on Weiss to get me into the PBI and find some way to stash me inside the execution room while keeping me hidden. I padded back to the bed and plopped down on it. My body felt different as I moved. Holding up a hand, I studied the way my muscles looked as I turned it on one side, then the other. I felt firmer, stronger. The soreness of my first change still tingled through my body, a strange sense of awareness that filled my heart. There was a new voice inside me, a wild, restless side I hadn't been aware of until now. Taking advantage of the silence and peace, I focused in on it. My wolf was itching to go out and run in a forest, to howl at the moon, to chase something down and tear its neck away. I shook my head, the impulse almost too strong to resist. The idea of being caged in didn't work well for this newer side of me. I flexed my hands, stretched out my feet.

This was a good plan, the only one I came up with. Freaking out wouldn't help us now. I closed my eyes, took deep, even breaths. My own energy shifted inside me, wrapping the restless wolf in blankets of comfort. He calmed down, leaving me with a clear sense that this was postponing his wishes, not giving up on them. Our wishes and feelings would slowly merge into one solid consciousness, I knew—I'd read up on that. It usually happened within the first few changes, and until it did, changed wolves could become dangerous if left unsupervised by their alphas. Well, I had no reason to worry about that, at least. Weiss would be hovering over me all the time, I had a feeling. After all his recent issues, he'd be terrified of allowing me to screw up.

I crossed my legs, tapping a lazy rhythm with my toe on the sheet. Singledom had officially ended tonight for me. From an outcast fey I'd gone into the terrifying and shifty terrain of mated werewolf, with a stepson to boot. My stomach tightened at the thought. Tomorrow morning, Alf would watch his mother's execution. No matter the bravado he'd put up, I was sure it would be devastating for him to go through. But he had to, those were the pack rules. These executions were public affairs, cautionary tales.

My heart froze as a sudden explosion of rage filled the space upstairs. Pain, shooting pain—someone was hurt. I jumped to my feet, my pulse spiking up immediately. I walked to the door before I'd even realized I was moving. Fear, waves of it shooting out. Holy magic wands, what was going on up there? I pressed my forehead against the cold door. Weiss was involved, I felt his anger reaching out and slapping everyone around. Oh gods, what was going on? I scanned the room for Travis and Rick, hoping to be able to pick up on some loose strand of emotion. Nothing helpful came up. Then I zoomed in on Alf's emotions, sure he'd be terrified if his father was in any real trouble. I breathed a sigh of relief as the kid's emotional grid showed some admiration, affection, and a little excitement. His father couldn't have been hurt, then. Maybe he was fighting with someone?

Fucking door, keeping me locked in here! I forced myself to walk away from it. My fingertips burned to scratch and tear at the walls, at everything just so I could get out there. I felt my wolf shiver with excitement at the thought of lashing out at something. My pulse spiked, muscles beginning to tingle. I had to calm down. Shaking my head again, I started pacing around in circles. It helped drain some of the tension, but not much. I did my breathing exercises, hoping to calm down the storm going on inside me. The wolf knew Weiss was involved in something upstairs. He itched to go out there, be with his mate, join in a fight. He was a nasty little critter, but I couldn't help the surge of affection for him. He was a loyal, brave wolf. I smiled and breathed in deeper.

"Sorry, buddy, it's not time yet," I whispered.

I imagined a lush green forest. The earth was damp under my bare paws, the cool night air sliding inside my burning lungs. I walked between tall trees. The musky scent of earth and the fresh air of the forest calmed down my furious pulse. In my mind, my paws slapped the ground faster and faster, turning my stride into a run. Leaves brushed over my face and fur. Every now and then, I hit a puddle, water splashing up on my paws and stomach. It felt glorious. My muscles burned with the effort of running, but in my imagination I didn't let it stop me—I didn't have to. The run appeased my longing for freedom, at least for now. I slowly opened my eyes and slowed my breathing down. The wolf inside me huffed out a long breath but stopped pushing me to lash out at my cage.

Walking back to the bed, I sat down and crawled back to lean against the headboard, stretching out my legs. The door's mechanism moved. I jumped to my feet and padded behind the door. If anyone was coming in to check on my body or make sure I was staying dead, there was little chance of hiding. I'd jump them from behind the door, maybe change and let my teeth sink into the intruder. Oh, my wolf liked that idea a lot.

As soon as the door opened, Weiss's scent drifted in. I took in greedy gulps of it, allowed it to calm down my nerves. He was wearing a robe and a tense expression as he closed the door behind him and punched in the code.

"What happened up there?"

He sighed. "Fucking horny bitches got into a fight right there, under my nose. In my fucking living room," he growled.

"Competing for your attention?"

He nodded and leaned back against the door. "Had to calm them down and let everyone know I wasn't interested... yet. That it was too soon after... the debacle of your changing."

"They bought into that?"

"What, that I might actually have some feelings?" he snapped.

I swallowed. "No, I mean into the whole me being dead thing."

"Oh. Yeah, they did. James looked so happy, I thought he might've creamed his pants." He ran a hand through his hair. "The whole fucking world is unraveling," he muttered.

I stepped closer to him, close enough to feel his body heat. "Sometimes, it's a good thing. Helps us settle things better."

"Come here," he whispered.

I pushed my forehead into his chest, felt the pounding of his heart.

"The plan is we get you into PBI tonight, like we discussed," he whispered.

I felt his chest vibrate with his voice. Damn, I loved the feeling.

"Bert will help me carry your 'body' in there. We'll set you up in a... secondary observation room. If you can make James lose it, we might get some fucking answers. Nothing else points in any direction right now, those five leaders, the lone wolf... nothing fucking showed up."

"Someone killed those leaders and arranged the bodies," I mumbled against his chest. Then I pulled back and looked up into those gorgeous and scary light blue eyes. "If someone on the Council is involved... one of the fey ambassadors could be in on it too. And they are the kind of fey who wield enough magic to cover up the traces for someone who did it."

He wrapped his arms around me. "If we can't squeeze James, we have nothing. You know what that means, don't you? Even if we survive tomorrow, or the day after that...."

I rubbed my nose against his chest. "No suspects for the latest Leader Murder case, you directly investigating it. It's in the Council's best interest to get rid of me, and now you too. They can't fire or demote you, which leaves a clear last option."

He lowered his nose into my hair. "Our lives depend on you making James spit something out tomorrow. My son's life," he whispered and his voice hitched.

I shivered. "I'll do whatever I can to make James talk."

"Maybe I should give you some incentive."

I snorted. "Not wanting to die is pretty stimulating, I promise you."

"All the same, I'm going to give you some incentive."

His hands traveled down my back and arched around my ass, squeezing.

I gasped. "What kind of incentive, exactly?"

He chuckled. "The very stimulating kind."

I swallowed thickly. "Don't."

His hands remained on me, warm and tempting. Oh, how I wanted him to touch me more. For him to let me touch, to taste his skin. I burned for it more than ever. *We* burned for it, my wolf and I, each of us with a fire of our own. Those flames combined to form a consuming need, powerful enough to almost take my breath away.

"You don't want me?" he asked with a wicked grin in his voice.

I gulped. "I want you so bad I can hardly breathe."

"Then?" he almost purred.

"Not like this. Don't use what I feel for you as a bargaining chip. Trust me, I'd die ten times over before allowing anyone to harm you… or your son. Or me," I mumbled.

His hands pulled me into him, his hard-on pushing against my stomach. "Would you?" he whispered.

I nodded and hoped very hard not to have a heart attack.

"Then why not let me enjoy you?" he murmured against my ear.

Electricity crackled between us; my skin zinged where he touched it. "Don't do it as… incentive."

"Why should I do it, then?"

Oh, gods. "Because you want me."

He pushed his hips into me, his hard-on burning hot through his robe. "Is there any kind of doubt in your mind about the fact that I do?"

"I don't know."

He pulled the robe open and let it fall to the floor. His glorious body had me taking in a shuddering breath. The wide expanse of his shoulders called to me, and my palms itched to reach out and touch his chest, to run through the gray hairs there. My gaze lowered to the happy trail going down from his navel, all the way down to the treasure of his hard dick. Sweet magic wands, I wanted to taste him. I wanted to feel his cum on my skin; I wanted to lick off sweat from his body. I whined, like a lost little puppy.

He chuckled and closed his arms around me again, allowing our chests to touch. His hair tickled my skin. I leaned into him, rubbed against that hair. It fascinated me, I couldn't help it.

One of his hands traveled up my arm, shoulder, neck, and tipped my head up. His lips brushed against mine. "Let me make it clear, then," he rumbled.

I felt the tip of his tongue flick out and wet his lips, then mine. He pushed a finger gently on my chin, urging me to open my mouth. I did. He rewarded me immediately, sliding his tongue in to touch mine, a tender, possessive caress that made my stomach clench tight. He hummed softly and slid his tongue in deeper. He tasted so rich, the warmth and hunger making my heart thump hard. I leaned into him, reaching between us to rub my palm against his dick. He rumbled deep in his chest and pushed against my palm. Right now, the only thing that was clear was that I was dying to feel as much of him as I could, whatever his reasons were for doing this right now.

His emotional grid pulsed with yearning, affection slithering through it like rivulets of light. I moaned into the kiss and squeezed his dick, loving the way he groaned at the pressure. Fuck his reasons for doing this. Fuck my worries and fears. I wanted him so bad it hurt, and tonight I would have him.

twenty

THE KISS went on for what felt like an eternity: my jaws burned from it, my blood thrummed through my veins, my heart was all aflame. Unlike our prior time fooling around, Weiss didn't seem starved. He didn't rush, didn't demand much. He offered me a part of himself I hadn't seen before: a tender, generous Weiss.

I pushed my fingertips along his neck, down his chest, the texture of his glorious hair ticklish under my touch. He hummed as my fingertips ran down to his pebbled nipples, down his clenching abs, then back up as I grinned.

"Mm, feels good," he whispered.

"Oh, yes it does," I mumbled.

My eardrums were clicking with the pressure in my bloodstream. My muscles quivered, my skin was hot all over. His scent pounded into my lungs, almost sensual enough to make me cum. I brought my mouth close to that dusting of gray hair on his chest, rubbed my lips against it. Mmmh, yes… it felt glorious. I moaned, turned my cheek into it, and rubbed my face against that rich texture.

He chuckled. "You more of a cat than a wolf, Tim?"

I hummed. "I love your hair."

My hands slid down his abs, my fingers widely apart. I didn't touch his dick as I slid my palm down. Instead I rubbed my fingertips through his neatly trimmed pubic hair, the sensation making me shiver.

"Fuck, *that* feels good," he mumbled.

I got down to my knees smoothly, my every motion now merging into the next one, a sense of endlessness I'd never had before. The scent of his dick had my mind spinning. I rubbed my nose into his pubic hair, caressed his dick with my smooth cheek. His hands shot into my messy hair, and he pulled me closer, rubbing that delicious-looking dick against my face. I cupped his balls and turned my lips against his burning hard-on. My tongue shot out, and I licked him from base to tip, pushing out a lot of spit. The very idea that my spit was on his skin made me even harder, if that were even possible. As it was, I felt my dick was about to explode, too hard, too hot, too hungry to bear. I covered my teeth with my lips and opened my mouth around his head, pushing against it. He rumbled and flexed his hips forward, the wet and tight orifice of my mouth opening slowly to allow his dick in. Once I felt him on my tongue, I couldn't play anymore. I swallowed him down eagerly, ignoring my gag reflex. My mouth was starved for him. Spit ran down the sides of my mouth, wetting my chin and dribbling down his balls in the process. He purred, positively purred, as I sucked him hard and fast. The taste of his precum made me rumble around his dick, the vibrations going through his hard flesh.

I looked up to find his burning hot gaze fixed on my lips, on the way they stretched around his dick. I swallowed around him, massaged the underside of him with my tongue.

"You suck like a hungry little manwhore," he rumbled, looking into my eyes. "Are you hungry, little manwhore?"

I moaned and swallowed around him again, then pulled his dick out of my mouth and dug the tip of my tongue into his slit. "I'm starving for you, for your cum. Will you give it to me?"

He groaned, then grabbed his dick and slapped it against my cheek. The wet slap made my dick twitch.

"You want my cum?" he asked in a low, gravelly voice.

I shivered. "Yes, please."

He grinned, his gaze going positively predatory. "Have to earn it first."

My mouth and throat went dry. "What can I do to earn it? Please, I want to deserve your cum in my mouth."

He groaned again and rubbed his dick in long strokes, his grip strong enough to leave pressure marks as his fist traveled along the hard flesh. "Get on the bed. Open those gorgeously long and lean legs of yours, open them wide for me."

I crawled over to the bed, did as instructed. Precum leaked out of my dick as I saw him watching my balls, his gaze trailing down to my hole.

He gripped the base of his dick and squeezed. "Find the lube, work a lot of it into that gorgeous hole. I'm going to fuck that hole hard, and I want my dick to slide in and out of you with ease."

I shivered. The lube was on the nightstand; I grabbed it with trembling hands. Fuck, I hadn't ever felt the way I did right now. The anticipation had me twitchy and nervous, my stomach feeling full of fluttering butterflies, my skin burning with the need to be touched by him. I worked a good amount of lube inside, slid my fingers in and pushed them apart as I stared at his hand working and squeezing his dick. "Please," I gritted out in a raspy voice. "Please, let me feel that delicious dick."

He grinned again and strode toward me. The way his body coiled with each step, every motion fluid and so well-choreographed, had me sweating. Nothing had ever looked as beautiful as he did right then. It was almost enough to make me cry, or maybe the anticipation and downright desperation running through my veins was at fault.

He settled between my legs, rubbed the head of his dick against my slick hole, but didn't push in. Instead he covered my body with his, dug his arms under my shoulders and gripped the back of my head in both palms while his hips flexed and the head of his dick kept rubbing at my hole.

"Flapping wings, just fuck me already, please," I whined.

"Shhh," he whispered against my lips. "I've wanted to feel you for five long years, Tim. Five years," he mumbled as he nibbled on my chin. He bit the underside of my jaw, making me jump under him and draw in a sharp breath. He suckled on the skin there, lapping at it gently. "I love your body, the smooth skin," he rumbled and sucked the spot again.

I moaned and closed my arms around him, pulling him to me like a drowning man would pull at his last chance of survival. I dug my nails into his flesh, blunt and small as they were. I dug them deep, drawing a hissing breath from him.

He gripped the back of my head harder with both hands and angled my face so he could suck my lips into his mouth, one at a time. By the time he was done tormenting them, the flesh was pounding almost as bad as my dick was, trapped between us, rubbed with his every motion. I was panting, breathing through my open mouth because I just couldn't get enough air in through my nostrils. He looked down into my eyes, that predatory gaze now mollified. There was a level of tenderness in that gaze, a degree of need that went beyond the physical, something of a desperation I felt mirrored in my own heart. I squeezed my arms around him as hard as I could, overcome with the need to press him into me until the point of meshing our skins together. He leaned down to my lips slowly, almost torturously so. When our tongues touched we both moaned. This wasn't a playful kiss. It was wet, wild, unrestrained, with our teeth clashing and our lips pressing together so hard that it almost hurt. I couldn't give a fuck if he'd pressed them flat. I wanted to get inside him, to crawl into his very soul as his tongue probed my mouth. I sucked on it, sucked hard, almost as hard as I had sucked his dick. The head of his dick rubbed at my slick hole at an angle, and finally, gloriously, pressed in. I screamed with glee as it pushed against my ring of muscle and slid slowly inside. The stretch burned beautifully, his thick meat soldiering in so very slowly but steadily. He kept kissing me with abandon, swallowing up my groans and cries and mewls until he was buried inside me, balls deep.

When he was finally all the way inside, he pulled back from my mouth, still holding the back of my head in both of his hands. "You feel fucking amazing," he rumbled. "Your hole is gripping me so hard, almost as hard as your arms. So hot and hungry…."

I shivered. "Starving for you," I whispered breathily.

He groaned and pulled out slowly, sliding back in hard. I cried out, rolled my head on the pillow. He'd hit the spot just right, causing an almost dizzying wave of pleasure, intense enough to almost touch pain, to explode through me.

"Rub your dick for me," he whispered as he pulled out and plunged back in. "Rub it hard, as hard as you're gripping my dick inside. I want to feel your cum on my skin."

Holy shit, I saw stars as he rocked inside me again. I slid my hand between us as he pushed my feet up on his shoulders. I felt him slide in deeper as I gripped the base of my weeping dick. The problem wasn't cumming. I barely stopped myself from doing it already. The problem was I didn't want this to end. I refused to let it end.

His gaze found mine as he fucked me, and the depth of the contact left me breathless. I couldn't blink, didn't dare break that connection. My eyes stung with it, but I didn't blink. I felt our emotional grids melt at the edges, blend together. It made my skin sing, my hole clench him tighter. He groaned and fucked me harder, the strokes more rapid but still as deep. He braced himself with one hand and gripped my dick with the other. I gripped the base of it tightly with my own hand as he rubbed his palm over the head. It felt so good, I hissed, threw my head back on the pillow, and opened my mouth widely, groaned out.

He let go of my dick and pulled my chin down, so our eyes met again. "You look me in the eye when you cum with my dick inside you," he growled. Then he gripped my dick in a merciless fist and rubbed me in time with his strokes inside me. Our gazes fused, the slick slapping sounds in the room beating in time with my pulsing heart. My whole body pulsed, a throbbing, quivering mess as I tried to hold back the blinding orgasm I felt trying to overtake me. I didn't want it to stop. I bit my lips until I felt the tang of blood in my mouth. His thrusts grew harder, almost punishing, making me cry out with each one. His fist never stopped pumping my dick, fast, hard, tight, and so fucking hot, I feared I'd find burn marks on me later.

"Want my cum up your ass, Tim? Do you?" he growled.

"Yes, please, please," I mewled out.

"Cum for me like a good little whore," he rasped as he pumped his dick inside me.

I swallowed a few times, my body tensing up. This was it. I'd lost the battle of wills. I felt the tide build slowly, almost leisurely, from my fingertips, my toes, the tips of the hairs on my head, growing, clawing at my insides, building, burning through my muscles, making my spine grow rigid and all my joints freeze. His fist pumped faster, his dick hammering inside me now, his gaze locked on mine. I felt him so deep inside it almost scared me, the connection too overwhelming to bear. The wave crashed into my stomach and exploded into my loins, burning hot cum shooting out of my dick in angry spurts that left my balls throbbing so hard it hurt. I cried out, my gaze still fixed on him. I saw stars with my eyes wide open.

He grinned and moaned openmouthed as my flesh tightened around him, my grip on him going even tighter as I shuddered. He swiped his fingers through the cum on my stomach and chest. I watched him, lost in rapture as he licked it off his fingers. I shuddered again, a body-wide twitch that had me moaning out. I felt his hips piston against my ass with punishing force, his thrusts going irregular and shaky as his moans went wild. And then hot spurts of his cum began to shoot inside me, the slight burn of them making me gasp. He felt bigger, wider, longer, big enough to almost expel me from my own body.

He leaned down on me, planting his forehead on the pillow, his face turned toward the side of mine. His lips rubbed against the shell of my ear, his breathing hard and hot. "Finally mine," he whispered between breaths. "All mine."

I closed my arms around him and squeezed as hard as I possibly could. "Finally," I whispered back.

Finally his, and he was finally mine. I refused to allow any other thoughts to fuck up my afterglow.

twenty~one

WE STAYED in bed, a tangle of limbs. I would have liked to fall asleep in his arms; feeling so sated certainly called for some rest. But I couldn't, and neither could he. I almost felt his thoughts buzzing, he was thinking that hard.

"What's the plan?" I asked as I stroked down the side of his chest, all the way down to his hip.

He sighed. "You keep doing that, the plan is gonna be another round."

I chuckled. "I'd like nothing more, but I have a feeling we don't have time to play right now."

He turned to look at me and angled my face up so our gazes met. "Play?"

I swallowed. "You know what I mean."

"What do you mean, Sands?"

I smiled. "Ah, you're pissed. It's always 'Sands' when you are."

"Is this a game to you? Any of it?" he asked, his gaze searching my face.

"I've been head over heels for you for years, Weiss. You can't possibly still doubt that at this point," I ventured.

"I don't doubt it, not after we got mated. You can always tell when the mating is sincere or not, as a pack alpha."

"So you know it's not a game."

He frowned. "I can also feel you're different after the first change. Your presence reminds me of your father's more than it did before."

I widened my eyes. "What?"

"There's a new feel to your presence, a new, darker layer. You feel like a stronger creature."

"I think I am more powerful as far as emotion and magic play are concerned, but you can't possibly think my character has changed. Not enough to compare me to *him*," I muttered and tried to pull away.

He wouldn't have any of that. He turned us over, him keeping me pinned down. "Tim, I'm fighting for both of our lives and my son's tomorrow."

"And I'm fighting for all three of them too," I snapped. "I get that you've been hurt, and betrayed, and unhappy, and maybe even lonely—no, don't give me that look! You might be a big, bad bastard of a werewolf alpha, but you still have a heart in there," I said, looking at his chest. "If you don't trust me, kill me. Kill me for real, right now, tonight. Because unless you trust me from here on out, we won't stand a chance. And neither will Alf," I added, half hating myself for playing that card.

He exhaled a puff of hot air and fixed those amazing light blue eyes on me. "I'm going to put you in a body bag."

My heart froze. "What?"

"A body bag. That's how we're getting you out of this room. Bert will help me carry the bag to the car, then into the PBI HQ. Lora at the morgue will swap your body with a real corpse, and we'll get you into that observation room after that."

I swallowed thickly and looked away. "My living body."

"Of fucking course!" he snapped and pushed his forehead down into my temple. "What the hell were you thinking?"

I swallowed. "I guess we'll have to take a leap of faith, both of us."

"I'd never turn on you," he whispered faintly.

"Neither would I. But I'm betting you don't really believe that 100 percent. Not yet, anyway. It's normal not to. We'll win each other's trust over time. If we have time," I added slowly.

He turned my face toward him and kissed my lips, a slow, tender kiss. Then he got to his feet. "I'm getting your clothes. Look in that drawer there," he said, pointing at what looked like a wall to me. "Take out a body bag, try to get used to the idea."

Turned out there was a drawer in there, built into the wall. I pulled it open and got one of those thick black plastic bags. A chill went down my spine as I looked at it, nicely unfolded on the floor at my feet. However alive I might be when inside it, the very thought of a body bag had my stomach churning.

Weiss came back in with my clothes and handed them over. "Get dressed. I would be supposed to get rid of your clothes anyway, right?"

I nodded. After I got dressed, I climbed inside the damned thing. "Close it up, but not all the way. Make sure I'll still have air."

He sighed. "This isn't my first time closing a body bag, Sands."

"Well, it might be the first time the body inside needs to breathe," I snapped.

"Might have a point there," he commented as he pulled up the zipper.

I saw some light through the very top, so it wasn't closed all the way. I heard some fabric rustling, probably Weiss getting the robe on, and then the security keys of the door beeped and the door opened. Not long after, I heard a second set of steps following Weiss's. They were both wearing shoes by the sound of it.

"I'll take the top corners," Bert said.

Weiss sighed. "I can carry it myself."

It? What the hell? I was still able to hear, and I most definitely wasn't an *it*.

"Boss, let me help you."

"Then help with the bottom half instead," Weiss snapped.

Bert sighed. "But it's heavier, and you're taller than me, so all that weight is going to…."

"I'm not that goddamn heavy!" I grumped.

Bert chuckled. "'Course you're not. Just making sure you hadn't fallen asleep in there. That would be awkward, wouldn't it?"

I sighed. "You knew I was okay before coming down here?"

"No," Weiss's beta replied as they lifted me up. "But unlike a dead body, you were still breathing," he whispered. "Now shhh for the cameras."

They lugged me up the stairs, then, I guess, out of the house and into the trunk of the car. I wanted to protest but figured supposedly dead bodies shouldn't be too picky about their means of transportation.

I breathed out a tiny sigh of relief as we stopped moving. When they carried me inside the PBI HQ I knew I was close to freedom. Weiss growled and snapped at someone, and then we got into the elevator that began its descent to the morgue. I braced myself for the moment those doors would bing open, though I suspected no amount of preparation would really help. Our medical examiner, Lora, was a thoroughly competent troll, but a troll nonetheless. Right now she smelled so bad, troll bards would compose odes to it. Of course, to them it smelled like fertile troll lady, sexiest scent in the world.

When they pulled that zipper open and the full force of the scent hit me, I almost asked them to pull it back up again, but by now the smell had gotten in, so it wouldn't have helped. I held my breath and reached out to Weiss, hoping he'd thought to pick up the jar of cream on the way in. Mercifully, he had. He smiled and plopped a good amount of it underneath my nostrils.

"Sweet wands and gods, I love you," I whispered on a sigh of relief.

He chuckled and kissed my temple. When I turned around, remembering we had an audience, I saw Lora dabbing a finger at the corner of her eye and Bert grinning like a maniac.

"What?" I stammered.

Lora shook her head. "I'm so happy to see you together, at last."

Weiss cleared his throat. "What's that supposed to mean?"

She grinned, showing those scary rows of teeth. "You've been yearning for each other for years now, my nose always picks that up," she said, tapping a fingertip to said organ.

I cleared my throat. "Right. Thanks. Now, how do we get into that observation room?"

Weiss crossed his arms. "What you're about to see will not leave this room, we clear?"

Bert and I nodded, though I noticed Lora only smiled. Then she turned around, pulled open the freezer's door and walked in. Weiss motioned to follow, so we did. At the very back of the room full of still-unprocessed cadavers, there was another door that I'd never noticed before. Not that one would normally spend any time in here, except Lora and maybe her assistants. When she tapped in a sequence of buttons on a tiny keyboard, I had a déjà-vu feeling.

"Let me guess," I ventured. "Nobody but Lora knows that combination?"

Weiss nodded. "This is her escape route. In case anyone gets in through the main elevator, thinking she has no other way out...."

Bert cleared his throat. "I hope you never have to use it, doc."

Lora chuckled. "You and me both, dear. You and me both. It does come in handy, though."

We got in, and she operated another set of keys, hit a code into the board, and then the elevator was moving.

"I have exit routes all through the building, hidden rooms. The director was kind enough to build the section plans. The architect we used and the secondary constructors were met with... an unfortunate incident. So were the plans. So if word gets out, boys, I'll know who to come after," she said in that raspier, pure troll voice.

I froze solid and so did Bert. Perfectly civil lady or not, she was an impressive female troll specimen, larger than male trolls and a lot more powerful. She could easily wring our necks, should she put her mind to it. It was easy to forget just how strong she was because of her impeccable manners and the lovely, though faked, very humanlike voice she used.

"You have my word your escape route will be safe," said Weiss.

She nodded and smiled. "Hope you won't drown in cobwebs, I'm afraid I haven't been using the corridors," she said in the singsong voice she liked to use.

Bert chuckled, and I joined in.

"You're saving our lives. I'm sure cobwebs, should there be any, won't be our main focus."

She smiled. "You're always such a smooth talker, Mr. Sands. Maybe it will rub off on the director too," she added sweetly.

When Weiss sneered, she went on, cutting him short.

"The blood test results are back for Tricia. You were right, she had a strange substance in her system. I've tested it and did some research. I remember reading a paper a while back on something of the sort. When combined with a tracker's and a target's DNA, it can render that tracker blind to that target. There's some fey doctor who patented the formula... a Dr. Strimmel, or Strommel... I can't quite remember."

"Dr. Vanda van Stromm, official research director at the Fey Institute," I cut in. "The King's concubine after he divorced my mother."

"Fucking damn fey bastards!" Weiss seemed to remember whose company he was in, so he added hastily, "No offense, Tim."

I smiled. "None taken. I'm a werewolf now, no longer fey at all. And I wasn't much of one to begin with."

The doors binged open, and we slowly stepped out. Lora waved good-bye and went back down to the morgue, the elevator doors closing behind us. They were hidden in the back of a small room, what I supposed to be one-way glass giving view to two separate rooms: the official execution room, and the main, and only public, observation room. I guessed this place was written in as a recording room. There was a table surface incorporated in the wall, though no equipment. There was another door that gave way into the main observation room, though it must be hidden on the other side, as far as I could remember.

"No recording devices in here, then?" I guessed out loud.

"It's a secret room," Weiss said. "You can pull open that door there and go through the drywall into the observation room, should there be an emergency. Other than that, you can use the elevator to go down a level, into a corridor."

I frowned. "Isn't Lora the only one who can use that elevator?"

Weiss shook his head. "Would I install a toy I can't use? You have to use her code to go into and out of the morgue's floor, but the elevator can be used by anyone with the security code for any other level. The security code I'm going to show you in a minute."

Bert scratched the back of his head. "Wouldn't it be better if he didn't get out of here, though? Might be at risk of being seen."

"True," I said.

"In case you have to leave, you will know the security code," Weiss proclaimed. Then he turned around, pushed some keys on the keyboard beside the call button for it, and shooed Bert inside, face turned away from us. I felt Weiss's palm press a small bit of paper into my hand as he whispered "9 4 2 0 0 5" into my ear. Then he kissed my cheek, said, "Try to get some rest," and turned around and left.

I pulled open the paper. It had another code scribbled down on it, and Weiss's scratchy handwriting below it proclaiming "Real code." I chuckled and put the paper into my breast pocket, then lay down on the floor, setting my phone to wake me up at 6:00 a.m. Good thing it was in my pants. People might start to show up into the execution room sometime after seven, preparing for Amanda's execution. Tricia would be held in custody until the Council and Weiss could decide whether she'd be up for a parole of sorts. But there was little hope she'd ever get out. Traitorous betas never made it out of custody alive, even if someone decided to release them. Pack members wouldn't take her treason lightly. Among werewolves, the punishment for it was usually death. And doubly so if they'd betrayed a mate.

I closed my eyes, trying my hardest to push out any stray thoughts. I needed to rest, and after some sleep, I'd have a better grip on my new emotional grid reading and manipulating skills. Or at least I hoped so.

twenty-two

MY PHONE chirped and woke me up at 6:00 a.m. I wasn't actually rested, but at least I didn't feel that burn in my muscles from yesterday. I got to my feet, stretched a bit. There were some sore spots; sleeping on the floor could only be so comfortable. First order of business was to mask and shield myself. Though after the bite I wouldn't register on any fey's radar as a fey myself, I didn't want to take any chances. Knowing my father, if he were in any way involved in these murders, if he'd gotten to someone in the Council for some fucked-up reason—he only had that sort—then he'd want his lackeys here to witness the grand event. At least one of the fey ambassadors would witness Amanda's execution, and what I assumed would happen as a result of it.

I expanded my awareness and did a quick reading of the emotional grids around. It was still early, so there weren't many people in, not yet. There might be a swarm of them here later on. After all, this was a big pack and everyone loved community events. Lots of people hated Amanda's guts by now, so her execution must've looked like a jolly occasion. To her credit, she'd been quite the hardass, not afraid to bust everyone's balls.

My wolf stirred inside me, an angry growl in my mind, a layer of his vicious nature trying to surface into my consciousness. He was afraid of what might happen, and being locked up in a room didn't suit him either. Another prison, only this time with a view. He wasn't fond of sitting around on our asses, not at all. I focused on a forested scene again, this time bathed in morning light. I walked through the wet, cold grass, buried my paws into the chilled ground. Birds were chirping in the trees, and I heard running water nearby. Zooming in on that sound, I slapped my paws into the ground, opened my snout to breathe easier. My heart pumped fast, muscles tingling with the delicious effort. When I reached the river, I stuck my forepaws in it and enjoyed the piercing cold of the water. Freedom—my wolf demanded it. I knew it in my bones that I'd have to change again today and let him loose, though not just yet. Not now, when I needed to keep my head in the game, to focus, stay alert. My wolf whined, but conceded the point and retreated deeper into my consciousness for now. He wanted Weiss and Alf to be all right as much as I did.

I decided I'd use the time I had to meditate, focus on my new abilities, flex my muscles. Today's outcome depended on how well I'd manage to use skills I didn't normally use. Growing up among fey had made me feel uneasy about manipulating emotional grids. Reading them had never been a problem; it was second nature to all fey. They all did it on instinct. Manipulating was tougher to do. You had to have a lot of will and considerable magic to achieve that. As a result, those I'd seen doing it were High Court members, my father, prominent figures at Court—so generally anything but nice people. The very thing that had made me want to become a therapist was my dislike of the practices I'd seen at Court. But it had also made me refuse to accept a part of myself, to deny a part of myself—the part that could do what they did.

The fact of the matter was I was part fey. It meant I was naturally drawn to read emotional grids and, in some cases, balance them. Since Weiss's bite, it wasn't something I leaned toward doing, but something I felt constantly compelled to do. My instincts ran the show, reading everything and everyone around without me willing it to happen. Perhaps with time I would learn to turn this emotional grid radar off. But right now I couldn't. What I needed to do was manage to focus it on only one person, or at most a group. And then, to do what I'd hated high rank fey doing: manipulate those feelings.

There would be no other way to make James confess. And there would never be any other proof of his, or anyone else's, involvement in the pentagram murders. Whoever the victims had been, and whatever they'd done, they deserved justice. The only way to get it for them was this: to amplify, yet temper down his emotions until he'd tell the truth. It had to be done, and only I could do it. All my years around Fey Court had prepared me for this. I just needed a little practice with someone's emotional grid, some harmless push into some direction they already wanted to go in. If I could do that, I had to hope I would manage to make James confess.

After a while of visualizing a wild forest, I reached out slowly and focused on the emotional grids nearby. Two people one floor below me, working on something tedious—probably reports, by their reaction to them. I focused on their desires, their needs, and amplified them once, twice, three times... there, mission accomplished. Their grids shone with raw sexual desire, the tedious work forgotten. I couldn't hear or see them properly, but their grids started going fuzzy at the borders and slowly fusing, so they were getting it on. I grinned—mission accomplished. Pervy, maybe, but accomplished. This was an easy exercise, though. Desire was the easiest to manipulate, especially when the subject had a baseline of it.

Manipulating James's grid would be somewhat easy too: he hated *a lot*. I wouldn't have to plant the emotion, to seed it into his grid, to force it to grow. Just redirect and amplify it, boosting his satisfaction. If I hit the balance just right, he would explode in a stupor of glee.

My joints started protesting, so I changed position. It must have been some time already; I didn't usually get sore after sitting one particular way, not that soon at least. I checked my phone—7:30 a.m. The main observation room door clicked open and shut. I got up slowly, careful not to make any sound, and peered through the one-way glass. Someone was arranging chairs, a lot of them from what I could see. So there'd be a big audience. That was either very good, or very bad for us—I couldn't quite decide. Many witnesses to what anyone would do or say, that was for sure. If the seats were all occupied, that was. A couple of agents started preparing the execution room, the table, the IV stand. Death by injection, supposedly a merciful way to go. Though nobody really knew, did they? Not like anyone had come back to tell us about it.

I would know, sadly. Witnessing Amanda's death, I would know just how it felt for her to die. I shivered at the thought. No matter how much I thought about it and tried to wrap my head around the execution, it just didn't seem right. The fey system, the official and lawful one at least, had life sentences as their harshest form of punishment. Execution was considered barbaric under lawful circumstances. Of course, that didn't keep anyone from killing someone else in unlawful ones. That was the thing with rules: the ones obeying them were the good guys. I took another glance at that IV and swallowed thickly. Alf would see his mother get killed this morning. How could a seven-year-old boy get over that? I had no clue. I still wasn't sure if Weiss had gotten over his mother's execution, though that one had been more old-school, considerably less civilized, some might argue. Though I didn't think death could be anything close to civilized, regardless of the MO.

At 8:00 a.m. I was already jumpy enough to break out in a sweat. Patience had been one of my strong suits until now, but I was running rather short on it. I crossed my arms over my chest and tapped my fingertips against my shirt. Gods and fey dust, why couldn't this go quicker?

The main observation room door finally opened again, and I saw Weiss walk in, holding Alf by the shoulder. *Of course they wouldn't be holding hands*, I thought and rolled my eyes. Mrs. Stein and her daughter, Naty, came in too, the Council members following suit. Behind them, of course, Leonard Hughes—fey ambassador and one of my father's favorites, at least he had been while I was still at Court. The man had the most reptilian eyes I'd ever seen, a chilling gaze that matched his heartless but efficient enforcement of my father's every command. If the King had sent him in, then he was very interested in what was going on here. I still couldn't grasp the why, despite my admittedly outdated knowledge of the Fey Court's matters. James walked in too, hands in his pockets, and the most outrageous joy in his gaze. I could read the glee all over his emotional grid, putrid joy at the thought Weiss would be hurt, no doubt. That I had been killed last night. A few others walked in too, among them Travis and Rick, until there was no more room to stand in there.

Weiss and Alf were at the very front of the bunch, side by side. My heart ached watching them both. Weiss was surprisingly calm, though he flared his nostrils when he breathed and seemed to seethe over everyone giving him the time of day. Alf was serious, a determined look on his face, his body rigid. Travis and Rick made their way close to the glass too, and Rick's outrage screamed at my senses. I paid a lot of attention to Leonard Hughes, hoping to catch on if he caught on to me. But I didn't dare read his grid; I just monitored him for any spike in magic. The room was eerily quiet. No one said a thing.

And then the door opened in the execution room, and a drugged Amanda was carried in, arranged on the table. I'd recommended the drugged measure as part of executions, my attempt at making the process easier on the convicts. This way, they wouldn't spend their last hours contemplating the fact they would die. It was part of the policy to keep that aspect quiet, out of any regular PBI agent's earshot. If they knew they'd be drugged beforehand, then the whole anticipating their death process would just start before the drugging instead of before the actual execution. Amanda might have known, as Weiss's mate. Her grid was muddled, but the rage and hatred shone out almost as much as James's, which was quite the achievement. But then again, she was somewhat justified to feel them: she was about to die.

Rick reached out and splayed the open palms of his hands on the glass. He was outraged, angry, too angry, and kept giving Weiss death glares. He blamed him for the whole Amanda fiasco, of course. He was partly right too, only there was no such thing as an only guilty party in things that went sideways, like Weiss and Amanda's mating had. Of course Rick would blame Weiss, though, the one playing some semblance of the abuser role. After Rick's ex, the man had a bone to pick with anyone exerting abusive authority over anyone else, especially in matings. And he was right to feel that way too. The new bill of recruit and leader mates' rights would help to even out the odds. Some changes would happen.

As they strapped Amanda to the table—an unnecessary precaution since she was also drugged, but good for show I guessed— I felt Hughes's magic spike. The wave of rage tried to hit Weiss, and despite my instinct to dismantle the attack, I thought it might be useful. After all, I'd plucked out the root of the conditional magic, so the rage wouldn't do the kind of damage Hughes was hoping for. It would help Weiss act like he was going mad, though. The steady stream built, coloring Weiss's grid in an angrier and angrier red. The doc pushed the poison into Amanda's IV bag and stepped back, crossing his hands before his groin. He felt defensive about what he was doing, maybe even shamed. But someone had to do it, and he was the one in charge of it.

"It's all your fault," Rick muttered venomously at Weiss.

Weiss exploded in an angry growl, his face morphing into wolf form. Travis grabbed Rick and more or less threw him out the door, following behind him. Most of the crowd present made a quick exit as well, Hughes among them. Weiss snarled, a terrifying sound, and went down on the floor, completing the change. James's expression positively beamed with joy, and Councilor Stein shook her head.

"Poor man, he's fallen prey to the rages. After what happened last night, I can't blame him."

The blood froze in my veins. That simple? It was that easy for her to declare the PBI director insane and sentence him to death? This wasn't going right. James was gloating but keeping silent as Weiss's rage exploded in angrier and angrier snarls. All wolf now, he kept his snout low, drool falling out of it in copious amounts. His gaze was aimed at Mrs. Stein, those icy blue eyes looking pretty set on murder.

Naty tried to get in front of her mother, her ears twitching and her tail jumping nervously underneath her lab coat. "Weiss, you need to calm down. This is tough, I know, but... but... please... calm down...."

Amanda screamed, a ragged, tormented sound that started out as a low moan and steadily grew into hysterical wailing. Her body spasmed and contorted on the table, the restraints barely holding her in place. Pain and horror washed through me, along with the sudden realization that the life force wasn't seeping out of her as it should have. No, she seemed to sober up, come out of the stupor of the drugs, in fact. The pain exploding through her system only spurred her on, and her face slowly morphed into the wolf one. She pulled at the restrains until she was free. The first one she jumped was the doctor who had injected whatever the hell he did inject into her IV. She ripped his throat out in one smooth motion, blood gurgling out of the broken mess she left behind. One of the others managed to run out of there and to close the door behind him, leaving the raving-mad Amanda in the room with another agent. He was a lycan and managed to shift in time to parry Amanda's first attack. But the odds were stacked against him if what I read in her grid was true. She hadn't been poisoned at all; whatever the fuck they'd given her was acting as a massive dose of adrenaline, making her stronger and meaner than ever.

In the other room, Alf pressed his palms against the one-way window as he watched his mother bite the lycan's hand and pull, tearing off some fingers. I heaved, the desire to jump in and the horror at what I was watching battling for supremacy.

Weiss snarled again, louder, fucking scary, and jumped. All hell broke loose.

twenty~three

COUNCILOR STEIN didn't change, and her daughter couldn't have, even if she would have wanted to try. James's fangs shot out and he grinned as he jumped at Weiss. The glee hadn't loosened his tongue, but apparently it did his fangs. Weiss whined as the vampire managed to bite him, and then James screamed as Weiss got in a solid bite into his shoulder too. At least he didn't have to worry about being changed: vampires couldn't change into werewolves. Naty tried to walk around and grab Alf's hand, but her mother grabbed her arm and pushed her out of the room, following. On one side, Amanda was tearing out bits of that lycan, on the other, James and Weiss were at each other's throats as a frozen Alf stared. No one was coming in to help, on either side. I could only imagine it meant at least Mrs. Stein was trying to get both Weiss and Alf killed. Once Weiss was a goner, Alf wouldn't stand a chance, not on his own. They'd kill Amanda, eventually. She had no way of getting out of the execution room; it was secured. Unless someone would open the door for her, of course. At this point, nothing would surprise me.

I wanted to remain calm, though my wolf was clawing at my mind from the inside. Each time Weiss snarled and jumped at James again, my wolf pushed harder against the restraints I'd managed to put on his wild nature. I had to stay focused, or I couldn't help. But all my energy was focused now on balancing out Alf, trying to keep him as not-terrified as I could so he could bolt at least, and calming myself so I wouldn't change. Fuck, what was I supposed to do? Calm Weiss down?

The rage helped him, and if James had acted under a Councilor's guidance, he'd never talk. Not against a Council member, and even if he wanted to, he'd never live long enough to manage it. Of that much I was sure. My mind was pounding. What the fuck to do? Alf finally snapped out of his daze and moved slowly toward the farthest corner of the room from the fight—the corner near the door of my room.

I had to go in. My hands trembled with tension, not fear, as I took my clothes off, then opened the door on my side of the drywall. I shook all over as my barriers were broken. My wolf howled inside my head, full of glee. Muscles burned and bones twisted. I felt the change settle through my body, and when I blinked my eyes again, I had paws covered in fur. I took a few steps back, then jumped the fuck through that drywall. My mate needed my help, and his son needed to get out of there. I barely felt the drywall give way to me. It was like a sheet of cotton candy. Alf screamed and crawled into the corner of the room, big eyes fixed on me. He didn't know who I was, of course. No one had seen me changed except Weiss, and the kid was probably too scared to sniff and recognize my scent. I bowed my head at the hole in the wall a few times, until I saw understanding glimmer in his gaze and his nostrils flare. Either he'd recognized me, or the fear was so big he jumped at the chance to get some distance between him and everything else. He crawled through the hole in the wall, into the relative safety of the next room.

James threw Weiss across the room, into the one-way glass between the observation and execution room. It cracked, but didn't break. I was stunned. There was no way James was stronger than Weiss. No way.

The bastard vampire grinned at me. "That's twice now you've escaped death, little fairy prince," he spat at me.

I growled and coiled tightly. At the smallest move he'd make toward Weiss, or the hole in the wall, I'd jump the bastard. My blood boiled with rage.

"It is you, isn't it, you wolf slut?" James barked.

Amanda jumped at the dividing glass, hitting it with her head. It cracked a little more, still not breaking. If she made it in here, we were all fucked. The thought seemed to cross James's mind too, because he stepped slightly in the direction of the door. Oh, he wanted to get out, did he? The little traitorous fuck. I inhaled deeply and jumped, my jaws wide open. When I caught a part of him between my teeth, I clamped down with all the might I had. A wet crunch filled the room and James shouted in agony. The back of his neck. I'd caught the back of his neck. His spine snapped in two under my jaws, and his body collapsed to the floor in a heap. He wouldn't die yet, not immediately. But he would die; I'd make sure of it. Short of a confession, he was of no use to us.

I changed and leaned down beside him. "What do you know about the pentagram murders?"

He spat blood at me. "Why the fuck… would I tell you?" he hissed, though barely breathing.

"I'll make it a quick kill if you do, spare you the pain. It's going to hurt if you die like this," I informed him and pressed my finger into the wound.

I flooded his emotional grid with fear and guilt, massive amounts that would bring him close to hysteria. This was my one chance, even though there wasn't anyone in the room capable of acting as a witness. But the surveillance system covered this room, and a confession would still count, even here and now. I pressed harder on his wound, gritting my teeth.

He gasped and his eyes widened. "I did it. The pentagram arrangement, I did it. All me."

"You're lying," I said and pushed my finger into the wound again.

He cringed, though he could only move his face. "Had help… fey pills… to throw off Rick….," he wheezed.

Of course he had. "Who gave you the pills?"

"Hughes," he panted out, his eyes going bleary.

I broke his neck, ending his suffering. Then I padded toward Weiss's slumped form. He kept trying to get up, and shook his head as if confused. Maybe dosed? Had they given something to him, to make him angry enough to attack? Thoughts rushed through my head. Why wasn't anyone coming into either of the rooms? Shit, had they planned this too? Get him to attack someone in the room, so his death would be fully justified? Amanda jumped and hit the glass again, and this time, it cracked and broke. I froze as I saw her supine wolf form fly over me as she jumped from one side to the other. Her fur was covered in blood and her yellow eyes were murderous as she snarled at me. I didn't look at the hole in the drywall. I wouldn't be able to take a raving mad Amanda down, I guessed. Weiss was in no shape to either, not at the moment. Maybe Alf would be lucky enough to have the sense and stay hidden, but even if he did, once Weiss, Amanda, and I were all dead, one way or another, he would have no fucking chance.

I had to allow the burn to run through my system now. Adrenaline must have pushed back the pain of turning into my human form. I couldn't risk it knocking me out all at once, so I relaxed enough to lose some of the adrenaline and allow that pain to slowly trickle through me. Slow and steady was better than an explosion of it. As soon as I could, I shot out tidal waves of calming energy at Amanda. She blinked a few times, as if trying to wake out of a stupor.

"Amanda, please, listen to me," I whispered, my throat strangely raw after the two shifts. "If you kill us now, you kill Alf too."

She squinted. The tidal wave of calming energy took a lot out of me, and she seemed to be a bottomless pit of rage. But I also amped up her maternal love, certain this was our only chance at survival. Weiss, her, Alf, and me trapped in a room, while Amanda raged and Weiss was out of commission, was a lose-lose situation.

"Just listen to me," I tried again in the calmest tone I could muster. "There's a traitor in the Council. They're trying to get Weiss killed, and they'll kill Alf right after that. Get rid of the alpha of this pack, maybe destroy the whole community with it. Stop to think about this. Maybe they framed you too," I added with moderate hope.

She stopped growling, those clever eyes of hers going speculative. It was working. The manipulation of her emotional grid was working; it had to.

I went on. "They framed you, most likely, to get easier access to Weiss. With you two killed, they can take Alf out easily. James was in on it too. Why else hasn't anyone stepped in to restrain you? To help Weiss out, or kill him if he's considered to be in the second stage of rages? They're trying to pin his murder and your son's on *you*. Think about it. The Council traitor would do that. Monday morning the Anti-Abuse Act is supposed to become law. With Weiss dead and chaos ensuing, it will be postponed, who knows for how long? They're trying to kill the act you fought for all these years. And they're trying to use you to get it done. Will you go back on your beliefs, your hard work for the freedom of leader mates?"

She shook her head. Her body wasn't poised for attack, but I wasn't fooled for one minute into thinking it would mean she wouldn't tear my fucking head off. I was buying us some time, hoping someone, Bert at least, would come in.

"Don't do this traitor's dirty work for them, Amanda. Don't go down as their lackey."

Her nostrils flared and she growled. Vanity. Yes, I played up on it. She was a proud creature, very independent. Even if she was in cahoots with the traitors in the Council, she wouldn't want to be remembered as their lackey. Wings and wands, where the hell was Bert?

Weiss changed back to his human form and lay slumped on the floor. Definitely drugged, but he hadn't been hurt badly enough to knock him out.

I stared at Amanda. "I can help you escape the building."

She changed into human form too. "You what?"

I took a deep breath. "Help you escape. If you just leave, right now. Without hurting us."

She snorted. "The two of you newly mated?"

I nodded. "I meant the three of us, though."

She frowned, sniffed the air. "What the fuck.... Alf is here?"

The little guy's face peeked out from the hole in the drywall. "Hey, Mandy."

Amanda blinked fast a couple of times. One of the things I had to get used to was the total lack of concern for nudity among werewolves. I would have cringed at the sight of my father naked, for instance. Alf and Amanda seemed perfectly at ease.

She smiled. "Came to see me?"

"Had to. Didn't want to," Alf replied.

"Didn't want to see me?" she asked.

"Didn't want to see you... die. Not like that," he said, staring toward the broken glass.

Amanda inhaled sharply, but kept her cool otherwise. "You have a way out of here?" she asked, still looking at Alf.

I swallowed thickly. Weiss would most likely tear me a new one for it, but what were our options? At least one Council member had said Weiss was in rages. If Mrs. Stein claimed Weiss had gone into rages during the execution and tried to attack her, they'd have footage that it had happened. From the outside, it kind of did. The only way to prove Weiss had been drugged would be to stick around for his blood to be analyzed, and once that happened, suspicion of rages would disappear. But we had to be alive long enough to get there.

We had no way to prove magic interference with Weiss's behavior, or to support any claims of treason within the Council. We were as good as dead, all in all. The only option was to help Amanda run. Weiss would absolutely hate me for it, but right now I had his life and his son's to worry about; his feelings would have to come second. I knew I'd have to face his rage later on for this, but seeing her out sounded way better than her turning on us now. She could take me out easily in a fight, I was sure of that. And whatever the fuck they'd injected in her was still going strong: I could see all the rage lurking right at the center of her emotional grid. She could snap at any moment. Frankly, I would rather have her snap at someone as she was trying to run, than at us while staying here.

I inhaled deeply. "Let's make a deal, Amanda. A fair one, not like what you've been dealt lately."

She grinned crookedly and turned to look at me. "You love the fucker, don't you?"

I nodded. "And if you agree to just leave, get out, you'll have your revenge on him too."

She squinted. "Oh really? And how exactly would I get my revenge on the bastard?"

"If you run now, you can attack him anytime you want, on your terms. He'll hate me for getting you out too. He'll be miserable and furious and frustrated and worried."

She smiled, her eyes alight with glee. Then she frowned. "But alive."

"Alive, and caring for Alf, until you decide to take proper revenge on him, one-on-one," I added, hoping I wasn't pushing that button too much.

She tilted her head to the side. "You know, Sands, I always admired your skills. You do know how to frame a clusterfuck, I'll give you that."

I smiled faintly. "Someone wanted you alive, Amanda. The injection couldn't have been a screw-up, it was intentional. Someone switched the poison with some stimulants. Whoever did that wanted you alive bad enough to take huge risks. I think people out there feel your... work... isn't done. That you can do more to help the... abused."

"You're sure they didn't poison me?" she asked.

Ah, so she didn't know who had helped her out. I could almost see the curiosity in her eyes. Interesting, disturbing, but also convenient for us at the moment. If someone wanted her alive, then she might have a chance at survival once out of the building. I planted hope into her emotions, lots of it.

"Positive," I said. "Do we have a deal?"

She grinned. "He'll hate you like a motherfucker. And you'll have to deal with his overbearing bullshit. I count that as fair punishment for your stupidity," she added cheerfully. "But you're trying to keep my son safe, so you're not as terrible as you might have been, I suppose," she added airily. "I do love my son, even if that fucker turned him against me."

"Do we have a deal, then?" I insisted.

"Deal," she replied. "Now get me out of this goddamn place."

twenty~four

AMANDA RAN into the elevator as soon as I gave her the code. She knew to go one floor down, and that some corridor was expected there. Beyond that, I had nothing to give her, and she seemed content with that much. I had no idea where the corridor led and how she might get out from there—or if she really could. Lora's floor was secured by her own code anyway, and I sincerely hoped Amanda wouldn't make it out of the building alive to tell the tale of her escape route. I'd told her about the code and corridor while we were in the secondary observation room, so it couldn't have been recorded. What was recorded in the official observation room wouldn't show a clear view of the wall I'd come out of. Cameras in the observation room were aimed at the middle of it, not at the walls. As far as the footage was concerned, I'd appeared out of thin air, and Amanda had vanished into thin air. If my gamble paid off, the Council would have some footage to use, even if it had to be edited here and there. A lot of today would have to be edited for us to make it out alive. But the cover-up had to be in the Council's best interest. Or in the best interest of one influential Council member, at least. It was all a matter of framing everything as in their best interest. I'd claim Amanda had disappeared with the use of magic, and as a new werewolf with magic powers, people would just have to believe me. After all, they would probably think I had entered the room by use of magic myself. The only ones able to claim I was lying would be fey, maybe Hughes, but he'd be otherwise engaged soon. I'd make sure of that. If things went the way I was planning them, the story of this whole debacle wouldn't make it out of this room, anyway.

Once Amanda had left, I put on the clothes I'd taken off in the room before changing, got back into the main observation room, and stood in front of the surveillance camera, while Alf sat beside his passed-out father.

"Amanda is getting out of the building. You'll find her somewhere in the building, a floor lower from this one or below. She's drugged and dangerous," I added for good measure. "As you can see, Weiss had been drugged before the execution, so anyone who had anything to do with him prior, anyone who gave him anything to drink or eat, is a suspect. Send someone in to take samples of his blood and test it, you'll see it's true. Councilor Stein," I said and made a significant pause. "The attack on you was drug-induced, not because of rages. I'm not dead, as you can see, and you can have any other therapist analyze Weiss to prove he's not in any way affected by rages of any stage. Someone targeted you, though. Someone set this up so he'd attack you. There's a traitor in the Council, I'm sure of it now. Someone working with Leonard Hughes to bring some of you down, and apparently to kill you. It's proof of your unquestionable loyalty to this Council and community that they'd resort to murder to get you out of the Council," I added sweetly, even if I didn't believe it.

She'd been overjoyed and relieved when Weiss had gone berserk and tried to attack her. As far as I was concerned, she was almost surely a conspirator in treason against the current Council. But by giving her such an alibi, I hoped to dissuade her attacks for now. She'd come out looking like a hero instead of a villain. She wasn't stupid enough to not benefit from such a fat opportunity. All her scheming and planning in the future would pose even less of a risk to her. Why she'd tried to take Weiss out, I honestly didn't know. But I was pretty sure she had.

"Morris James confessed to the arranging of the bodies in the pentagram murders, as you've heard," I went on. "He named Leonard Hughes as his accessory. I believe we now have a good bargaining chip in negotiating with the Fey Court. Their King wouldn't permit anything to happen to Hughes; the man is one of his most loyal and treasured subjects. Those protectorate signatures in exchange for the freedom of such a loyal subject seems a fair trade to me," I added, smiling.

Now all I had to do was wait, and hope that my spin on things would work. I'd thrown in a bone for Councilor Stein and for the rest of the Council. Though I couldn't quite be sure they'd decide to play ball, I extended my reading to the whole building, located the Council's conference room where they were all gathered, and gauged reactions. The emotional grids from that room were in turmoil: worry, some fear, hope, annoyance. They fluctuated, as though discussing things, perhaps, exchanging opinions, settling courses of action. If they'd trust Weiss as the alpha of their sanctioned werewolf pack, mistrust Leonard Hughes since he was fey, and half trust me and my thinking, then they'd have to take my side, run with my version of events. It was in everyone's best interest, well, except for Hughes, but he wasn't everyone's primary concern. This would buy us some time, even if the real traitor might have been, for instance, Mrs. Stein.

I went to sit beside Weiss and Alf, in front of them, and waited. Any moment now, the door to the observation room would unlock, open, and someone would walk in. They'd be carrying either a gun, or an olive branch—so to speak. I projected a wall of kindness and affection around us, hoping it might delay anyone from, say, shooting us as soon as they stepped in. My wolf howled inside me, frustrated and anxious about what would happen next. He wanted to come out again, guard his family. But I could use my magic skills and emotional grid manipulations better in human form, and I managed to calm my wolf down by projecting waves of calm onto him. I couldn't wait for our thoughts to blend properly; this two-voice thought process in my mind was becoming exhausting.

The locking mechanism on the observation room's door clicked. Then the door opened slowly. My heart lurched in my chest, my temples pounding. This was it, the moment of truth. Either they'd kill us, or help us.

The first one to walk in was Councilor Stein herself, with Naty right behind her. Though Naty's ears were twitching, and under her lab coat, her tail was too, she smiled in reassurance, and I felt relief wash over me.

Mrs. Stein cleared her throat. "Amanda was captured two floors down, running down the emergency exit staircase. She was killed on sight. I'm told she claimed you helped her out of this room, but convicts would say and do anything, wouldn't they?" she said, smiling in a chilling way.

So would traitors, I thought bitterly.

Mrs. Stein sighed. "This whole debacle will be… adjusted in our records. We can't have anyone outside of our circle of trust think Amanda escaped our custody, after a failed execution attempt to boot. For all concerned, she died in that room," she said, pointing at the broken dividing glass. "Weiss's… episode never happened, though Naty here will take some blood to find out what he was given, and we'll investigate who might have drugged him. I'll handle the investigation myself," she added sternly.

Most likely it had been her, then. I smiled and nodded, feigning relief at the news. If she was a traitor, she had to believe her act was fooling everyone or she'd become truly dangerous… or more so than now, anyway.

"What about Morris James's confession about the pentagram murders?" I asked.

Naty came over and took some blood from Weiss. She patted me on the hand when she was nearby and smiled fondly at Alf. "It's recorded, and he's responsible for his crimes. I'm told there were some audio issues with the surveillance system in the room, so parts of what happened and your discussion might be harder to understand. But thank God, his confession is on the good part of the data," Naty said in a sad voice. "Tricia confessed to being his accomplice after some… persuading," she added on a wince.

"Needless to say we're chagrined that our Downtown chief and one of Weiss's betas turned out to be traitors," Mrs. Stein proclaimed haughtily. "You'll personally interview and read all personnel, Mr. Sands. Everyone who's anyone in this community will have to be personally vetted by you."

"Read? You mean… read their emotional grids?"

She nodded. "We trust you completely, as we do Weiss. You're both responsible for the safety of us all," she added gravely.

I smiled, pretending to feel touched. Personally interviewing everyone who was anyone meant keeping me swamped for a while. The real traitors would have more room to maneuver, I ventured to guess. Though right now it wasn't in their interest to attract any attention.

I inhaled deeply. "What about Leonard Hughes?"

Mrs. Stein's lips stretched into a devious grin. "The Council very much agrees with you, Mr. Sands. The King's most loyal subject for those protectorate signatures is more than fair trade, considering Mr. Hughes is an accomplice to treason against this Council and to six murders."

"Councilor, if I may speak freely…," I said.

"Please, do."

I shut up as two medical care center assistants pushed in a gurney. Naty directed them to set Weiss on it and take him back there to do a full blood workup, and she went out with them.

Alf walked up to me, standing a step or two away. "I'll stay with you until Dad recovers," he whispered. "Someone has to take care of you until he's better, yes?"

I smiled. "Thanks, Alf."

He clutched my pants leg, and I reached down to hold his hand. Relief washed through him as he took my hand, and I projected even more of it into him as I held him. Future alpha or not, he was just a seven-year-old kid right now, and kids needed love and comfort, even if they might claim otherwise.

I cleared my throat. "Councilor Stein, the doctor who prepared the poison in the IV—"

"Dealt with," she shot back.

"Did he say anything of use?" I asked, frowning.

"Mr. Hughes offered him some… benefits to change the substance in the syringe. One more damning fact about our dear fey ambassador," she said and tutted with glee.

I wouldn't have been shocked to find out Mrs. Stein herself had gotten to the doctor about that syringe. But blaming Hughes worked for her, and right now, it sure worked for us. Bringing her down would need a lot more than I was able to do on my own, and it would take time and effort. In the meantime, having a pretty strong feeling about who your enemy was, but living with them, seemed better than not knowing at all.

"About the wall…," I muttered, cocking my head to the side in the direction of the hole I'd jumped through.

She crossed her hands in front of her middle and smiled. "What about it?"

"Well, I mean the hole...." *And the room, and elevator in it, and everything else.*

She smiled wider. "There's no hole in our walls, Mr. Sands. No hole at all, are we clear?"

I nodded. If we were covering up Amanda's escape, the route would be covered up too, of course. Though anyone covering the actual hole up would see.

I looked at that hole, then back at her. "Would it be all right if I remodeled this room a little before Weiss recovers? I don't like to sit idly when I'm... waiting," I added carefully.

"Of course, be my guest," she replied. "I heard there's a new one-way type of glass on the market anyway, we'll have to replace our old ones. The rest of the room should match, hm?"

Then she turned and walked out. Of course, it wasn't lost on me that everyone who'd walked into this room had seen the hole there. Considering the other room was dark, and there had been a passed-out and naked Weiss on the floor, maybe they hadn't paid it much attention. But Mrs. Stein had. So even if I covered it up right now, her, Alf and me, at least, knew there was something of interest back there, behind the drywall I'd put up.

I looked around for my phone with Alf's help, and once I found it, called the supply room of the Bureau. They brought me up a few sheets of drywall and the supplies to set them up, no questions asked. After setting up sheets to cover the hole and the entire wall, I called back the supplies department and let them know I'd accidentally messed up the divider glass of the execution room while I was playing around, so it would need to be replaced and the whole room cleaned and set to order.

Then I took Alf by the hand and we walked to the medical care unit to see his dad.

twenty~five

WEISS RECOVERED in about two days. The mix of adrenaline and other stimulant substances had hit his system pretty bad, and it took a while to flush it all out. Once he was well enough, though, of course he wanted to get back to work, because that was the kind of alpha he was.

He stood at his desk, leaning back in his huge directorial chair, and glanced at me. My old office was now a therapy sessions room only, where I also kept my records due to the security setup there. But I spent most of my time in Weiss's office when I wasn't interviewing or counseling anyone. The stubborn man wouldn't have it any other way.

"Fifteen leaders convicted of abuse against their mates, and the matings dissolved," he announced. "This week."

I smiled. "Good. I'm happy to see the Act in effect."

He sighed. "I'm not. Between the interviews to vet everyone nontraitor and the counseling sessions, I barely get to see you."

"During work hours," I added, smiling.

He squinted. "The point of having you in my office was to have you around, during work hours."

"Small sacrifice, considering all the good the Anti-Abuse Act is doing."

"I'd rather not have to make sacrifices," he countered, looking out the window. "But so far hierarchy hasn't suffered from what I can tell, so at least there's that. Though inflicting therapy upon the leaders proved to abuse their mates seems quite cruel," he muttered, looking at me from the corner of his eyes.

I rolled my eyes. "I'm not cutting their balls or tits off with a pair of gardening sheers, you know."

"I'd like that better. Would be done quicker," he grumped.

I smiled again and turned back to look over my notes. This somewhat clingy, needy Weiss was a total revelation to me. He'd started acting that way a few days after he recovered, and those walls he so liked to keep around his feelings had slowly gone down. It was still weird for him, and he felt vulnerable, which was why he wanted me around pretty much all the time. Which, of course, resulted in him feeling even more emotionally vulnerable. Despite him asking me to balance that out with my "fey trick," I refused to. Some feelings had to be worked through the regular way, or there'd never be any progress. I wasn't trying to soften him up. On the contrary, I was trying to help him be even stronger. Ignoring his feelings didn't make him strong, but weak, in fact. At least that much he'd agreed upon, so we were making definite progress.

"Are you keeping your suggestion about our ambassador?"

I nodded. "I trust Bert, and so do you. The Council might not like it, because of the whole Tricia situation, but that's in the past. He's loyal, he has some connections there already, and he volunteered for the job. Makes him the perfect candidate, in my opinion."

"I guess. I don't like not having him around, though. And neither will Alf," he added in a soft voice.

"I know," I replied. "But he'll have his favorite aunt, Tish, around."

"I like that even less," Weiss confessed bitterly.

Our family dynamics were difficult at times, but I loved them both to bits. Aside from loving Alf because he was Weiss's son, the little guy was irresistible all on his own. I would really have appreciated it if he stopped chewing on my shoes, but he was so fond of them, he'd even drawn a pair into our "family drawing" of his dad, me, and him. We had that on the fridge now, and though he wouldn't admit it openly, Weiss made more incursions into the kitchen since it was up there. The fact I fitted into the whole alpha-planet of those two made my heart swell. Sure, it was difficult sometimes, all family life was. But we loved each other. I knew that for sure, and that was what really mattered. That, and security, and Tish helped provide that while we were in the office—which was a lot, I was sad to say.

I grinned. "Your big sister is a riot."

He squinted. "'Sister' would be enough."

"Well, I do like to be thorough," I quipped.

"One of your less annoying qualities," he said airily as he picked up a pile of files from his desk and deposited them on mine. "Deal with those by the end of the week, please."

Well, at least he'd said "please."

I sighed. "Will you ever do your own paperwork?"

He snorted. "Of course I fucking won't. You came up with the Tish idea, so you owe me this much at least for the kind of damage you've done to my life."

"Oh, stop it. She's a joy to be around."

Especially since she loved to rub it in that she was bigger than Weiss, and she teased him relentlessly when we were alone. She'd never dare do that in front of the rest of the pack, but big sister liberties were taken when it was just the family.

"For you, maybe," he replied as he leaned against the edge of his desk. "Alf and you like her, and that's what matters most. But I still don't like the idea of Bert out there, among the fey assholes."

I leaned back in my chair and looked up at him. "He wanted to go. Felt like he had to prove himself all over again, because of his sister's betrayal. It was what he wanted to do, we have to respect that."

Weiss sighed and crossed his arms over his chest. My mouth went dry, as it usually did, as I watched his muscles bunch. Sometimes I thought he did that just to shut me up, because he knew the kind of effect he had on me. Of course, two could play at this game. I turned my chair around halfway, facing his desk now, and crossed my legs as I leaned back in the chair. His gaze shot to my ankles, and slowly went up my legs, over my groin, up my chest, then settled on my face. My throat went even drier.

"We're close to finding out who the second beta will be," he commented distractedly.

"Any day now," I answered in the same tone.

"Have any favorites?" he asked as his gaze went back down to my legs.

"I like Christopher Dutton and Celia Reed best."

He smiled crookedly. "Chris just got his ass kicked. I'm pretty confident it's going to be Celia. We'll know by the end of the week."

She had two more contenders to fight, if Chris was out. With Bert going into the Fey Court as ambassador of the Council, and his other beta turning out to be a traitor, Weiss had to take on another beta. Tish was acting as Alf's security, but pack politics required a beta. Most likely it would be Celia starting next week. Bert's position as beta wasn't over, simply suspended while he was away. Of course, the official story was he was covered in disgrace for his sister's actions, and booted out as ambassador as punishment. It was a good cover, and it would help him into actual Court information if he managed to play his cards right.

Weiss walked around my desk and leaned down to brush his lips against mine. "When's your next appointment?"

"One hour from now," I replied as I nibbled on his lips.

"I know just the thing to pass that time," he growled.

Liv Olteano is a voracious reader, music lover, and coffee addict extraordinaire. And occasional geek. Okay, more than occasional.

She believes stories are the best kind of magic there is. And life would be horrible without magic. Her hobbies include losing herself in the minds and souls of characters, giving up countless nights of sleep to get to know said characters, and trying to introduce them to the world. Sometimes they appreciate her efforts. The process would probably go quicker if they'd bring her a cup of coffee now and then when stopping by. Characters—what can you do, right?

Liv has a penchant for quirky stories and is a reverent lover of diversity. She can be found loitering around the Internet at odd hours and being generally awkward and goofy at all times.

Stop by her website for the latest news or visit her blog for occasional rants. She also regularly spamificates Twitter and Facebook. For The Win.

Be afraid. Be very afraid.

Website: http://liv.liviaolteano.com/
Blog: http://blog.liviaolteano.com/
Twitter: @LiviaOlteano
Facebook: https://www.facebook.com/LiviaOlteano

The Heracian Affair

Space Files R: Book One

By Liv Olteano

Even years after Rizzo Berg's lover and Dom died in combat, the memories torment him. Following a particularly disappointing date, Rizzo goes to sleep in his apartment only to wake up on a spaceship with tall, gorgeous, alien Captain Conrad D'Ollet of Heracia, a man so deliciously dominant Rizzo's knees turn to jelly.

Apparently the Heracians need help, and Rizzo is a humanitarian through and through. Spending more time around Conrad is totally not one of the reasons he wants to lend a hand.

Soon Rizzo finds himself completely conquered and blissfully owned. But neither he nor Conrad is willing to risk his heart, let go of the past, and dare to believe in a future that won't end in catastrophe.

Sandstorm Heart

Space Files R: Book Two

By Liv Olteano

Ron Vid is a Celian soldier with some personal demons. Hoping for respite, he deserts his squad and leaves his planet. Working as a mercenary on Asai, planet of sand and wind, he has a reprieve, until the Haffa named Zaoh joins the mercenaries. Celians and Haffas have a history of strife, but when Ron and Zaoh are paired on a mission, their chemistry crackles. After they fight together for survival, it's clear Zaoh wants Ron. Zaoh can be a fierce and dominant lover, but Ron's secrets, and his fear that the Haffa might uncover them, could keep Zaoh from getting his man.

http://www.dreamspinnerpress.com

FRIENDS
WITH *Benefits*
CHEYENNE MEADOWS

http://www.dreamspinnerpress.com

Brian's Mate

HOLLIS SHILOH

http://www.dreamspinnerpress.com

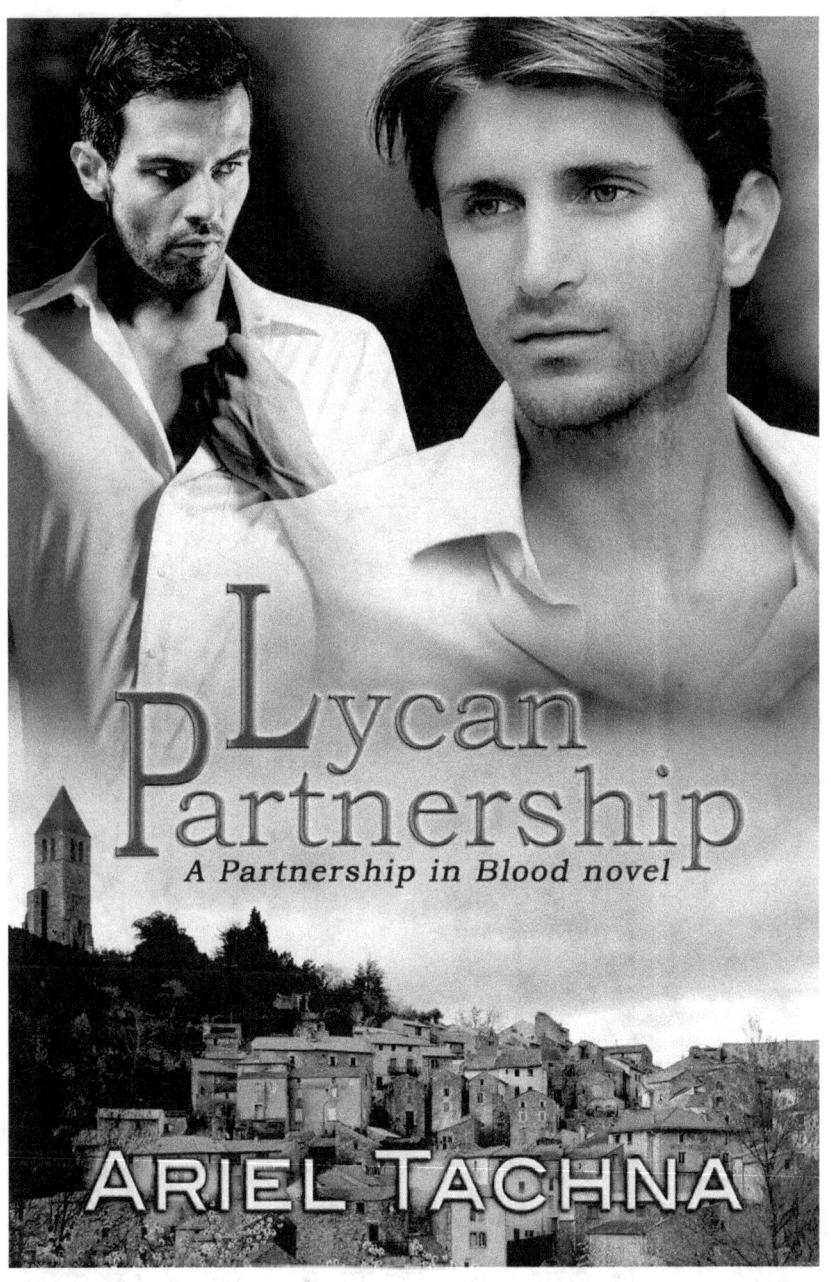

Lycan Partnership

A Partnership in Blood novel

ARIEL TACHNA

http://www.dreamspinnerpress.com

www.ingramcontent.com/pod-product-compliance
Lightning Source LLC
Chambersburg PA
CBHW070107260626
47160CB00004B/1358